CYRANO

H. BEDFORD-JONES

CYRANO

H. BEDFORD-JONES

COVER ILLUSTRATION BY

PAUL STAHR

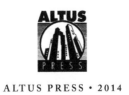

ALTUS PRESS • 2014

EDITED AND DESIGNED BY
Matthew Moring

PUBLISHING HISTORY

"Cyrano" originally appeared in the November 16–December 21, 1929 issues of *Argosy* magazine (Vol. 208, Nos. 1–6). Copyright 1929 by The Frank A. Munsey Company. Copyright renewed 1957 and assigned to Steeger Properties, LLC. All Rights Reserved.

THANKS TO
Joel Frieman, Everard P. Digges LaTouche and Gerd Pircher

TABLE OF CONTENTS

CHAPTER I

—MAKES ENGAGEMENTS
WHEN DRUNK.

A DUST-COVERED, TRAVEL-WEARY cavalier dismounted from a very lame horse at the Tavern of the Three Kings, toward noon of a warm Spring day. He had obviously ridden far and hard, for he was spent with fatigue and stiff in the knees. He yielded his reins to the host and pointed to his lame beast.

"A stone—I cannot dislodge it," he croaked. "Have it attended to at once. Fetch me wine, a bite to eat. And quick about it, you rascal!"

The surly rider staggered across the little courtyard and vanished in the tavern. The host shrugged and called angrily for a groom. Little did any of them imagine that upon this lamed foot of a horse hung the lives of men, the fate of kingdoms, the destinies of unborn generations. This stone wedged between hoof and shoe created invisible circles which reached out and out, lapping at the years to come.

Destiny, however surprising, is never illogical. True, the Three Kings was a shabby tavern, haunted by grooms and lackeys and cutthroats and loose women, but it lay just within the Barrier St. Jacques. A rider coming into Paris by the Orleans route would quite naturally stop at the Three Kings—if forced to stop by thirst and a lame beast.

Not that Paris cared for riders from the South. In this Spring of 1642, Paris was ruling itself in happy-may-care fashion. Paris was its own little world; the court was a separate world entirely, and now the court was out of Paris. King Louis XIII and Cardinal de Richelieu were both in Narbonne, directing the war against Spain, and the court had been moved south to Tarascon; another army was in Savoy, pushing the war against Italy. Paris, which loved the careless king for his vices and hated the too-patriotic cardinal for his virtues, was content to have them both far away, for it could go about its own business unconcernedly.

The cavalier who entered the dark wineshop, blinking, was of the court. This was very obvious in his garments and bearing and face; a thin-featured, intolerantly proud man who looked about him in unconcealed disgust.

The place was empty except for a shaggy, tattered man who sat at the only window-table, bending over among empty wine bottles, writing furiously; at his elbow were ink-horn and sand-box. He did not so much as glance up at the visitor.

"Out of the way, fellow—I desire this table," said the arrogant noble.

THE WRITER looked up abstractedly. He was of most extraordinary appearance. He had long, uncut hair, a finely sensitive mouth, liquid dark eyes and a very large, hooked nose; his face was much cut about by sword-scars, lending him a most bizarre look. His once-rich clothes were shabby rags; his unkempt hair was a filthy mat. He was unshaved. His hands left smears on the paper whereon he wrote. He was very pale—a sure sign that he was drunk, had the cavalier known it. But the cavalier knew nothing of Paris or its characters.

"You heard me!" snapped the weary, haughty noble. "Out of the way, gutter scum!"

The two eyes, like stars set in a mass of dirt, peered up at him. A maudlin laugh broke from the writer.

"Ha! M. de Luynes, grandson of the great marshal, gentleman of the court, noble, warrior, in all his splendor. And Cyrano de Bergerac, grandson of the great fish monger, wastrel of the back alleys, poet, gambler, in all his squalor! Here's contrast for you!"

"Eh! You know me?" exclaimed Luynes.

"I know every one," muttered Cyrano, and with shaking hand reached for his wine cup and drained it. Luynes regarded him with insolent disdain.

"Move, *canaille!* Dog, make way for your betters. Writing, indeed! Since when did gutter cats learn writing? Away with you!"

As he spoke, with his gloved hand he swept paper, ink-horn and sand-box to the floor. Then he started back a step, hand going to sword, swift, startled alarm in his face.

Cyrano had come to his feet suddenly. His eyes blazed; in his scarred countenance was such unspeakable fury, such a wild and reckless burst of rage, that the cavalier drew back before it.

Hot words poured from the poet-warrior's lips.

"Beast that you are—to touch a letter to *her!* Oh; foul hands!"

Luynes perceived the drunken menace, and half bared his blade—but too late. Cyrano had snatched up an empty bottle; his arm moved with the rapidity of light. Struck above the ear, the hapless noble coughed and collapsed in a limp mass, as the bottle smashed.

Cyrano blinked, then stared down in gaping, slack-jawed realization; upon the instant, he was half sobered. Dimly the penalties pierced to his brain; the archers of the watch, imprisonment in the Châtelet, perhaps the scaffold or gibbet. His hand groped for a full wine bottle, and he lifted it to his lips, gulped down the wine, then lowered the bottle and stared anew. After a moment he leaned over and touched the fallen man. There was no mark where the bottle struck, but Luynes was dead. His skull had been broken.

The eyes of Cyrano darted about. They were alone; the swift incident had passed unseen. He staggered, then stooped and with an effort lifted the limp body, placing it in the corner of the window-seat. He arranged it there in a natural position, and pulled down the wide-brimmed beaver over the eyes of the cavalier.

A part of his brain was clearly enough at work. Now he stooped and retrieved his scattered writing materials, picked up his unfinished letter, and stood swaying as he eyed it drunkenly.

"Ha, my good Bergerac—my good poet, my good lover, my good rogue!" he muttered. "What though she will never read it! This is little short of sublime. But now—"

He thrust the letter into his pocket, sagged down into his seat, poured more wine.

THE HAPLESS Cyrano was already in the depths of debt, drunkenness and dissipation, with all his future a hopeless blank. Cursed with a nose larger than that of other men, a hooked eagle's beak that gave him the look of a bird of prey, he had entered the guards.

Pretending to be a Gascon noble, and taking the name of Bergerac, he had won a place among the swashbuckling Gascon fighters. He served the sword well, becoming the deadliest rapier in all Paris, so that men laughed at him and his nose no more, but feared him, and wisely so.

However, the sword served him ill. He was repeatedly wounded on campaign.

But that was nothing; the tragedy came in Paris. One day,

embroiled with a crowd of lackeys, he mistook a trained monkey for a man and killed the animal.

Thus ended Cyrano the guardsman. Laughed out of his world by mirth that would not down, he forswore the sword. Vowing he would never wear rapier again, he turned to the philosopher Gassendi at the College of Lisieux, and took up the pursuit of letters. For the past year, gambling, dissipation and the dregs of Paris had claimed him. Money he had none, save what he could borrow or win at dice. His family shunned him. Thus, at the age of twenty-three.

There was, however, this peculiarity about M. Savinien de Cyrano; what he lacked in scruple, he made up in roaring mirth, and he had respect for no man.

The host came into the place with a tray of wine and stopped short, looking around for the cavalier. As it chanced, Cyrano was not known at this particular tavern; his own haunts were across the Seine. He looked up and beckoned.

"Here we are—your man has gone to sleep. Leave the wine. I can use it."

The host came to the table, glanced at the apparently sleeping cavalier, and set down his tray. He regarded Cyrano dubiously.

"As to payment, *monsieur*—there is already a matter of three crowns for wine."

"Leave it, leave it," and Cyrano waved his hand grandly. "I have not finished."

The host, being impressed by the fact that his drunken and questionable customer could write, decided to chance payment, and departed. Cyrano poured more wine and gulped it down. Then he stared at the limp figure opposite.

"Think, M. de Bergerac, think!" he murmured. "Think yourself out of this in a hurry, my poor Savinien! This man is a grandson of the great Marshal de Luynes, who sprang, it is true, from the lesser *noblesse*; but you spring from no *noblesse* whatever. Now you must use your wits, or you'll end like poor Villon on the gibbet! Come, wits, come! Pox on me! If I were not so drunk—let's see, now."

He leaned far over the table, and his long arms sent prying fingers over the body of Luynes. It was true that the latter came of a renowned family, but for a year or two past had fallen into some disgrace and had been exiled to his estates. This would not avail his slayer, however.

Cyrano pulled forth gold pieces, silver coins, a fat silken purse, papers, a sealed packet and an unsealed letter. He sat blinking at them for a moment, dizzily, until his eyes focused upon the letter. It was addressed to M. d'Effiat, at his chambers in the Louvre.

"*Mordious!* What's this?" Cyrano clutched at it, spread it open. "Effiat? That will be the cousin of M. le Grand Equerry Cinq-Mars, favorite of the king! Here, now!"

The portion of his befuddled brain which was a trifle sober, slowly comprehended the lines of writing that greeted him:

> DEAR COUSIN:
>   Make use of the bearer. He is not acquainted with our plans,
> but is favorable to our cause. He has great ability, and can be
> of extreme value to us. As yet no further news.
>   CINQ-MARS.

Cyrano did not attempt to pierce beyond externals. The instant he read this epistle, he perceived salvation in it. Effiat obviously was not acquainted with M. de Luynes, who was not named in the letter. A wide grin showed Cyrano's large and even teeth, and his sudden roaring laugh shook the glasses on the table.

"Ha!" he exclaimed, sweeping coins, purse and sealed packet into his pocket. "Quick, now! M. Savinien de Cyrano, you are no more; I baptise thee M. le Marquis de Bergerac! Aye, a marquis at the very least. Off with you, before they examine yonder clay! Here's a friend, shelter, money—a whole purse of gold pieces! But you can't appear at the Louvre in this shape. Stop on the Pont Neuf, aye! A barber, a decent suit; half an hour at most. Then to the Louvre, with honest lies ready to hand. Ha, there's fortune in it! On with the game, Cyrano!'"

He perceived the host at the door, called to him, drained a last flagon of wine.

"Here, my good man," and Cyrano gave him a gold piece. "Keep the change, I beg of you. Let this gentleman sleep; he said not to waken him for an hour at least."

The inn-keeper bowed and scraped. Cyrano gathered his rags about him, and sauntered forth. Once in the street, he turned and made for the Pont Neuf as rapidly as his unsteady legs would bear him. Oddly enough, his muscles were seldom affected by liquor, but it fired his imagination, stimulated his brain—and usually ruined him completely.

IN HIS room on the second floor of the Louvre sat M. Claude d'Effiat, Sieur d'Ernonville, titular Abbé of the great fortress of Mont St. Michel. He was the only gentleman at present occupying the Louvre palace of the Kings of France. Three years with the embassy in Venice had ended a few months since, when he found himself invested through Cinq-Mars's influence with the splendid fief of Mont St. Michel, which had been stripped from the Duc de Guise.

A touch of fever had kept Effiat from going south with the court; and now he was the picture of a great noble, with his frills and laces, his pomades and dogs and horses, his daintiness and his lechery, as became the cousin of the royal favorite. But in the eyes of Claude d'Effiat was a steely glint, in the set of his long and narrow jaw was a firmness, such as his debauched cousin Cinq-Mars never knew.

He was a handsome gentleman, not well known at court. When the rebellion of Guise, in the previous year, sent that prince into exile, many men had desired that marvelous abbey of wealth and beauty, the impregnable fortress of Mont St. Michel; Effiat had obtained it. True, he had never seen his abbey, but he enjoyed its net revenues of 20,000 livres, which was the main thing.

"*Monsieur*, a gentleman with a letter. The Marquis de Bergerac."

Mervaut, Effiat's lackey, stood in the door. He was a wide-shouldered rogue with heavy, sullen features, but had a way with women, and had served Effiat well.

"Admit him," said Effiat carelessly, and surveyed himself in his mirror. If M. d'Effiat was handsome, his raiment was superb. His suit of scarlet silk, slashed with silver and sewed in patterns with seed pearls, had cost nine thousand crowns. His narrow features held pride and arrogance, with some reason; also, he could be charming when he so desired. Hard and cold as steel were his gray eyes, yet at times, as those who had faced his rapier well knew, they could glow and scintillate with sparks of cruel light.

Cyrano entered and bowed—not the same man who had sat in the Three Kings, but a Cyrano cleansed, shorn, shaved, clad in passable garments, with a magnificent silver-hilted poniard at his girdle. The silver hilt bore, after the fashion under Henri IV, very elaborately chased arms, and Cyrano had paid two livres for it at a booth on the Pont Neuf.

"You seek me, *monsieur?*" asked Effiat, surveying his visitor curiously. Cyrano bowed and presented his letter.

"This will speak for me, *monsieur*," he rejoined. He was apparently quite master of himself, but his glassy eye and thick tongue told a different story. "I have but just reached Paris; my fool of a lackey took my spare horse and portmanteau to my lodgings, and I hastened here without awaiting a change of clothes."

"You did well," said Effiat dryly. "At this hour to-morrow I shall be gone. Ha! The hand of Cinq-Mars! You are from the South?"

CYRANO ASSENTED and twirled his mustaches with his best Gascon air, as Effiat scanned the paper. If his assumed manner of Gascony had fooled all the Gascons in the guards, it was assuredly good enough to deceive Sieur d'Effiat.

"Alexandre Hercule Savinien de Cyrano, Marquis de Bergerac, at your service, *monsieur!*" he declaimed grandly. "I have been for some years with the army in Italy, and have had the honor of commanding a regiment for His Majesty the King of Hungary; but upon coming into my estates returned to France and had the pleasure of meeting your very excellent and worthy cousin. Since my time is my own, he suggested that I might settle certain business in Paris and—"

"Pray be seated, *monsieur*. I am charmed to make your acquaintance," said Effiat. "Most unfortunately, I am compelled to leave Paris to-morrow. It would give me great pleasure if you would accompany me to my abbey of Mont St. Michel."

"There or to the moon," said Cyrano, refusing the proffered chair. "No, no wine, I beg of you! I have drunk too much already. I am mortified at appearing in these miserable garments, *monsieur*, and beg of you to excuse my appearance and lay it to my anxiety to present myself."

Effiat was somewhat astonished at the words of this strange marquis, but they showed him the truth—or a little of it—and he broke into a laugh.

"A frank confession, M. de Bergerac; you are absolved!" he exclaimed. "You have lodgings, then? Or may I offer you hospitality?"

"Thank you, *monsieur*, I am provided," said Cyrano.

"Very well. You are weary, you have business—suppose we appoint a meeting for the morrow? That is to say, if your affairs will permit a departure."

Cyrano gestured magnificently. "My affairs are not many. Chief of them is the excellent Barsac they used to have at that tavern behind the Palais Cardinal, at the corner of the Rue des Bon Enfants—the *cru* of '35. An admirable wine, *monsieur!* It is like the ichor of the gods. No, that's not the word either. Nectar and ambrosia—eh?"

"Correct." Effiat chuckled softly. "Shall we meet there at noon to-morrow, then?"

"With all my heart, *monsieur*," and Cyrano bowed profoundly. "Ready for campaign."

"Agreed, then!"

Cyrano left the Louvre in a most confused state; yet, at the
back of his head, he remembered what had happened. He was
to meet Effiat on the morrow and leave Paris with him; excellent! Meantime, he had a few debts to pay and must have clothes
worthy of his new estate. The better to ponder this, he dropped
into the first wine shop on the quay, one of many which catered
for the gentlemen of the guards, and ordered something to eat
and more to drink.

The meal steadied him if it did not sober him, and two more
bottles of wine served to bring him into a very singular condition indeed. In the midst of his meal he felt something hard in
his pocket and drew it forth. It was the sealed packet he had
taken from M. de Luynes. He set it on the table, looked at it,
turned it over, looked at it again.

A queer sort of sobriety seized upon him; a frozen sense of
most deadly peril.

A silk cord tied about the packet was sealed, and with the
seal of Cardinal de Richelieu. On the other side was an address:
Père Hugo Carré, at the Novitiate of Preaching Friars, in Rue
St. Jacques.

Founded by Richelieu for his own purposes, this establish-
ment of Dominicans embraced the whole system of espionage
and news reports started by Père Joseph, the "Gray Cardinal,"
and greatly developed since his death. Cyrano, like every one
in Paris, knew that it were better to stand as a felon before the
high court of Parliament than to incur the anger of Père Carré.
What was more to the point, he now understood that M. de
Luynes had carried a private letter, and also dispatches from
Richelieu to Père Carré; and these dispatches now lay under
his hand!

"Devil fly away with me!" swore Cyrano, hastily putting the
packet out of sight. "I only wish he would! What now? If I

destroy these letters, every spy in France will seek to unearth the slayer of Luynes; were I hidden in the Bastille, they would uncover me! If, on the other hand—by the saints!"

A startling idea had come to him, an amazing idea; it was fraught with peril enough, but it was his only chance. He seized his wine flagon and drained it, staring wide-eyed at the wall. Of course, he dared not lie to Père Carré, who could discover all about him within an hour's time; yet, why not?

Cyrano ordered another bottle of wine.

WITHIN THE long gray building in Rue St. Jacques there was a large and curious room. Books and manuscript cases lined the walls. At the head of a huge and massive table where four secretaries were busy among documents and ink-pots, sat a man with long and shrewd visage, probing eyes, tight lips. To this table and this man came letters, reports, messengers from all France and half the world besides.

The armies of Richelieu were poorly trained rabbles; his victories were won in Rue St. Jacques. Daily couriers departed thence, bearing the gist of this far-flung news system, boiled down into succinct words by the worthy father superior, Père Carré. In these latter days the great cardinal was wasting away, dying by inches, and all details were left to others; even his letters were to go unsigned until his death at the year's end, thanks to the ulcers which left him helpless.

Père Carré opened documents, scanned each with swift gaze, and spoke. One secretary took down the summary to be incorporated in the daily report to the cardinal at Narbonne. Another took down the reply to the epistle itself. A third took down any further letters occasioned by the paper. The system was swift, sure and comprehensive; it gave Richelieu a great advantage over his ill-informed foes or rivals for power, such as Cinq-Mars, who worked often at cross-purposes.

A bell tinkled. A monk entered.

"Reverend father, a courier with dispatches from Narbonne."

The superior made a gesture and the secretaries, dropping

their work, left the room. A moment later Cyrano was ushered in. He was deadly pale, and made a profound bow as he fumbled in his pocket with shaking fingers.

"*Monsieur,*" he said, "by chance I have come into possession of certain dispatches, which I believe should be placed in your hands. By your leave."

He stiffly extended a paper. Père Carré took it, opened it, and stared up again at Cyrano in startled astonishment.

"What's this, *monsieur!*" he exclaimed. "It appears to be a letter addressed to Mlle. de Gisy; from the opening sentence, indeed, a letter which—"

A deep groan burst from Cyrano.

"Your pardon, your pardon—oh, the saints deliver me! What have I done? Here, *monsieur,* is the proper packet."

He held out the sealed packet and repocketed his own letter. Père Carré eyed him sharply and perceived something of the truth.

"Who are you, *monsieur?*"

"M. Savinien de Cyrano de Bergerac."

The brows of the father superior lifted a little. He had, obviously, heard of M. de Bergerac. Then he gestured to the table.

"Be seated, *monsieur.* I have ordered refreshments; you will honor me by partaking of them while I glance through these documents. You did not bring them from Narbonne, I gather?"

"No, *monsieur,*" said Cyrano in a dead voice. He was perspiring heavily as he sat down.

A lay brother entered with a tray and set it on the table, and Cyrano was not averse to the excellent wine which greeted him. None the less, he was aware of his peril, and kept a sharp eye on the father superior.

PÈÈRE CARRÉ ran through the papers with practised eye, then picked up one for closer reading; unsigned, it was in the writing of Cardinal Mazarin, the secretary and most trusted confidant of Richelieu. As Père Carré read, his expression changed; his eyes widened in astonishment and alarm, and his thin lips were pursed up. Then, with a swift glance at Cyrano, he swept all emotion from his face and read on.

At length he pushed aside the papers and regarded his guest with a certain intent appraisal. He knew the virtue of the maxim *In Vino Veritas;* but he did not know M. de Bergerac, whose brain was never more nimble than when half drowned in the proper fluid.

"Your hospitality, *monsieur*," declared Cyrano with gusto, "deserves my warmest thanks! I don't know when I've tasted rarer Chambertin."

"No matter, my son. Regarding these letters: how came you by them?"

Cyrano swallowed hard, "*Monsieur*, I sat in a tavern writing a letter—the very letter which I handed you in error. I do not know what tavern it was; I confess that since yesterday noon I have been drinking with Chevalier d'Harcourt and others, and have no remembrance of my whereabouts. Well, a gentleman entered the tavern, where I was alone. He was offensive. He was fresh from the South, said that M. de Richelieu was dying, said other things which I do not recall—about M. de Cinq-Mars and *Monsieur* the Duc d'Orleans. I have always had profound respect for His Eminence, *mon-sieur*, ever since certain verses of mine received his approval, and I became angry at the slurs cast upon a great man by this cavalier. I am not certain what happened, but I believe that he is dead."

"What!" Père Carré's eyes widened sternly. "Dead? You killed him, miserable man?"

"At least, *monsieur*, I resented his disparagement of the cardinal. I found myself sitting there; certain papers had fallen to the floor. One was this packet, addressed to you. Another was a letter to one M. Effiat—"

"Eh? Effiat? You are certain?" demanded Père Carré sharply. "Where is it?"

Cyrano gestured vaguely. Great drops of sweat stood on his forehead.

"I do not know, *monsieur*. The tavern—ah, I recollect now! It was the Three Kings, in Rue St. Jacques. I brought here the packet addressed to you, and resolved to confess everything and throw myself upon your mercy, reverend father."

"One moment," said Père Carré, and struck a bell. A secretary entered. "Send to the tavern of the Three Kings in Rue St. Jacques—send a party of archers from the Châtelet. See if a traveler is injured or dead there; have all his papers and effects brought here at once. Hasten!" The secretary left. Père Carré turned again to Cyrano. "*Monsieur,* this is a most serious matter. You, if I recall, are in the guards?"

"No, *monsieur*." Cyrano opened his doublet to show a ragged scar at his throat. "I've served, been wounded, and resigned. I'm now a philosopher, save the mark! That is, if Gassendi can make me one. I strongly doubt it."

"He is more apt to make you a heretic," said the friar dryly. "I have heard of you, M. de Bergerac; a swordsman, I believe. Hm! And a gentleman, since you have served in the guards. What is more to the point, you have intelligence. It pleases me."

Cyrano breathed more freely. He perceived that he was saved, and instantly his spirits rebounded in exuberant relief.

"Ah, good father, give that recommendation of me to poor Gassendi!" he cried. "Perhaps he will have some hope of me, if you vouch for my intelligence! Regarding this cavalier—"

"Let be, let be," said Père Carré, pursing up his lips. "You have rendered me a great service in bringing those papers here. A letter to Effiat, eh? Yes, my son, a great service! Had those documents fallen into the wrong hands—hm!"

Cyrano drained a bumper of wine at a draught. Père Carré looked at him, and suddenly spoke in a tone of decision.

"*Monsieur,* the letter you first showed me was addressed to Mlle. de Gisy. You know her?"

"No, my father," said Cyrano, astonished. "I—one day I saw

her pass in the street. I looked after her, asked who she might be. I saw her but the once."

THE OTHER frowned, eyed him sharply, saw that he spoke the truth. "Well, my son, I have something to propose to you: a very honorable engagement in the service of His Majesty."

Cyrano took instant alarm. He knew very well that he was dealing with a more subtle and deadly antagonist than any swordsman.

"Alas, how could I refuse such an offer!" he exclaimed earnestly. "Yet I have close relatives in the church, and religion holds the first place in my life. I am leaving Paris to-morrow in order to fulfill a vow that I have too long postponed. I am making the pilgrimage to the abbey of Mont St. Michel, father."

"Indeed! That is most singular, my son, most singular!" Père Carré studied him with odd intentness at the mention of this particular destination. "And you leave to-morrow?"

"About noon, *monsieur,*" said Cyrano.

"Hm! Would it be possible for you to pass this way to-morrow morning, my son?" said the good friar, with his most friendly air. "I recollect that in the chapel treasury we have a blessed amulet containing a fragment of feather said to have fallen from the wing of the archangel when he appeared to the holy St. Aubert and commanded the building of his church at the Mont. It is true, the authenticity of this relic is somewhat in dispute, but none the less it is a precious possession. We are in your debt for these dispatches, and if you will allow me to present this amulet to you, I shall be obliged. Upon your pilgrimage, you may well find it of benefit."

Cyrano was delighted, but he was by no means blinded to the facts in the case. Finding himself dismissed, with no further mention of M. de Luynes, he lost no time in leaving the building with all possible speed.

No sooner had Cyrano departed than Père Carré summoned a secretary and gave him explicit instructions regarding the late visitor.

"Discover everything!" he concluded. "Get men to work on the instant! The chief thing is the attitude of this Bergerac toward His Eminence. If he has been concerned with any plot, I must know it. If not, he can be of inestimable use. He is of loose tongue, and inquiry at the College of Lisieux, perhaps from Gassendi, will soon determine the matter."

"Reverend father, you will have the conclusion in a report to-morrow morning."

Satisfied, Père Carré turned to his neglected dispatches, while he awaited further word about M. de Luynes and the letter to Effiat. Of the letter to Effiat, naturally, no trace was found.

CHAPTER II

—AND KEEPS HIS ENGAGEMENTS WHEN SOBER.

OVERNIGHT WAS born a new Cyrano, a brave Cyrano, so altered that none who had known the beard-blurred, sunken features of his hopeless days would know them now, despite the eagle beak of a nose; for the drowned dark eyes had become fiercely proud, and as by miracle the whole man was filled with youth and eagerness. Here indeed was one who laughed and sang and fought; a lute in silken case was slung about his shoulder, and the pistols at either side of the ornate saddle were of chased and fluted brass. Cyrano carried no sword, however.

Here was one, too, who had fallen overnight into sober reflection. The Marquis de Bergerac had a clear memory of what had passed on the previous day, he knew he was treading a desperate, slippery path—and embarked upon it with a gay and confident abandon.

Nobly had he scouted the pawnshops. Now he was perfumed and scented as any Valois, brave in the most gorgeous Genoese cut velvet imaginable. The suit was richly glowing purple, edged and pointed with gold, and the cloak was cut to match.

True, it had not been cut for Cyrano, as certain bloodstains might testify, but genius had triumphed above this sorry witness. Upon the velvet cloak were sewed seven stars in cloth-of-gold, forming an irregular pattern which quite concealed the stain and rent; a worthy dame had spent the entire night at this work, and had been well paid. Hat and plume were new, of the finest quality, and so were the high boots of red cordovan. At Cyrano's girdle shone the magnificent silver-hilted poniard purchased on the Pont Neuf. His horse was a splendid animal, worthy a duke at least.

Since the days of the great Bassompierre a more magnificent lord had seldom been seen, and those in the street stopped and stared after him, wondering what prince had come to Paris. And they had some excuse; Cyrano bore himself with majesty, while the proudly arrogant flash of his eye was a danger signal. Gold in his pocket, intrigue afoot—he was living, in thought and deed, the new self he had assumed. Here was, in sober truth, the Marquis de Bergerac.

It was two hours before noon. Cyrano rode across the Pont Neuf, twirled his mustaches at the glancing ladies, grimaced at Briocci's puppet show, where he had spitted that abominable, unlucky monkey, and turned his horse toward Rue St. Jacques. He was more than ready now to match his wits against those of the cardinal's chief agent; a creature of impulse, M. de Bergerac had discarded with his old personality all fears and hesitation.

He found Père Carré in the same room where he had been received the previous day, and the father superior greeted him most cordially; whereat Cyrano took instant warning. The promised reliquary, a handsomely chased locket of gold in the shape of a star, upon a golden chain, was produced and placed about his neck with an appropriate blessing, and was devoutly received by Cyrano.

"I have heard good words of your devotion to the king and the church, *monsieur,*" said Père Carré. "Has your recent business with M. d'Effiat resulted to your satisfaction?"

Cyrano blinked. "That remains to be seen; you are aware of it, eh?"

"I am aware of many things, M. de Bergerac. Come! I have a reason for asking you to be frank with me," and the penetrating eyes bored into him. "That letter to M. d'Effiat—"

Cyrano gave no sign of his inward alarm and consternation. To impersonate a marquis was fully as grave an offense as to kill a nobleman; and he had announced himself at the Louvre under his assumed title. Spies had been set upon him, evidently—

"*Monsieur,*" he said gravely, "I confess that yesterday I was drunk; I am not well aware of what I did or what I said. I can only beg of you to ascribe to my intentions the merit they deserve. As I recall, I have an engagement to meet M. d'Effiat at noon, and to ride with him to Mont St. Michel. The reason, I do not know. Have I said enough?"

"Enough to hang you, my son, if need were." Père Carré was silent for a moment; in this moment, and in those shrewd appraising eyes, lay deep peril. Then the father superior smiled. "However, *monsieur,* I believe you; and I know your devotion to His Majesty, of which you bear honorable proofs upon your body. You are a gentleman by training, if not by birth. So, I am going to risk a little in order to gain much, and give you an errand at Mont St. Michel."

HALF IN relief at these words, half in deeper alarm, Cyrano remained silent; for once his dark gaze was intent and piercing. He knew that his entire destiny might well be hinging on this interview. Now Père Carré went on speaking, in a low and purring voice, and Cyrano girded himself for a battle of wits.

"My son, in the very household of France are traitors. Rebellion and treachery threaten her from within and without—that is to say, as a very present possibility. There is even some fear lest the most impregnable jewel of the crown, that fortress against which all the might of England was shattered, may be handed over to enemies. I speak of this same royal château and abbey of Mont St. Michel."

Cyrano looked wide-eyed. "But we are not at war with England!"

"We are at war with Austria; with Germany, Spain, Italy! The Huguenots are ready to rise in new rebellion. France itself rose in revolt last year under the princes of the blood, and is ready to rise again."

"Oh! That is true," said Cyrano, as though impressed by the fact.

"Further, the state is upheld by one man, at present; and against him, lesser men conspire. You are not a fool, my son."

Decidedly not. Cyrano knew now whither all this tended. It was generally enough whispered that Cinq-Mars plotted against Richelieu—and with Cinq-Mars were the Duc d'Orleans, the Prince of Sedan, and others. The Red Minister had enemies, more enemies than friends.

"And M. d'Effiat," murmured Cyrano thoughtfully, as if realizing it for the first time, "is a near relative of the Grand Equerry, M. de Cinq-Mars!"

"Exactly," said the father superior, watching him with close scrutiny. "You go with him; excellent! I ask you to inspect Mont St. Michel. Regard its defenses, its guards, the possibility of the Mont or of its sister isle, Tombelaine, being delivered to an enemy. This service can be performed only by a gentleman of intelligence, of action, of initiative, by one who has the eye of a soldier. I know your record, *monsieur*, and am satisfied of your loyalty. Hence, I ask your aid."

"The matter," observed Cyrano as though to himself, "would of course depend upon the action to be pursued, were action necessary."

A trifle startled, Père Carré pondered this speech for a moment. Cyrano, as a matter of fact, had leaped from alarm to vast self-confidence. Instead of facing a cell, he was becoming an agent of Richelieu. Being an extremist in all things, it was natural that he should at once dart to the offensive.

"Hm!" said the friar. "Your exact meaning?"

"A question of scruple, good father." Cyrano twirled his mustache, gave Père Carré look for look. "Come, we are alone; let us be frank! I cannot ride with a man as his friend, and act the spy, make reports upon him, betray him. No, no! But, once convinced that this man was a traitor to his king—ah, that's another matter! That would call for action."

"So!" The thin lips of the friar curved slightly. "If there were cause for such action, as you have hinted—"

"Then, naturally, I should be in position to act," said Cyrano, with his engaging smile.

"By all means, by all means," said Père Carré. "However, we need not anticipate any emergency; this is merely a trip of inspection. We deal with the abbey, not with the abbot; the essential thing is a report upon the Mont and its condition."

CYRANO BOWED in his best guardsman's manner. He did not intend to be put off in any such fashion.

"*Monsieur*, I thank you for the honor you do me! As you may be aware, the monks of Mont St. Michel have a manor in Paris, in Rue St. Etienne-des-Grecs. I have talked with certain of them and understand that they are inclined to be jealous of their prerogatives. Also, I believe that at the present time their prior holds himself as only a little less than St. Michel himself." Cyrano paused reflectively.

"So," he continued, "being compelled to use my intelligence, it is still possible that I might be required to take action. And in case of this emergency which we do not anticipate, it were very sad if I did not have anything to show that I held a cardinal higher in the scale than an abbot or a prior! As you so truly said, *monsieur*, one must risk a little if one desires to gain much."

Père Carré regarded him half sourly, half admiringly, then broke into a slow smile.

"Upon my word, you should be a diplomat!"

"Thank you, *monsieur*. A diplomat requires rhythm, however; being a poet I have only rime." And Cyrano twirled his mustache, his black eyes dancing and glowing.

The superior nodded amusedly, opened a drawer, and sat down at the table, quill in hand. The quick eyes of Cyrano perceived the paper to be some sort of ready-written form, which Père Carré was signing. Then, sanded and cleaned, the paper was folded, and with the aid of a candle already burning, the superior sealed it. From the drawer he took a purse and extended paper and purse to Cyrano.

"There, *monsieur,* this will serve your purpose should emergency arise. And His Eminence is not niggardly; this will serve your ordinary expenses. There is but one thing I require of you, M. de Bergerac, at all costs. At all costs, you comprehend?"

Thus speaking, Père Carré rose, and his gaze became piercingly intent.

"And this one thing?"

"Is that the impregnable western bulwark of our beloved France should not pass into hostile hands."

Cyrano bowed.

Two minutes later he was in the saddle again, riding for the Pont Neuf, He was extremely satisfied with himself, as he well might be.

"Worthy father superior, how well the Marquis de Bergerac fitted into your purposes—and how well you fitted into his! Moreover, you expected to send forth a spy, and instead you dispatch an ambassador! I'm afraid M. de Richelieu would not be pleased to know you'd given me this little paper, whatever it is. Decidedly, you'll never step into the shoes of that sly little Mazarin. So Cinq-Mars conspires, and Richelieu cannot catch him at it, but hopes to catch cousin Effiat, eh?"

The thought sobered him. Effiat, he knew well, was a powerful man; Cyrano was playing with fire there.

PRECISELY UPON the stroke of noon the tavern behind the Palais Cardinal witnessed the meeting of two lordly gentlemen. Sieur d'Effiat, garbed in superb riding clothes, the Cross of St. Michel blazing on his cloak, had just arrived when the magnificent figure of M. de Bergerac swung into the courtyard and dismounted.

"Greetings, my friend, greetings!" exclaimed Cyrano gustily. "Would you believe it, that rascally lackey of mine has absconded with half of my effects? I've just seen the provost about it, and they're astir at the Châtelet. There was a diamond worth above a thousand pistoles, a gift from His Eminence himself, not to mention certain jewels presented to me by grateful ladies, and a superb rapier which I had from the King of Hungary. Well, let be! I'm ready to ride with you to Mont St. Michel or the devil. Ho, there! Wine! The Barsac of '35!"

Effiat settled down at table with him. The lackey Mervaut brought them wine and commanded dinner, and after an approving drink Effiat fell into talk. Cyrano's grandiloquent personality quite fended off any doubts as to his estate; besides, his tale of service in armies abroad was plausible enough, and not uncommon.

"*Monsieur,*" said Effiat with a certain deliberation, "I understand from my cousin that you bear the Cardinal no great love."

"Nor he me," and Cyrano's laugh rang out. "*Mordious!* That's why I left Paris in the old days, just between ourselves! A question of a lady, who favored a handsome guardsman rather than a stingy minister of state—you comprehend?"

"Good," and Effiat chuckled. "However, *monsieur,* I have a purpose in my westward journey which is not concerned with cardinals. We ride into the country to visit a lady who is a sorceress. She rides on with us—of her own will or against it. We carry her to my abbey of Mont St. Michel and talk pleasantly by the way. That is all."

"All?" Cyrano's jaw fell. "There is a sequel to that sort of comedy, *monsieur,* and it is not a comic sequel. Me, I do not care to be broken on the wheel for abduction!"

"Bah!" Effiat shrugged. "A sorceress has no protection from the law. And what's the law to me?"

True enough, and Cyrano nodded. While Cinq-Mars was Grand Equerry, favorite of the king and most powerful man in France after Richelieu, what indeed was the law to his cousin Effiat!

"Do you, by any chance, know the Tour de Gisy?" said Effiat.

There was a short silence. The home of Mlle. de Gisy! Effiat's words stunned Cyrano, but he gave no sign of it.

"Hm!" he returned at length. "Wasn't there some old scandal about Sieur de Gisy—he was a lover of Chevreuse, I think?"

"He is dead. His daughter, who is a sorceress, occupies his place. Now, she has inherited an old dispute with Mont St. Michel over certain lands which she and the abbey both claim. It may be that she will ride willingly with us, to settle this matter. In any case, I have ordered a coach to await us at Palaiseau, which is not far from the Tour de Gisy. Is it clear?"

"Not altogether," said Cyrano. "If she's not willing to come, how can we use force against a sorceress?"

Effiat looked at him, found Cyrano's dark eyes twinkling, and broke into a laugh.

"Bah! Sorcery troubles me little, nor you! She lives there almost alone, and studies the stars. She has red hair, therefore is a sorceress. It's simple."

Cyrano shook his head. He waited until Mervaut had served their meal, then drained his winecup and turned to Effiat earnestly. As a matter of fact, he knew all the gossip about Marianne de Gisy; he knew that she studied the stars and was therefore reputed a witch.

"FROM A philosophic standpoint, the experiment of mating with a sorceress would be most interesting," Cyrano observed, whereat Effiat smiled thinly. "But, *monsieur,* I gather that you

are in love with this lady? Then, I assure you, reflect! You are
making a grievous error."

"Eh? In loving her?" demanded Effiat amused.

"No; in forcing her to ride with you. Now, then, suppose I
ride to the Tower without you! For you to use force would be
fatal; for me to use force, if need be, would in no way involve
you. You might dispatch a courier at once, saying that you are
sending me in your place, being forced to post for Mont St.
Michel at once, and so forth. You comprehend?"

Effiat stared at him rather blankly.

"No; devil take me if I do!"

Cyrano broke into his hearty laugh, and stretched one hand
across the table.

"Come! In me you have found a friend, a poet, a troubadour,
a magician. I guarantee that if you leave the lady to me I can
bring her willingly to Mont St. Michel. The land dispute; over
and above that, a dozen other reasons—bah! It's the easiest
thing imaginable. Besides, the devil himself couldn't make love
in a coach."

"True," said Effiat with a laugh. "You think you can bring
her willingly, eh?"

"Upon my honor! Of her own will, and in your coach. Come,
my dear Effiat, have faith! Leave these matters to me. You see
these seven stars of my escutcheon! I'm something of a sor-
cerer myself. We shall ride, she and I, take what comes, sun or
rain or wind, love or hate! With a lady to serve, a road to ride,
a lute to pluck, a sword to swing—devil take all buts and ifs!
Leave the thing to me, and do you play the fine lover when the
time comes. You want her at the Mont; I'll have her there for
you!"

The swift blaze of those dark eyes, the infectious burst of
laughter, kindled a responsive spark in the cold gaze of Effiat.
The brain of Cyrano went dancing on in a furious gust of elo-
quence, his eyes aflame, until Effiat checked him.

"Say no more, Bergerac! You have the right of it. I'll give you a letter to the lady, telling her—"

"That I'm a student of the occult sciences," cut in Cyrano.

"Eh?" Effiat grimaced. "You cannot trick her!"

"Nonsense! I know more about wizardy than she does, I warrant!" and Cyrano's laugh filled the place like a trumpet blare. "There's never been a Bergerac burned at the stake for magic; but all the same I'm not so simple. I learned a bit of it in Hungary, and more when I accompanied an embassy to the court of Poland. So why not?"

Effiat shrugged, then put out his hand and smiled as he gripped that of Cyrano.

"Good. I thank you, and am in your debt! Willy-nilly, you'll bring her?"

"Upon my honor—if I must bundle her off neck and crop."

Effiat rose. "Then I'll to the Louvre. Wait here, and Mervaut will fetch you back the letter. He'll also accompany you as lackey, since you have no man. The coach will await you at Palaiseau. You're ready to ride? Good. You can reach Berny to-night, the Tour de Gisy some time to-morrow. Agreed?"

"With all my heart!"

"Then *au revoir*, until we meet at the Mont. Mervaut! Follow me."

And, bowing to Cyrano, Sieur d'Effiat departed in all haste.

"SOUR DEVIL—AND I must ride with you, eh?" muttered Cyrano, eying the lurching back of Mervaut. He filled his cup again and drained it, set it down, felt in his pocket, and drew forth the crumpled letter he had written on the preceding day. "Come, this will bear copying, and while he's writing his precious epistle I'll be doing mine."

Writing materials were brought by the waiter, and Cyrano set about copying out his letter which had been addressed to Marianne de Gisy. Nor was it the first letter he had ever written her, though she had seen none of them. When he had finished he leaned back and inspected it.

"Ah, sublime!" he murmured admiringly. "Better than the others—and this seems like to be delivered, for a miracle! Curious that it should come about so. I see a face pass in the street, and straightway become a fool! Well, I may not find her so pleasant on closer acquaintance. Probably her teeth will be bad or her person foul-smelling—it's usually so. Alas! Must a sorceress lose the love of Cyrano because she does not use perfume?"

He broke into a peal of harsh laughter which betrayed the irony in his words and in his heart toward all the world, including himself. Undoubtedly the ancestors of Cyrano in their native isle had eaten of that Sardinian herb which engenders bitterness of spirit.

His letter pocketed, his meal finished, his horse fed, Cyrano applied himself to the bottle until Mervaut returned to the tavern, riding a good horse. He dismounted and gave Cyrano a sealed letter addressed to Mlle. de Gisy.

"You are riding with me?" demanded Cyrano.

"Yes, M. le Marquis," said Mervaut respectfully.

"I perceive you're well trained, Mervaut. See that you don't forget it; because if you do I'll take a stick to your back in proper fashion. You comprehend?"

"Certainly, M. le Marquis!"

"To horse, then!" and Cyrano rose from the table and called for his own mount.

CHAPTER III

— DELIVERS A LETTER.

THE TOUR de Gisy was an ancient, half ruined keep, where had once been a great château and open park; house and trees had the air of things blasted. In past years the pride of Gisy had indeed been smitten to the quick, and the place now stood uncared for, looking at the world from blank eyes; despite the presence of a woman, it still bore the bitter and fiercely aloof aspect of its dead master. Solitary amid its few trees, the tower stood bleak and black, shunning men and shunned by men.

The woman dwelt here alone, with her father's two old servants; rumor said she was a sorceress from Brittany, whence came the family, and where the family lands lay. That she had the evil eye was no secret. Thus the Tour de Gisy assumed a still blacker hue in the sight of men.

There were no tenants. Those who must needs come this way of an eventide looked at the lone dark turret against the sky and signed themselves as they scurried past. The only hamlet was two miles away; hereabouts was a lonely countryside, scarred by the wars of the League.

Upon a late spring afternoon, Marianne de Gisy sat in the sunlight upon the flat roof of the old tower. At one side stood a covered telescope on its stand. Before her was a table, piled with huge tomes; she was working over a volume, copying out the figures of some long dead student of the stars. About the roof ran a parapet, breast-high.

The heiress of Gisy, to a casual eye, might have been twenty-six, or forty; as for beauty, that was a matter of opinion. The king detested red hair, and the king set the fashion. Common folk saw no beauty in hair like raw gold, shimmering with a halo in the sunlight. The face below was not lovely; it was sad and strong and weary in repose—all but the eyes. These leaped out in quick lightning blue, transformed the whole face; and when they fell into sleepy reflection the vivid eagerness was lost.

Few men sensed the peculiar wise sweetness of this face, its grave kindliness, nor even the fair rippling womanliness of the body below; they saw the mass of flaming hair, and swiftly looked away, and that was the end of it.

A startled cry from somewhere caused Marianne to lift her head sharply, staring at the opening of the stairs that ran down to the entrance court. The cry came again; then a clatter of wooden shoes on the stairs, and at the opening was revealed the head of an old woman.

"*Ma'm'selle!* They have come back, those men who were here! I said they were bad ones. Pierre has gone out to send them away, but they are bad ones, those!"

Marianne came to her feet and went to the parapet of the roof. She knew that a rabble of disbanded soldiers had passed that same morning, but any trouble was, to her, inconceivable. And yet, as she looked down, she beheld the incredible come to pass under her very eyes. Absorbed as she had been in her work, it was all as sudden and sharp as the bursting of a summer storm.

Out there in front of the tower was Pierre, her father's old servant, running, staggering, hand pressed to side as he made for shelter of the entrance. And close behind him half a dozen ragged figures pursued with shouts and curses. The afternoon sun flashed on steel. Pierre faltered. One of the ragged men leaped and struck, and Pierre fell. The others were upon him like wolves, and their blades took the life out of him. Far behind, two men on horses were just coming into sight.

THE WOMAN, watching, uttered a swift, piercing cry. Then they looked up and saw her there at the parapet.

"Sorceress!" The yell leaped up at her, wolfish in its intensity. They shook their fists, brandished crimsoned weapons, leaped in the air and hurled imprecations. "Come down to us, sorceress! Come down and play with us!"

Marianne shrank back from those faces, all aflame with passion, with greed, with cruelty, with lust. So they had heard tales of her! They meant to pillage and slay—

The hollow crash of the iron-bound portals weakened her, caused her to turn hastily to the stairway. The old crone had swung the massive doors shut; a few moments gained, at least!

Marianne was down the stone stairs lightly as a dancing flame, and, in passing, snatched from the wall her father's sword.

She came into the lower hall, where the old dame now crouched in moaning terror. Outside they were smashing at the sturdy doors, hammering, yelling maudlin curses. Drunk, then! This explained it. They had obtained liquor and had come back here to seek her out.

Abruptly, the blows and voices fell silent. There was a new voice, ringing loud and clear; then a sharper, keener yell swept up from the pack. A pistol crashed out, followed by a second. A man screamed. What was going on out there? Without hesitation, Marianne leaped at the door and swung away its massive bar; the old servant protested wildly, frantically, but she wrenched open one of the doors, unheeding.

Outside— She remembered the two cavaliers now. One of them was sitting his horse, looking around, laughing, a pistol in his hand. Three silent figures lay sprawled before the entrance. The others were running, in wild flight, pursued by the second horseman. Now Cyrano, putting up his pistol, dismounted. He turned and saw Marianne standing there in the opening.

He caught his breath sharply; the sight of her burst upon him like a vision. For an instant he stared at her, eyes wide, and before his ardent, quivering eagerness a slow tide of red crept up her face. Then he swung off his hat and swept its plume in the dust with a low bow.

"Surely this is Mme. Thessala, she whom Horace sung, whose beauty drew down the moon!" he exclaimed. "Daughter of the sun, gloriously crowned with fire and ruddy gold, I salute you! I came hither, seeking no goddess, but a mortal woman, one Mme. de Gisy—"

"Who stands before you," broke in Marianne, "and who owes you gratitude, *monsieur.*" If the grandiloquence of Cyrano tempted a smile to her lips, it was banished by his very earnestness, by his astonishing and impulsive ardor. He produced a sealed paper and handed it to her.

"Here are my credentials, *mademoiselle*. M. d'Effiat prayed me to stop and make you his compliments and to place myself at your service. I am indeed honored that our arrival was timely. My lackey is attending to those rogues."

Marianne regarded him for a moment, then smiled.

"Ah! I had a courier from M. d'Effiat last night," she replied. "You are, then, M. le Marquis de Bergerac?"

"True, dear lady!" broke in Cyrano, a sonorous ring to his voice. "I cannot look into your eyes and live a lie! No, I'm called Marquis de Bergerac indeed, but my name is Cyrano. By the seven stars, Cyrano is name enough! And if it must bear title, then in God's love a title o' some meaning! Marquis of Poesy—Duke of Wine-bibbing—Prince of the Seven Stars. Aye, there it is! Marquis of the Seven Stars, *mademoiselle,* at your eternal service!"

If Marianne did not comprehend the mad words, at least she perceived a certain wild earnestness behind them, and with a quiet smile, held out her hand to Cyrano.

"Enter, *monsieur,*" she said. "The house is yours; make yourself at home. I pray you, excuse me a space until I get my old nurse calmed. I have no other servants."

She vanished inside. Cyrano turned, as Mervaut approached, and ordered the lackey to take care of the horses, remove the bodies, and make himself useful. Then he followed Marianne into the building.

NOW, FIERCELY exultant over the fortune which had brought him here at such a moment, the Marquis of Seven Stars strode up and down a somber room whose walls were adorned with tattered tapestry and old portraits. The furniture in the room consisted of but a large table, loaded down with books, and a few chairs. Laughing suddenly at some thought, Cyrano strode to the table, seized on the topmost book, and whistled amazedly when he had opened it. Then, fumbling under his doublet, he produced a folded letter.

When Marianne came into the room, Cyrano was standing at the window, and swung about to meet her.

"*Monsieur,* I owe you deepest gratitude," she said earnestly. "Pray consider yourself and your lackey as my guests. He must help us with the service, for we live simply here, but we can make shift. Sieur d'Effiat—"

"Has been called to his fief of Mont St. Michel," said Cyrano. "I am also bound thither, with pilgrimage in mind—and other things more important. But what's this I see?" He broke off, took a step to the table, and opened a book there. His astonished gaze went to Marianne. "The 'Clavicule' of Solomon! And beneath it the work of Rabbi ben Chomer. Ha, a miracle, no less! To find these books of witchcraft and magic—"

Marianne looked a trifle startled. "There is much of interest in them, and no witchcraft," she said, and watched him turning over the leaves of the book.

"Aye, interesting," said Cyrano. "Nicetas mentions it in his life of Comnenus, and—"

She put out a hand and checked him. "There is something between the pages; what is it? A paper? A letter? Strange!"

Cyrano carelessly removed the letter and she turned it over in her hand, with an air of puzzled wonder.

"Addressed to me—and I never knew it was there! Your pardon, *monsieur.*"

She broke the seal, opened the letter, glanced swiftly through it. A little color came into her face, then she looked up and smiled.

"It is nothing. Pray be seated, *monsieur;* we shall have food and wine shortly. So you go on pilgrimage to the Mont?"

"Well," said Cyrano, when he had placed a chair for her and taken another himself, "I go on pilgrimage, of a sort." His gaze was whimsical, his dark eyes were laughing. "My real aim is less worthy. Look at the books there on the table; each book represents a man, you comprehend? A legacy to the world. Well, if Cyrano were to write a book, what then? Look you! These

many months I've been studying with Gassendi in the College
of Lisieux, and what's the end of it all, of these learned doctors
and professors? Talk, talk, talk! A man can make no impression
on the world by talking. Either he creates, or he vanishes
utterly!"

"Why make an impression?" Marianne regarded him
amusedly. "Vanity of vanities!"

"True, yet the urge is in us," said Cyrano soberly. "What good
in talking, scribbling, philosophizing? A man has hands and
brain. If he can combine them, whether in book or painting or
what not, he leaves something in the world he found not there.
Did you ever hear of Lady Tiphaine of Brittany?"

Marianne shook her head, watching the ardent, impulsive
Cyrano with thoughtful gaze.

"She was wife to Bertrand du Guesclin," he went on. "While
Bertrand was fighting the English, and was prisoner in Spain
for five long years, Lady Tiphaine sat in her house atop Mont
St. Michel and studied the stars, and wrote books about them.
Her manuscripts are all in the library of the monks. Well, I go
to see what she left to the world."

"What?" Marianne's eyes widened. "She studied the stars—
and left manuscripts?"

"Aye, one of the monks told me," said Cyrano. "Does this
interest you, who also study the stars? Well, well, go on pilgrimage, too! Simple enough. I'll have a coach at Palaiseau, and you
shall share it with all my heart."

Marianne made no response to this. The old crone hobbled
in, bearing a tray which she set on the table.

WHEN THE wine was poured, the Lady of Gisy studied
Cyrano, appraising him with her quiet eyes, those eyes so gravely
kind, so wise, yet so filled with a girl's laughter. As they sipped
the wine and sat in talk, Cyrano was aware that she was searching out the depths of him, weighing him in the balance of her
mind. And he was aware of the subtle power that emanated
from her, wakening his pulses.

So, abruptly, being a man of no tact and great impulse, he brought up the question of Sieur d'Effiat. In reply to his query, Marianne scrutinized him thoughtfully.

"What do I think of him? A strange question, *monsieur*. He is your friend."

"He is not," said Cyrano flatly. "I'd put sword into him with pleasure. He means you no good, let me tell you."

"Oh! I know that already," said she, and looked at him all smiling. Now he was confused, perceiving that there was a great deal this woman knew. "Cyrano—a singular name! And a singular device, if those stars are a device!" And she indicated the seven stars on his cloak.

"Ah, *mademoiselle!*" said Cyrano. "You, who study the stars, know not this device?"

"Not I, indeed."

"Why, look you!" With his long finger, Cyrano followed the design of those seven stars until he had connected them in lines. "They are my device indeed and my symbol, but more, they show the fate of all France, of this great kingdom! There is the word, *Caah* in the Hebrew," he went on swiftly, eagerly. "It signifies a man struck down, ill, without hope. Well, that is my own case! But look at the astrology of it, at the inner meaning read by Rabbi Chomer in that very book on the table there! The letter Aleph, in the center, is given numerically the number one, or one thousand; the first letter in this word is numbered twenty, the third, five. Thus we have one thousand and twenty-five years which this Realm of France will endure from its foundation. And granting it was founded in 768 A.D., then in the year 1793 the kingdom will fall—"

Marianne de Gisy broke into laughter so unassumed that it silenced Cyrano.

"My dear marquis, do you expect to live another hundred and fifty years to prove your astrology true? Surely you place no faith in this sort of star-divination, in this superstitious mummery? Why do you indulge in such foolish nonsense?"

Cyrano grimaced, then broke into a frank laugh. "Oh, it is amusing at times," he said with his air of naïve gayety. "Besides, those stars stand for many other things, dear lady."

"Who are you?" she demanded, quietly persistent. "Come, tell me. From what part of France are you; where did you learn your wizardry?"

Sudden misery leaped into the dark eyes—misery so acute, so terrible, that the sight of it blanched the cheeks of Marianne.

"Dear lady," said Cyrano in a low voice, "ask me that question again, some day—but not to-day. Lie to you I cannot and will not, yet I would know you for a little day or two, be your friend if I might, help you if it lies in my power; I do not want to tell you the truth lest the cup of sweetness be taken from my lips."

"Very well," she said quietly. "At least you are a true magician, since your touch brings unguessed letters to light! But you have interested me with your mention of Dame Tiphaine. I study the stars in my own poor way, having a taste for it. If it be true that the wife of Bertrand du Guesclin left manuscripts—"

"True, indeed," broke in Cyrano. "The monks have a house in Paris, in Rue Etienne-des-Grecs, and I have talked with them at times. These Benedictines of St. Maur are historians and writers; they delve into old matters and ancient books. Yes, I assure you it is true."

"And you go to the Mont? I am indeed tempted," she returned thoughtfully. "However, I have the feeling that behind all this is something you have not told me; some purpose you have left unsaid. Is it so, my dear marquis?"

FOR AN instant Cyrano hesitated; then, as though her kindly, quiet eyes stripped away all defenses, he flung caution to the winds and burst forth in swift mad impulse.

"Yes, it is true. This rascal Effiat is behind it! Figure the thing for yourself, dear shining lady! He had certain intents, certain plans all laid. He told me of them. 'Nonsense!' I said. 'Leave the matter to me. If you desire this lady at the Mont, then I'll fetch her there to you! I will bring her.' I told him this to throw him

"Come! A kiss, little pagan!" they jeered.

off the track, dear lady. You will not go there, of course—oh, I had fine dreams about it! I thought I might escort you there, preserve you, lay down my life for you. Bah! All folly. Rank madness. Better for me to tell you the truth, thus, and then bid him to the devil if he asks why you did not come."

Her eyes, resting steadily upon his face, showed no astonishment at this disclosure.

"The truth is always better, my friend," she said softly. "I think that I may go with you to Mont St. Michel."

"Eh?" Cyrano opened his eyes wide. "But no—not at all! You misunderstand. I have told you the truth. Do not be tempted, dear lady, by my talk of manuscripts—oh, I am a fool, a bitter fool! Let us be sane. Sieur d'Effiat is lord of the Mont, a great noble, a powerful man.. You would run risks with the rascal."

"I? You do not know me," and Marianne laughed softly. "I would run risks with most men, though I do not like this man Effiat. When balked, he would not be a man but a devil. Still, there is the old dispute over lands, which might be settled. Then, the manuscript of Dame Tiphaine."

"Do not go," said Cyrano curtly. She eyed him for a moment.

"Perhaps I shall go," she said. "If so, then what?"

"Then you go against my advice and warning."

"What I do, I do of my own advice," said she, calmly. "Besides, you have promised Effiat to fetch me to the Mont."

"Bah! That is nothing," broke out Cyrano earnestly. "Now that I have met you, it is another thing entirely. You are more than I ever dreamed you could be. My promise to him meant nothing."

"I really think that I shall go," said Marianne de Gisy. "This Effiat has no real love for me; he does not know the meaning of the word. His pride is the only emotion involved. Because I refused him my favor, he is resolved to conquer me; like many of these court gentry, he considers a woman an inferior being. Perhaps he may learn a lesson! So, then; supposing I do go with you—would you be my friend?"

Cyrano read in her eyes that she would indeed go, that his protests were unheeded, that his warnings were less than the winds of heaven to her calmly poised spirit. So, being the man he was, he instantly swung over to the other extreme. If she would go, good! Why not? He warmed to the thought.

"Would I, indeed!" he exclaimed eagerly. "Excellent! It is settled! I am more than friend, dear lady—a very troubadour who would lay his devotion before you, who would gladly die in your service! Let us go adventuring, then. You, to run your risks, settle your dispute with the monks, get the manuscripts of Dame Tiphaine. I, to protect and watch over you."

Laughter shone in her eyes suddenly. "But," she said, flinging back his own words at him, "this Effiat is lord of the Mont, a great noble, a powerful man."

"Bah!" Cyrano twirled his mustache. "What is that to me? I am—Cyrano! And you are the daughter of the Sun. Such as we accept risks to gain our ends. You have lands and wisdom to gain; I, the honor of being near you for a little while. So—it is settled?"

"Not quite." She laughed a little at his eagerness. "Let us seek advice from the stars to-night, my dear marquis-astrologer! If the sky be not overcast, we shall see. And Pierre must be buried in the morning. May I send your lackey to seek the priest?"

S O I T was arranged, and neither of them showed any surprise at this very surprising conversation. Marianne de Gisy had few contacts with the artificially polite world, and, like Cyrano, was a person who spoke with slight pretense or concealment. They had known each other a scant hour, and were at ease.

That night, however, Marianne sought no advice from star-calculations. Alone in her own chamber, she opened the letter so magically produced from the "Clavicule" of Solomon, and spread it in her candle-light. The writing was large, scrawled, filled with character. The words were singular in the extreme:

MADAME:
I stood in the street and saw you pass, a daughter of the Sun. And you will never know me.

Should I weep, should I write, should I die? Better to write; my ink-horn will supply more ink than mine eyes would furnish tears. Did I seek solace in death, it were vain; Paris is closer to Gisy than is Gisy to the Elysian Fields! But what can I write you? Nothing, Goddess of the Flaming Hair—nothing and everything! Despair flows from my quill; you looked at me there in the street, and in your eyes I saw that were I of your world you would know me—but there are seven stars, and I have drowned them all.

Good! Let me serve you. Send me your commands; address your letters to the St. Jacques cemetery. Your messenger will always have news of me there. He may learn my lodging from the grave-digger or from my epitaph. He will there read that, as I had no hope of meeting and knowing you in this world, I have departed for the other—being well assured that you will come there. It may serve as some consolation, that to guarantee you from the impertinence of the Devil, you will there find this poor devil
YOUR SERVITOR

Marianne lifted puzzled eyes.

"Strange words—yet a certain something glitters through them!" she murmured. "Written by a madman, or by a genius. 'Seven stars, and I have drowned them all!' And he, down below, with his odd whimsical talk about seven stars—of course he put the letter there and uncovered it. Queer, impulsive man! What is his purpose behind all this nonsense? Why did he come here? Did he tell me the truth about Effiat, that cold, debauched, crafty creature?"

So she pondered the letter of Cyrano, and Cyrano himself, and the "adventure" to which he called her; yet she did not reread Effiat's letter, urging her to come to Mont St. Michel and adjust the land dispute, and introducing the Marquis de Bergerac. There was nothing in his letter to demand rereading.

But for a third time she read the letter of Cyrano, and then stared into the candle-light, and her eyes were very sweetly thoughtful, and smiling.

CHAPTER IV

—IS ELSEWHERE.

EVENTS OF considerable bearing on the distant Cyrano were transpiring in the south of France, in ancient Narbonne, whence the rabble army of France was driving the Spaniards back beyond the Pyrenees.

Armand Jean du Plessis, Cardinal and Duke de Richelieu, minister and virtual ruler of France, was closeted with one of the secretaries of state, Chavigny.

"How much time have we, Chavigny?" asked Richelieu, weary of dictating letters. His sharp, ascetic features were wan and worn with suffering, and the gray hair fell lank and sweat-thick about his head. His right arm, covered with ulcers, was useless.

"His majesty will not arrive before an hour, *monseigneur.*"

"Good. Will you have the kindness to send M. de Mazarin to me?"

Chavigny gathered up his papers, bowed, and withdrew.

Richelieu lay in his great traveling-bed, whose scarlet curtains were drawn back for air. These curtains were embroidered with the cardinal's hat and arms, as though in mockery of the wasted figure on the pillows inside. Since the minister at this time dreaded assassination, and with good reason, the doors were guarded and the antechambers were filled with his adherents and guards.

Dying, Richelieu might be; but to the dismay of those who thought him moribund, his will was unshaken. As though to deny approaching dissolution, never had his genius been so savagely alert to the peril surrounding him. He himself, and all France, were approaching a crisis with each fleeting moment; and he was preparing to meet it undismayed.

Louis XIII had left the court in Tarascon and had come to Narbonne, himself carried in a litter. The king, also dying by slow degrees, had no suspicion of the intrigues, the gathering treachery, the rising menace threatening to overwhelm minister, king and country. Richelieu kept grim silence about these things; he must first have conclusive evidence before he attempted to bring the greatest nobles in France to scaffold and exile.

At this period Richelieu was enjoying one of those brief respites from physical torture which enabled him to keep in his own hands all the threads of statecraft. From Narbonne he ruled France, conducted the war with Spain, menaced all Europe, and kept his finger on the pulse of the court in Tarascon, where his bitterest enemies were centered.

The door opened. The implacable gaze of Richelieu fell upon the sleekly handsome figure of the Italian secretary who alone possessed his entire confidence, and the cold eyes warmed a little.

Four years previously, at the age of thirty-seven, Giulio

Mazarini had become a naturalized Frenchman. With this act he opened his very simple campaign—to make himself so indispensable that, when Richelieu died, Mazarin must take his place. He possessed a perfect poise, a shrewdness which nothing could disturb, an ambition which nothing could satisfy, and an ability which none could equal. Richelieu trusted him.

Bowing profoundly, Cardinal Mazarin came forward and arranged his papers on the table beside the great bed.

"The Paris courier has arrived?" asked Richelieu.

"Yes, your eminence," lisped Mazarin. He had never rid himself of the soft Italian accent which infuriated so many people. Now, settling himself at the table, he took up the papers and began to go through the reports.

"OF THE utmost importance, *monseigneur;* our London agent states that two ships have been secretly outfitted at Falmouth and are on the point of sailing. It is supposedly a private enterprise for the New World, backed by certain Puritan leaders, among them a M. Cromwell. That is all."

A savage gleam lighted the cold gaze of Richelieu.

"Ah, these Puritans!" he murmured with distaste. "I knew it, I knew it. You comprehend, M. Mazarin? Two ships—more than enough to seize the fortress! Cinq-Mars has arranged with Montgommery, the Huguenot chief. A private enterprise can always be disclaimed by London. But go on."

Mazarin proceeded with the reports already summarized in barest details by Père Carré—reports which covered the world and touched on all the politics of Europe. When he had finished, he waited in silence, caressing the goatee which he wore in imitation of his master.

"As you foretold," said Richelieu, "this is why Effiat went to Paris. He will go to Mont St. Michel—the Montgommery is already at its gates with his Huguenots—and with the two English ships—hm! Yes, we did well to warn Père Carré two days since."

"But, your eminence, we merely told him to obtain a report on the Mont. In the light of this present information—"

"Which comes from the hand of Père Carré himself," broke in Richelieu. "Trust our good father superior! Now let Effiat hang himself with his cousin's rope!"

"He is a man who stops at nothing, and he is powerful," persisted Mazarin gently. "The garrison of Mont St. Michel and of the sister island, Tombelaine, are commanded by M. de Coalin, a distant relative of the Effiats. The abbot, Effiat, is a cousin of Cinq-Mars; the garrison is composed of serfs from the mainland fiefs of the abbey; either or both might well betray the place. But the monks—ah, that is another thing entirely!"

"So!" murmured Richelieu thoughtfully. "I see! The royal commandant Coalin is the strategical point, eh? Yet it is a delicate matter. I would not give any cause to think that we suspect anything."

"Oh, *monseigneur*, it is very simple!" lisped Mazarin. "There is the position in the king's household which M. de Chavigny has solicited for his cousin. We will contrive to have M. de Cinq-Mars solicit it for his relative M. de Coalin this very day. The letters of recall will be sent Coalin by special courier, post-haste, to-night. Meantime, I can get a courier off for Paris within an hour, bearing the appointment of commandant in favor of M. le Marquis de Salignan who is at his estates near Caen. The chancellor will seal the appointment and send it on at once to Marquis de Salignan with imperative orders to assume the post as swiftly as he can reach the Mont. Thus, by the time M. d'Effiat reaches his abbey, he will find an unpleas-ant surprise awaiting him. We should, of course, give Salignan full powers and a free hand to act."

"Excellent!" approved Richelieu, leaning back. "Upon my word, *monsieur*, you have conceived an admirable solution! Handle it as you suggest. Salignan is an excellent man."

MAZARIN MADE a note or two, smirking to himself. He had put a spoke in the wheel of Chavigny, who was his only possible rival for power, and had at the same time placed a strong and loyal man in command of Mont St. Michel. Now he looked up.

"*Monseigneur,* I have myself gained interesting news to-day. Cinq-Mars is in communication with the king's brother, the Duc d'Orleans; he not only anticipates your death, which may God forfend, but he would like to hasten it."

"Yes," said Richelieu dryly. "M. le Grand Equerry is ambitious; but there is no room in France for ambitious men—at present."

Mazarin discreetly lowered his eyes. "We know that Cinq-Mars and M. de Thou are behind this activity," he went on. "We know they are in touch with Madrid. We know they, and the princes, would not hesitate to make peace with Spain, to intrigue with the Huguenots, and to overthrow your eminence at any cost to France. Unhappily, we lack proof."

"Exactly; we lack proof," said Richelieu with asperity.

"His majesty may not be a wise king," murmured Mazarin, "but he has the greatest abhorrence for traitors."

"Ah!" Richelieu was watching his secretary intently. "You know something?"

"I hope to know something very soon, and have already learned a little," returned Mazarin with his usual air of deference, as though he were uttering something quite commonplace. "Perhaps your eminence already knows that the Spanish Cortes has approved a secret treaty which has been brought from Madrid and is now in possession of Cinq-Mars?"

"What?" Richelieu turned on his pillows, his eyes widening. "A secret treaty with our enemies?"

"Yes. Madrid will not trust Cinq-Mars's agents, but demands that the document be signed by Gaston of Orleans, by the Duc de Bouillon, and by—her majesty the queen."

A flash of terrible joy crossed the features of Richelieu at thus discovering how his bitterest enemies were delivered into his hand, and he lifted his eyes, as though in mute thanks to

Heaven. Then, looking again at Mazarin, a thin smile touched his lips which had not smiled for a year past.

"M. de Mazarin, we must secure this document—after it has been duly signed. You do not know its contents, of course?"

"Only in brief summary, your eminence." And Mazarin, with secret triumph, passed a slip of paper to the astounded figure on the bed. Richelieu looked it over, then let it fall, incredulous.

"IT IS past belief!" he murmured. "Well, *monsieur*, you must now lay aside every other task and devote yourself to obtaining this treaty—after it has been signed, remember."

Mazarin started slightly. "Is it worth the risk to let it be signed, *monseigneur?*" he inquired. "If by any chance it eludes us, if it is smuggled out of France—"

"If it eludes us or is destroyed, M. de Mazarin," said Richelieu, "no one would be sorrier than you, I assure you."

Mazarin turned pale. "And the means?"

"I leave to you," said Richelieu, sinking back and relaxing. "So! French territory is to be occupied by Spanish troops, and Sedan handed over to them; a Huguenot uprising, with all our blood and treasure which was spent in crushing them gone to waste; the rebellious princes back in power. France disrupted, Gaston of Orleans appointed regent in event of the king's death! All these things can be averted, M. de Mazarin, by diligence on your part. Do not fail, I warn you most solemnly!"

"I shall not fail, *monseigneur*," said Mazarin, but in his voice there was more despair than hope. "If we but knew when this document would be signed, who would carry it—"

A knock sounded at the door, which opened to disclose the austere features of the secretary, Chavigny.

"Your pardon, *monseigneur*—Père Syrmond asks for immediate speech with you."

Richelieu made a gesture of assent. The king's confessor was more important than all the gentlemen of the court put together.

Into the room came a black-robed figure of dignified, rather kindly features, and very deep-set eyes. The Jesuit saluted Richelieu with great respect.

"*Monseigneur*," he said, with a troubled air, "my only excuse for disturbing you at this hour is that I have certain information of the most urgent nature, which should come to your ears without delay."

"To you, my father," said Richelieu with his most urbane air, "my doors are always open. If you desire that we be left alone—"

"No, no, let Cardinal Mazarin remain," said the Jesuit. "As your eminence is aware, there has been in the past a certain amount of most regrettable friction in certain departments of the government—let us say, as between church and state. Unhappily, the church herself is not always at unity, thanks to her zeal in the propagation of the faith."

At this, M. de Mazarin smiled discreetly down his nose. More than once, in matters of political policy, had Richelieu been close to open breaks, not only with the Jesuits, but with the Vatican itself, And it was not Richelieu who had capitulated.

"Friction should ever be removed if possible," said Richelieu suavely. He knew that the Company of Jesus had cast longing eyes upon New France, where the Recollet fathers were developing astonishing strength and results.

"My present errand," went on Père Syrmond, "is of strictly private nature—with the minister, not with the cardinal."

"The minister is entirely at your service, my friend and father," returned Richelieu.

"The information I have for you comes from authentic sources, but I cannot quote them," said the deep-eyed Jesuit. "This information concerns three gentlemen. M. le Duc d'Orleans is at Moulins, awaiting news of certain events. M. de Cinq-Mars, the Grand Equerry, is at Tarascon. M. le Duc de Bouillon, the third gentleman, is in his city of Sedan."

Richelieu, his eyes very bright, made a slight gesture.

"In fifteen days," pursued the impassive Jesuit, "a document of most interesting nature will be sent from Tarascon to Moulins. From Moulins I believe it will be sent to Sedan. I strongly recommend that you take measures to secure this document, *monseigneur*."

"*Monsieur*, you are most kind," said Richelieu, a fierce and devout joy illumining his wasted features. "If I but knew who was to carry the document—"

"It will be carried," said Père Syrmond, "by one of Cinq-Mars's gentlemen, the Comte d'Aubijoux."

At this, Mazarin in turn raised his eyes in thankful relief.

"I do not know the nature of the document," went on the Jesuit, "but I have reason to believe that it is of great importance to the state, *monseigneur*."

"AH! BUT I know its nature!" exclaimed Richelieu. "The document was brought from Madrid. It provides that the King of Spain shall provide twelve thousand infantry and five thousand horses; this army will be given possession of Sedan by the Duc de Bouillon, who with M. de Cinq-Mars will then lead it upon Paris. At the same time, M. de Thou and others will have acted here in the south, with the army."

At these words, the features of the Jesuit became pale as death.

"But this—this is treachery to France!" he said in a low voice, staring at Richelieu. "It not only means your overthrow, it means the overthrow of France! And the king's brother, Gaston of Orleans—"

"Will prove an excellent witness for the prosecution," said Richelieu acridly. "And there is one thing more, my dear father. You may not know that in the west of France lives the grandson of that Constable de Montgommery who killed Henri II while jousting?"

"Montgommery? Yes, an arch-heretic, a leader of the Huguenots, I believe. He is said to be a trifle mad."

"He is not mad," and Richelieu's lips curved thinly. "Let us suppose, my dear father, that ships were to come from England into the Bay of Cancale, and that this Montgommery were to meet them with a Huguenot army and were to be given possession of the fortress of Mont St. Michel?"

"Heaven forbid!" The Jesuit's pallor became more accentuated. It was evident that he had known little of the treaty's contents. "Spaniards on the south, Savoy on the east, French revolutionaries marching on Paris, and English in the West? I had not imagined such things—they are incredible!"

"Their success, at least, is incredible," said Richelieu firmly. "In fifteen days; and Aubijoux carries the document! You hear, Mazarin? My father, I owe you great thanks for the information you have just given me. By the way—a curious coincidence—I was on the point of asking Chavigny to visit you. I believe there is some mention of friction in New France, or in regard to New France—some lack of coordination between the Recollet fathers there and the Company of Jesus?"

The eyes of Père Syrmond sharpened a trifle.

"*Monseigneur,*" he said humbly, "the way of those who carry the Gospel to heathen lands is not always a smooth path. It is true, the Company has envisaged great plans for work in the Canadian field, but to carry these plans out it must not be hampered by a divided responsibility."

"Have the goodness to confer with M. de Chavigny," said Richelieu. "I promise you, I shall indorse absolutely the position of the Company of Jesus in this respect. In fact, I am firmly of the opinion that they should be placed in charge of all the mission work in New France."

Joy darted across the face of the Jesuit. Next moment, Richelieu and Mazarin were alone. The Italian regarded his master with a reflective air.

"*MONSEIGNEUR,*" H E ventured, "may I bring to your recollection what you have promised madame your niece, the Duchess d'Aiguillon? As you know, she had established the Recollet fathers in New France."

Richelieu's lips twisted grimly. "*Monsieur,*" he retorted, "the sole fact to be remembered is that the Company of Jesus has saved France, which is worth everything; therefore I can well afford to give them New France, which is worth nothing. Now, *monsieur,* put all other duties aside. When this treaty has been signed by her majesty and the others, bring it to me."

"It shall be brought, *monseigneur,*" said Mazarin, and there was no longer any hint of despair in his voice.

Again a knock at the door. The captain of the cardinal's guards entered, saluted and reported that his majesty was arriving.

A singular scene ensued. Louis XIII, his life flickering, was sustained by a cruel persistence to outlive the minister whom he feared, respected, envied and admired. His traveling bed or litter was carried into the room and set down beside that of the cardinal. Wasted and pale with his own illness, the king put back the curtains and held forth one hand to Richelieu, who turned on his pillows and touched his lips to the thin fingers.

"Sire," he murmured, "you overwhelm me with kindness! That you should thus visit me—"

"Is but your due," said Louis. There was almost affection in his thin, cruel, utterly selfish features. "Good news, my friend! Perpignan is under siege and will soon be entirely invested. My physician promises that I may visit the army next week, and then return to Tarascon. And you?"

"Apparently I am in God's hand, as ever," said Richelieu. He spoke to one and another of the king's gentlemen, who had entered and who now made their compliments to him. Then, as these retired and left them alone, he bent his coldly inflexible gaze on the king.

"Sire, may I ask a question?"

"My dear Richelieu, you may ask a thousand!"

"Then, if by the Divine Mercy I were enabled to lay in the hand of your majesty the signed and written proof that certain nobles had conspired, not against me, but against France—what would you do, sire?"

The king frowned. "More talk of plots and intrigue. *Ventre St. Gris!* It wearies me. I tell you I don't like it!"

"Nor I, sire," returned Richelieu firmly. "Therefore I ask you, if I give you full proof that certain nobles have conspired to bring the enemies of France to the gates of Paris, and to place French cities in their grip—"

"Then, upon my word, they shall go to the scaffold, though they be the highest officers of the realm!" exclaimed Louis XIII sharply. "And I shall be the first to demand the full penalty, I promise you! But come, now; let us talk of more pleasant things."

So they fell to talk of more pleasant things, chiefly physicians and remedies.

CHAPTER V

— ACQUIRES A WHIP.

IT WAS a very merry morning of late spring, and the road was not a long one to Palaiseau, whither Mervaut had been sent ahead to have the coach ready. Cyrano and Marianne de Gisy rode side by side, with much laughter and gay talk.

Cyrano uncased his lute and tuned it with snatches of song, as they sighted the silver thread of the Yvette in the valley. And in this pleasant intimacy Marianne turned to him and looked at the seven stars glistening on his cloak, and asked of them.

"Come, troubadour, what are these seven stars? It seems to me there is a meaning in them and in your words that is not wholly of astrology."

"True enough, daughter of the Sun!" exclaimed Cyrano, his eyes dancing. "My faith, they stand for many things! Are there not seven stars in the heavens? And what said the sage of Israel: 'Seek ye him that made the seven stars and the Hunter Orion'?

But the seven stars of Cyrano—alas, lady, they're sad stars and beyond computation. Each star a virtue that is no more; or, if you like, each star one of the deadly sins! There's food for thought in the stars, as you should know; but why talk of these things on such a morning?"

And he swept a chord on his lute, his voice lifted in a gay lilt:

> "Oh, the road is very good to see,
> And full of hidden minstrelsy,
> For all the little green trees make
> music in the wind!
> And as we ride to Palaiseau
> With sun above and stream below,
> There's laughter all the way we go,
> and care is left behind!"

He checked himself suddenly, and blinked around; a thin, high, terrible sound had come piercing across the sunlight, so that the horses jerked up their heads, and the smile was stricken from the eyes of Marianne.

"What—what was that?" she murmured, staring about.

"That," and Cyrano hastily thrust away his lute into its case, "was a man dying—and not far away, indeed."

Now the road and countryside were deserted, but it was a winding road, full of turns and sheltered by copses of trees, and anything might lie around the next bend. Voices came in sudden outbursts as the two riders swung about a sharp turn and drew rein. Almost before knowing it, they found themselves in the midst of a surging throng.

An orchard wall bordered the road. About this wall were grouped a score of men, their jests and laughter rising cruel on the sunlight. Among them, at the foot of the wall, lay a dead man with a poniard-haft protruding from his back; his gay rags and tatters, his swart skin, proclaimed him an Egyptian, as those of the wandering race were known. Bayed against the wall, dagger in hand, was a woman, the wife or daughter of the dead gypsy.

At sight of the strangers, the crowd eddied out. Most of them were rustics, but two, judging by their swords and garb and saddled horses near by, were travelers. Cyrano sat motionless, his eyes wide, all astare. This Egyptian woman, panting, flushed, clothes half torn from her body, dagger flashing no more brightly than her eyes, was a thing of savage and piercing beauty. Swart and eager as the dark sea under clouds, she menaced the pack of them and gave them pause.

ABRUPTLY THE throng closed in upon her again, and Cyrano caught a half-gasp, half-groan from Marianne de Gisy. He put out a hand, checked her horse.

"Wait here, dear lady," he said, as he dismounted.

"Come, little pagan!" went up the shout. "Come, Egyptian! A kiss from those red—"

The dagger flashed, and with a cry, a man reeled backward and fell. A harsher note leaped into the curses and cries of the men around. Sticks struck at her, hands reached out. She stood immobile, as though spent by that desperate blow. For one flashing instant Cyrano, crowding forward, met her eyes and found them striking into his. Then, as a hand gripped at her clothes and tore them, her stiletto darted out. The hand dripped blood, the owner howled.

One of the two men with swords drove in at her from the side; a deadly stroke dealt by a brutal-faced ruffian. The woman screamed once as the steel went into her, then twisted about, trying to strike as she reeled against the wall.

A wilder, terror-stricken note suddenly shrilled up from the men around, for the silver hilt of Cyrano's poniard flashed in the sun and flashed again. The man with the sword pitched down upon his face, and Cyrano swung upon the others, his voice roaring at them.

"*Canaille;* To your kennels, dogs! Vile scum that you are! Cowards and murderers!"

He advanced upon them, transfigured by fury, in his whole aspect all the terrible savage blood-lust which had aforetime made him so dreaded a swordsman. They were, for an instant, appalled by his action, by his wild and terrible look. He seized a stick from the nearest peasant and swept at them; they broke in terror, deeming him some noble, swift to punish them. All, that is, save one.

The companion of the dead man threw up his sword, and with an oath bore in upon Cyrano. Laughing, Cyrano engaged the blade with the poniard in his left hand, and looked into the eyes of his furious opponent.

"Oh, fool that you are!" he cried. "Thrice fool, to draw steel upon Cyrano!"

And suddenly the sword was wrenched from the man's grip, to fly away and fall clattering. The stick in Cyrano's right hand lashed in a blow that stretched the swordsman senseless in the dust. The others had fled hastily from the scene. Turning to the Egyptian, Cyrano swung off his hat; it had remained on his head, although the lute was broken.

"Mademoiselle, or madame," he began, "if—if—"

His voice faltered. The woman was leaning against the wall, her eyes fastened upon him; blood was streaming from where the sword had bitten her side, and a deathly pallor was in her swarthy face. Then Cyrano was aware of Marianne de Gisy passing him, running to the woman, catching her in strong arms. He flung himself to her aid, and they let the woman down gently, Marianne holding her head. She was dying, as Cyrano now perceived.

There was a moment of dread silence. The sunlight was hot, the dust-laden air was stilled. The two dead men lay with blood black upon the ground, the senseless man stirred not, the horses were cropping at the wayside grass. The Egyptian woman opened her eyes, looked from Cyrano to Marianne, and her gaze held on the latter's face; but this gaze was wild as the faint words that came from her lips.

"Folly, mad folly—I tell you, they know that we carry it! Here, take it quickly—keep it from him!"

HER HAND lifted, her fingers tore at the string of a small leather scapulary about her neck—strange object to be worn by a woman of the Egyptians—and she thrust the thing into the hand of Marianne. Wonderingly, Marianne accepted it. Then the woman's hand flashed out, pointing to Cyrano, and a shrill laugh came to her lips.

"Ah, *gros-bec!*" she said, speaking in the argot of Paris, which Cyrano comprehended readily enough. To Marianne the words meant nothing. "Leave her, fool, leave her! Beware of him—he brought death—he carries death perched upon his shoulder."

"Beware of whom?" exclaimed Cyrano sharply. "Quick!"

"Of him—the cleft chin—the cleft chin!"

A shiver passed through the body of the woman. Her head fell back. Marianne let her rest gently on the ground, and looked up at Cyrano, perplexed.

"What was it she said? The poor creature."

"Nothing; warnings—warnings against some man," said Cyrano, and rising, gave Marianne his hand and brought her to her feet. "I did not understand it all. These Egyptians of Paris have no business wandering about the countryside."

"It is terrible," Marianne glanced around, moved a little away from the dead woman. "If we go on quickly?"

"No hurry," said Cyrano. "I sent that accursed Mervaut to fetch the coach; he'll bring it soon. I think I'll look at these two gentlemen."

He regarded the man whom he had poniarded, the murderer of the Egyptian woman. Yet this dead face did not correspond to her description. It was rather the face of a servant, of a lackey. Cyrano looked at the horses of the two men, and saw that they were very good animals indeed, of some value. He was about to approach the second man, when there was a shout, and with a whirl of dust their coach appeared, Mervaut riding before it.

"So, we start!" exclaimed Cyrano. "Dear lady, you will occupy the coach now?"

Marianne assented. "Yes. Where do we stop for the night?"

"At Versailles, and then to the western highway. I'll send you ahead and catch up in a few moments; I want a word with that rascal of a lackey."

With the coach had come a driver and a groom. The latter dismounted and, with Mervaut, was excitedly looking over the scene; Cyrano gave the coachman his orders, and then, taking the reins of his horse, watched the coach depart. Marianne, he perceived, was glad to be gone from this place of death.

Almost at his feet, Cyrano perceived something in the dust—a whip, and a very handsome one, of leather braided with gold and silver wire. He picked it up; some one in the throng must have dropped it, but no peasant would bear such a thing as this.

The butt was a round disk of gold, in which was chiseled the initial "A." Cyrano inspected it curiously, then shrugged.

"It perhaps belongs to the rogue who drew sword on me," he reflected, and glanced around. Somewhat to his surprise, he saw that Mervaut and the groom were now kneeling beside that same unconscious man, attempting to revive him. Cyrano approached, and caught a look of scornful contempt from Mervaut which quite infuriated him.

"Come, come, sirrahs, are you robbing the dead?" Cyrano asked ironically.

"No, *monsieur*," rejoined Mervaut. "We are succoring the injured."

The tone was insolent, and Cyrano, who did not love lackeys at all, turned slightly pale.

"This injured man is a friend of yours, Mervaut?" he demanded in a low voice. The lackey rose and met his eyes boldly enough.

"I think, *monsieur,* that he is a gentleman," was the response. "I have seen him in Paris."

CYRANO LOOKED down at the face of the man, who was just opening his eyes. Then he started. Here was the face the Egyptian woman had described—a strong, wide face with a prominent and deeply cleft chin. What did her warning mean; could it have meant anything? Did she, in the very grip of death, have some prevision of things to be?

"You know this man's name, Mervaut?" he asked.

"I think he is the Sieur d'Avillon, *monsieur*." The lackey was about to say more, when he turned, saw that the coach was gone, and swung upon Cyrano with hot anger in his eyes. "*Monsieur*, did you send the coach away?"

"What is it to you?" Cyrano was astonished by the man's boldness.

"My master has ordered me to watch over the safety of Mlle. de Gisy," said Mervaut, and scowled. "She is in my care, and—"

"You insolent dog!" said Cyrano, disdainfully, forgetting that the servant doubtless set great store by the estate of his master. "Do you want a whiplash over your shoulders?"

Mervaut gave him a sour and impudent grin.

"Come, come, M. le Marquis," he said. "You forget that a woman is a woman the world over! It is true that my master has certain pressing need of your services, but do not impose upon the trust he reposes in you. I've observed your looks and actions with *mademoiselle*, and I'm warning you—"

"Those who warn me are usually paid," said Cyrano.

His eyes gave the lackey no hint; the little whip lashed and Mervaut staggered back with a red weal springing across his face. The whip was heavy enough, meant for service; and for the second time, with astonishing effect, it lashed the face of Mervaut. Then Cyrano, in the midst of his contemptuous laugh, felt a hot breath on his neck—the groom was in the very act of driving a dagger into his side.

A sheer miracle of agility saved him from the blow. He leaped sidewise, as a cat leaps, and caromed full into Sieur d'Avillon, who was just rising. Flung off balance, he stumbled, fell to hands and knees—then caught up the whip in his hand and threw himself to one side, and came upright.

"Kill!" rasped the voice of Mervaut. "Kill him!"

Cyrano glanced around. Mervaut had rapier out, the groom was plunging in with his long poniard, and Avillon, likewise gripping a dagger, was rising to attack him from the other side. For a breath Cyrano stood motionless—then, swift as light, he became a thing of flowing action. Disdaining to use steel against such adversaries, he trusted instead to the footwork which had helped make him the first swordsman in Paris.

The groom screamed and fell writhing in the dust as the whip smote him square across the eyes, blinding him. Avillon lunged in, but Cyrano's riding boot caught him under the chin, and for the second time he plunged down into the dust and lay quiet. At this instant a thin tongue of steel drove between Cyrano's side and arm, touching the skin yet not breaking it. Mervaut was upon him, recovering, leaning in for another and more deadly thrust.

At the instant of lunging, Mervaut stumbled across the writhing body of the blinded groom. The whip slashed across the wrist of his outflung arm, and the sword fell from his hand.

"Now for your punishment, rascal!" exclaimed Cyrano. "When you are next tempted to be insolent to a gentleman, remember this!"

A terrible cry burst from Mervaut as the bloody whip lashed him across the face. He attempted to rush in upon Cyrano, but the latter kept his distance, and time after time drove home his biting weapon. Streaming with blood, helpless, cursing, Mervaut flung his arms across his face and dashed away at a blind run.

He had not, however, begged for mercy, as Cyrano later recalled.

LEFT MASTER of the field, Cyrano laughed and picked up his hat from where it had fallen. Then he paused, as something recurred to him.

"What 'certain pressing need' does M. d'Effiat have of my

services, eh? Come, there's something to ponder! He doesn't need me to take the lady to the Mont—this rascal was ready enough to fling me in the ditch and conduct her himself. My faith, it looks as though there were far more in this affair than I suspected. Ah, here is our good Sieur d'Avillon! Good day to you, *monsieur,* and kindly leave your sword alone, since you don't know how to use it."

He beamed genially upon the dazed and bewildered Avillon, as the latter rose. Mervaut had disappeared; the groom was groaning and holding his eyes as he writhed. Cyrano was under no illusions as regarded Sieur d'Avillon, whom he knew all too well by reputation as one of the most dreaded Cardinalist agents.

Richelieu's man, in truth, did not inspire dread at this moment. Avillon was dusty, his mouth was bleeding, and he seemed anything but certain of his whereabouts. He stared at Cyrano.

"Ah!" he exclaimed suddenly. "I have seen you before!"

"Very likely, since I am no dwarf," and Cyrano chuckled. "The Marquis de Bergerac, very much at your service, Sieur d'Avillon. May I have the impudence to inquire why you were so lustily engaged in murdering two Egyptians?"

"Devil take you!" said Avillon, blinking and coming somewhat to himself. He seemed jerked to life by mention of the luckless pair, and his eyes swept around and came to rest upon the body of the woman. "Ah! She is dead!"

"Thanks to you, murderer," said Cyrano.

Avillon turned and looked at him as though perceiving him for the first time.

"So, M. de Bergerac!" he said slowly, putting a hand to his bleeding mouth. "You've interfered with me, have you!"

"No; you've interfered with me," said Cyrano coolly, "and you'll answer to Père Carré for it when you see him."

Avillon started. His eyes widened.

"You?" he exclaimed. "You, rake-hell, alley cat, *bretteur* of the gutters—you speak of him?"

Cyrano realized that Avillon knew him for what he was, had perhaps met or seen him in Paris. However, he was too full of contempt and disdain for the man. He shrugged, turned his back on Avillon, and went to the hapless groom.

"Rogue, take your master's horses and go home," he said, kicking Effiat's groom to his feet. "If you meet that scoundrel Mervaut, tell him to hide his face from me henceforth or I'll have him flawed alive. Up with you!"

Cyrano turned to his own horse, swung up into the saddle, and set forth in the wake of the vanished coach. His smashed lute was tossed aside. Dusting off his hat and plume, Cyrano twirled his mustache, put in his spurs, and passed through Palaiseau with all speed.

"So that rascal Avillon knew me!" he thought, as he cleared the town and discerned the dust cloud left by the coach. "I forgot what the woman said; I should have killed him. Yet, to what end? I put a handsome flea in his ear, and if he goes to Père Carré he'll learn a thing or two. Why did that rogue Mervaut presume so far? Strange! There's something behind his impudence; he seemed to know Avillon, too. What could lie between the lackey of Sieur d'Effiat and the confidential agent of Richelieu? And I should like to know just why Avillon should be drawing the blood of two Egyptians in the highway!"

Had he been back at the bend in the road where the two Egyptians lay, at this moment, Cyrano might have wondered still further. For Sieur d'Avillon, going to the body of the dead woman, had fallen upon his knees and was searching it swiftly. He rose, with an oath, and went to the man, and searched his ragged garments with the same ill luck. Then, suddenly, he began to scan the road for his own whip, and found it not—since it was being carried by Cyrano. Avillon kicked up the dust, searched hither and yon, and finally, realizing that the whip was gone, shook his fist at the sky with passionate despair in his dark face.

Truly, very singular actions to be indulged in by a gentleman and a confidential agent of the great cardinal!

CHAPTER VI

—HAS AN ADVENTURE.

A SINGLE MAN riding posthaste, with change of
horses at every stop, and ample authority, can certainly
travel much faster than any coach. This very simple and obvious
fact might be the explanation of many puzzling things.

It might, for example, explain why the coach in which Marianne de Gisy was riding suddenly broke down two days after
leaving Palaiseau. The breakdown occurred during their noon
halt at a roadside tavern—a pleasant Norman inn with the not
uncommon name of the White Horse. The whole front of the
coach, springs and all, was certainly unfit to go a mile farther
without repairs, and there was no other vehicle to be had. The
innkeeper, however, stated that repairs might be made if men
were summoned from Morthange, a village some five leagues
distant. Cyrano, accordingly, sent on the coachman, disposed
his charge in very comfortable quarters above the tavern, and
made the best of a bad affair.

"We shall certainly be here until to-morrow," he said as he
handed Marianne de Gisy to her room. "That rascal will take
his time about bringing men or another coach, be sure of it!"

She stood smiling at him, in a way she had.

"Time was made for slaves, my dear marquis," she responded. "I shall sleep for an hour or two, and then rejoin you. Why
worry?"

Why, indeed? Cyrano had not a worry on earth; he was filled
with a joyous bursting happiness that took no heed to actuali-
ties. When Marianne smiled at him thus, he saw only her eyes,
and they gripped his very soul.

"Dear lady," he said earnestly, as he bent over her hand and
then looked again into her eyes, "remember only one thing of

me, I pray you. Do not say: 'Cyrano loves me!' for this is not true. Say this: 'Cyrano worships the Queen of Heaven, for whom I was named—a dear shining lady so far above, so far away, that her presence is a sacred thing, a glorious revelation of beauty to his poor starved spirit.' *Au revoir,* my lady. Rest, and when you talk with the angels, say a little prayer for Cyrano."

So he left her and sat in the stone-paved wine room over a bottle, and wondered what it was in this woman which so drew him. Why was Effiat, that cold debauchee, so drawn to her in like manner? Not for mere beauty—there were others more beautiful by far in the externals—but for the spirit which lay behind and above all beauty; the spirit which Cyrano himself could not define, yet felt so deeply.

"Shining lady—aye, there it is!" he muttered. "Her eyes speak of peace, of happiness, of a high surety. And I, a poor monk, wandering aimless about the cloister, look to her as my Madonna."

Three cavaliers came stamping into the place, stopped short at sight of Cyrano, and exchanged a word among themselves. One of them stepped forward and bowed.

"*Monsieur,*" he said—he was a young man, a provincial noble from his appearance—"may I have the impertinence to request a favor? I am M. des Essarts; my two friends are M. le Baron d'Yvert and M. de Frontard. We find ourselves at a point of disagreement. It becomes important to find a fourth gentleman, one who may accompany us to a quiet spot and assist us by his presence to untangle our knot of discord. We find you here; excellent! If you will have the goodness?"

Cyrano rose, bowed magnificently, gave his name, and called for more wine.

"With all the pleasure in the world!" he declaimed. "I am under a vow not to bear sword, my friends, but that assuredly does not hinder me from assisting a gentleman not under vow. And I may claim some little experience in the niceties of the duello, by my faith! Come, let us drink together, and I am at your service with all my heart!"

THE OTHER two gentlemen joined them, emptied a bottle apiece, and in ten minutes all four went out to the court-yard. Cyrano obtained a horse, and they rode forth in great gayety upon their errand. Frontard and Yvert were at odds over some lady, it seemed; and if the matter had singular aspects, Cyrano was in mood to overlook them all.

A couple of miles from the tavern they came upon a grassy roadside glade, and the spot being approved, Cyrano swung out of the saddle. It was the last act of which he had any memory. Frontard's horse sidled in upon him, and next instant there was a crash—the pistol butt in Frontard's hand came down, and Cyrano knew no more.

"Well done!" exclaimed Baron d'Yvert. "Now for the whip."

He dismounted, caught up the braided whip which Cyrano had carried, and swiftly examined it. A nod and he pocketed it, then leaped into the saddle.

"*Adieu,* my friends!" Yvert cried. "Dispose of him as arranged!"

In this wise did the Marquis de Bergerac become separated from his lady.

When he wakened to himself he was sitting in a huge oaken chair in a strange room, a vile pain in his head, and candles alight on a table before him. It was night. A fire burned in a hearth at one side, and across the table sat M. de Frontard, reading a book.

"The devil!" exclaimed Cyrano in astonishment. "Where am I?"

"Not in purgatory, at all events," and Frontard, flinging aside his book, laughed a little. "My dear Bergerac, you are the victim of circumstances. A shabby trick was played upon you; in the morning you shall be free to go. Until then, you remain as my guest."

"Eh!" Cyrano stared at him. "But why? What does it mean?"

"It means"—and suddenly the eyes of Frontard bored into him—"that you had something belonging to another man. Need I mention the name of Avillon? Compose yourself, I beg of you; here I am master, force will avail nothing—ah, have a care, *monsieur!*"

Cyrano came to his feet and found himself looking into a pistol's mouth. He stood motionless an instant, then sank back into his chair.

"Very well, *monsieur,*" he said quietly. "But I was traveling with a lady—"

"Who has by this time been supplied with another coach and escort," said Frontard.

This jerked Cyrano sharply out of his whirling chaos. Servants entered, bringing an excellent dinner and superb wine; without a word more, Cyrano accepted the situation. The whip? This explained the matter in part. Let them have their little game, then; with morning there would come a new day. Desperately, Cyrano forced down impulse, conquered his mad urge to be up and repairing the wrong; and accepted his rôle. He looked across the table and smiled at Frontard.

"*Monsieur,* I am your guest, on your promise that I depart freely in the morning," he said. "Only, let me tell you one thing; at our next meeting I shall assuredly kill you. Until then it shall be as you desire."

"Your word, *monsieur?*"

"Faith of a gentleman," said Cyrano, and Frontard at once threw aside his pistol.

CYRANO GATHERED that he was in Frontard's house, and in no danger whatever. He yielded to the urge of hunger, and over the dinner table became rapidly acquainted with his host, a man of forty, who had served in the army and who knew the court. Frontard, he concluded, was a Huguenot noble, and Cyrano here ventured one question.

"Your pardon, *monsieur,* but curiosity urges! You have upset my plans, I gather, at the request of this Avillon. He is an emissary of the cardinal; yet you are a Huguenot."

"I happen to be his cousin, also," and Frontard smiled. "I have regained his lost property, not for love of Richelieu, but because my cousin requested it. You comprehend?"

Cyrano nodded. He perceived that the little whip must have been for some reason highly important—and suddenly he recalled the golden plate in the butt. Dispatches, of course! Inclosed in the whip were papers. This explained everything—or much, at least. Not the matter of those Egyptians . . .

"*Mordious!* I've been a fool!" he exclaimed, and broke into a laugh. "If you'd asked me for the whip I'd have given it you and saved a lot of trouble. Here's a health to the king, and—"

"And damnation to his eminence," said Frontard.

Dinner over, the fire was built up and Cyrano was delighted to see a chess table carried in by two servants. He loved the game, though he was none too apt at it, and an hour passed swiftly over the board. Suddenly a servant came hurriedly into the room and spoke a low word at his master's ear. Frontard started up.

"Here? Impossible!" he cried, a singular agitation in his features.

"With a single gentleman, *monsieur,*" said the servant.

"Wait—I'll come at once." Frontard turned to Cyrano. "*Monsieur,* will you accept my excuses? A gentleman has arrived to speak with me—I shall return shortly."

Frontard hurried from the room, and Cyrano, thinking little of the matter, relaxed, rubbed his sore pate, and poured another glass of wine. He did not like Frontard; the man was a gentleman, yet was possessed of a certain coldness of manner, a hard and inflexible spirit, a puritanical air distasteful to Cyrano.

The door opened, and two men came into the room. In advance of Frontard walked a tall man, carelessly attired, whose extremely handsome features at once drew Cyrano's attention.

Pride was stamped in them, yet with the pride was something savage, unutterably harsh and cruel and intolerant.

Sieur de Lorges—what name was this? Cyrano bowed to Frontard's introduction, and cudgeled his brains hard. He knew the name, had heard it; this was no ordinary man, this Sieur de Lorges! Then the visitor turned to Frontard.

"Rest until midnight, then ride. To Doucy, first; there is much to do at the château. You are ready?"

Frontard assented, with a gesture of caution, and addressed Cyrano.

"*Monsieur,* important business is afoot; you comprehend? I beg you to excuse me. Your room is prepared; if I am not here in the morning I shall have you escorted whither you may desire to go."

"To the tavern where we met?" demanded Cyrano, and the other shrugged.

"If you like. But may I venture one word of advice, even if it be impertinent? Ride not to the west, *monsieur.*"

"Thank you, *monsieur,*" said Cyrano. "Is Sieur d'Avillon in the west, then?"

At the mention of this name, he saw Sieur de Lorges turn and stare at him.

"I do not know," said Frontard. "If he is your enemy, avoid him. He is no friend of mine, yet I have paid a debt and discharged it by this day's work."

"You have gained another debt, *monsieur,*" said Cyrano gravely. "And when you told me that the lady was already provided with another coach, you told me still more. M. d'Effiat is then not far away? He is, doubtless, a friend of yours?"

Frontard looked hard at him for a moment. Sieur de Lorges frowned and spoke.

"I do not comprehend this conversation; but it seems to me that you speak of certain gentlemen very carelessly. Names, *monsieur,* are dangerous."

Cyrano looked at him and laughed a little. "Exactly; but men are more dangerous still. I am glad to have the honor of your acquaintance, *monsieur;* perhaps we shall meet again in the west."

ONCE ALONE, Cyrano sank down on a chair, staring at nothing. That cruelly proud face, those bitter eyes—yes, he had seen it pictured somewhere, but not by such a name! And so Frontard had been in touch both with Avillon and with Effiat; singular fact! Those two men were not friends; Avillon, the Cardinalist agent, Effiat, a potential rebel.

"Ha!" exclaimed Cyrano suddenly. "I have it now. Jacques de Lorges? Aye, I know you now—Comte de Montgommery, son of the Huguenot Montgommery, who nearly captured our western fortress of Mont St. Michel during the religious wars—grandson of the Grand Montgommery who killed Henri II during a tournament and was executed for the deed. Ah, Montgommery, leader of the Huguenot party—so this is the man! And now what the devil is afoot, I wonder? Where does Effiat fit into this picture? And Avillon? Does this Montgommery think to surprise Mont St. Michel as his father did, with better luck this time? Well, with Huguenots and English together— ha!"

Rising, he crossed to the fire and stared down into the leaping flames. Conjecture could lead him nowhere, he had no clew as yet, but he felt something deep was afoot. Not for nothing had he himself been summoned to Mont St. Michel by Effiat. Not for nothing was the Montgommery riding about Normandy. Perhaps things were closer to a crisis than even Père Carré had supposed.

Cyrano's thoughts flew back to his own situation, not without a little sting of hurt pride. He was considered of small account, not even worth the killing, They had tricked him, got him out of the way; Avillon wanted that whip back, nothing else. But Avillon and Sieur d'Effiat would certainly not be working together.

Ah, the lackey Mervaut! There was the answer. Cyrano swore

Commandant Salignan acknowledged the
introduction to Cyrano with an air of hostility.

a deep oath of regret that he had not killed that lackey at the roadside. Mervaut and Avillon had probably joined forces and had planned this little affair; Avillon, to get back his lost dispatches, Mervaut to get rid of his master's friend. Cyrano's cheek burned, and he flung up his head.

"So Avillon, knowing who I really am, thinks me not worth the killing! We shall see about that, my friends. He is not so easily lost, not so easily discouraged, this Marquis of the Seven Stars! No, for there is something shining afar that leads him on—a shining lady whose eyes remain always with him day and night."

He began to undress, and suddenly broke into a chuckling laugh as his fingers touched the star-shaped reliquary Père Carré had hung about his neck.

"Ha, worthy father superior, your excellent Dominican ear must be burning to-night! Well, it's a pretty thing enough, but didn't save Cyrano from a devilish sore head, and perhaps a sore heart to boot, thanks to separation. Decidedly, St. Michael is not my patron; not when there's a Madonna who smiles at me, with blue eyes all gleaming like stars."

And Cyrano, pinching out the candles, knelt for a space in the flickering firelight.

Morning sunlight wakened him. A lackey responded to his call, and he found that his host had indeed departed during the night. Frontard, however, was as good as his word; an hour later beheld Cyrano mounted on an excellent horse, a groom at his side to guide him back to the inn of the White Horse, and all his personal belongings intact.

T O T H E tavern was only a matter of two leagues. Arriving there, the groom departed and Cyrano rode into the courtyard. A glance showed him that the coach was gone; the host came forth, threw up his hands, and in reply to Cyrano's questions stated that the vehicle had been repaired the previous afternoon. Two gentlemen had arrived with a letter for the lady, who had departed under their escort.

Pressed for a description of the two cavaliers, the host complied readily. Neither of them, Cyrano discovered, had been Effiat; one, with a wealed and angry face, must have been Mervaut. The lady had betrayed some agitation, but had departed willingly. More than this, Cyrano could learn nothing at all.

Thus baffled, finding his worst fears come true, Cyrano exchanged Frontard's horse for his own, loaded his pistols, and set forth upon the western road toward Mont St. Michel.

He rode with the sole purpose of overtaking the coach, finding Marianne de Gisy again, and continuing at her side. How she had been tricked or intimidated into leaving, he could not understand; the letter would explain it readily enough. Since she was not the sort of person to be easily deceived, he inclined to the belief that she had gone with Mervaut as the part of wisdom.

"Aye, that's it!" he concluded, plucking up his spirits. "The letter said that I was drunk or detained, and that Mervaut would take my place. Who wrote the letter? Mervaut and Avillon between them, forging Effiat's hand. Hence, it's clear enough that Mervaut will betray his master to Avillon, or has already done so—if there's aught to betray! And Marianne went, knowing that if I were alive I'd meet her again at Mont St. Michel. There's a woman for you, a blessed shining lady on the mountain top! She may well stand beside the Archangel St. Michael himself and beckon me to the mount!"

So Cyrano rode on into the west. But of his shining lady he had found no trace.

CHAPTER VII

— MEETS HIS LADY.

EXCITEMENT REIGNED in the little village of Pontorson, half a league from Mont St. Michel. While the Mont might be reached from various points along the coast, the gleaming expanse of sand which surrounded it at low tide was highly dangerous, since quicksands existed at many points, and the tide came in with a speed which had more than once cut off hapless pilgrims or fishermen and swallowed them. From Pontorson, however, the sands might be safely traversed, and this was the route usually taken by pilgrims and by the public in general. Hence the hospital and hostelries and other buildings which had made the village a place of some importance.

The advent of pilgrims in their fantastic garb caused little excitement in Pontorson; but others than pilgrims had arrived. It was rumored that the new abbot, Sieur d'Effiat, was now at the Mont; and certainly the prior had been summoned thither in all haste from his pleasant summerhouse, the Manor of Brion. Also, an hour before noon there had arrived at the inn some great lady in a coach; the tide would not be out for another two hours, so she was forced to wait.

However, it was of the prior, Dom Charles Ratran, that folk talked most. Those who were of the village, being serfs of the abbey, talked not at all; but a pilgrim who had been here a fortnight talked very readily with the dark-faced Mervaut.

"Scandal enough," said the pilgrim, a Lorrainer. "Do you know what they call the prior? Dom Charlatan—a play on his name. When you see him you'll understand. What with wine and wenches, he lives a holy life! He's the first prior who has disgraced his station, they say; but nothing can be done about it. We'll see what M. d'Effiat has to say—I fancy Dom Charlatan will walk into some hot water!"

"Perchance," said Mervaut, with a slight smile. "And perchance not. I have not heard that this M. d'Effiat was any saint himself."

"Oh, he is a gentleman, and that is different," said the pilgrim. "A prior is a prior. I heard yesterday that the royal commandant, M. de Coalin, has been appointed to a high post at court, and departs to-day. A new commandant has arrived or will soon arrive to take his place."

"Eh?" said Mervaut, sudden interest in his dark face. "A new commandant? Who, then?"

The pilgrim shrugged. "How should I know? It's a soft job at all events; nothing to do except to receive salutes, drink good wine, and entertain a pretty girl now and then. No lack of wenches at the Mont, let me tell you! The pilgrims' taverns are full of them."

Mervaut turned away, frowning a little in wonderment at the ousting of Effiat's kinsman, Coalin. At this moment there was a clatter of hooves, a trundle of wheels, and into the courtyard of the tavern turned a plain and very dusty traveling coach. It had no attendants save a lackey, who sat beside the coachman, and who quickly leaped down and held open the door for his master—an elderly man, this, severely attired, yet by his proud and arrogant features a nobleman of some rank. His quick, bright eye touched on Mervaut, and swept the courtyard.

"A foul-smelling place," the newcomer said to his lackey. "Ask when we can reach the Mont, and obtain a guide. We shall have to await the ebb tide."

He stopped short, staring upward. Mervaut, following his eye, turned and saw Marianne de Gisy descending the stone stairs that led down into the courtyard from the upper rooms of the tavern. Unmistakable recognition leaped into the face of the new arrival.

With a frown, Mervaut advanced to meet the lady; suddenly his arm was caught, he was thrust aside.

"Out of the way, fellow," said the nobleman in a tone of imperious authority, and himself met Marianne as she descended. He bowed low before her, and with her swift, flashing smile she extended her hand to him.

"S O Y O U remember me, M. le Marquis! After five, six years, is it not?"

Marquis de Salignan's severe features were suddenly warmed.

"Remember you, Mlle. de Gisy? Faith of a gentleman, the memory of you would be a bright and glorious thing after five years or fifty! I am a soldier, *mademoiselle,* and my tongue is not attuned to the flattering melodies of courtiers and fine gentlemen. Let me say bluntly that to meet you here, of all places, is no less than a miracle! To-morrow St. Michel shall have a taper of the finest wax, I swear."

Marianne broke into a laugh. "Alas, *monsieur,* you have a most convincing tongue, whether that of a soldier or a courtier! I almost believe you are glad to see me. You must be bound for the Mont, then? Not on pilgrimage?"

"No, on duty," returned Salignan, with a grimace. "I've been ordered to act as royal commandant here, temporarily. I was not overjoyed, I can assure you—but now all is changed. Is it possible that you, also, are for the Mont?"

Mervaut, with an expression of the utmost concern, quietly departed.

"Yes. Sieur d'Effiat, the abbot, is there now, I believe. I am trying to settle an old dispute between our family and the monks over certain lands near Brion; also, and more important, I want to inspect some manuscripts in the abbey library."

"Good!" exclaimed Salignan. "If my services can avail you—but you are escorted?"

"By a lackey who was here a moment ago," and Marianne glanced around. "Also by a gentleman, M. de Bergerac, who was unfortunately separated from us some days ago. He will, I think, arrive shortly."

"Bergerac? A Gascon name, that," said Salignan, frowning slightly. "I should know it, but cannot place such a man."

"Marquis de Bergerac, I should have said," amended Marianne. "A most extraordinary person, I assure you, and a very dear friend."

"H-m!" said Salignan. "Well, well, you shall not lack for friends, service, and help. If you desire the entire abbey, I shall be honored to back you up against all the sour-visaged monks in France! Shall we stroll down to the beach before our meal? You will, of course, do me the honor of joining me at noon meat? This is an evil-smelling place, but I understand there is no better place in the village."

"Most gladly, my dear marquis," said Marianne, her blue eyes very gay. "And like two worthy pilgrims, we shall go down below the cliffs and look out at the sacred Mont, and make believe that we can see St. Michel himself in the sky above!"

As she took his arm, Salignan pressed her hand slightly in warning.

"Careful, Huguenot!" he said in a low voice. "I know you're of the religion, like your father; but have a care. I understand there is much bitterness hereabouts. The Comte de Montgommery is at feud with the monks, and you'll get neither manuscripts nor lands if any religious difference becomes accented."

"Thank you," she returned, and patted his arm. "You were one of my father's best friends, and I spoke for your ear alone, my dear marquis. Oh, I can be most careful, I assure you! But I sha'n't tell any lies. I'm an honest sort of person."

"Then appoint me your high ambassador, and leave diplomacy to me," and the marquis laughed softly as they left the courtyard.

Things were not going to the liking of Mervaut, obviously; he stood out in the narrow street, and with a dark frown watched the two saunter down toward the cliffs, arm in arm. Presently he came back to the inn, demanded writing materials, and scribbled a hasty note which he sealed with his dagger hilt. He addressed it, then sought the host and gave him the missive, together with a broad silver coin.

"Within a few days," he said, "a Sieur d'Avillon will inquire here for any message. You will give him this letter. If you fail or make any error, my master, M. d'Effiat, will have something to say to you. It will be most unpleasant."

THE HOST, who depended on the abbey for his favor, was sufficiently impressed. Mervaut went back to the street and idled about, conversing with one person and another, picking up any news or idle gossip that came his way—until of a sudden came cries and warnings that caused him to turn toward an astonishing sight.

A most imposing procession was sweeping down the street; one would have said that at the very least, a prince of the blood had arrived in Pontorson. An ornate coach, drawn by seven horses, and escorted by a score of armed cavaliers, came into sight with great cracking of whips and creaking of wheels. Behind followed two mules, housed and caparisoned, whose bells tinkled gayly; a number of valets and lackeys brought up the rear.

A sudden roar of laughter in a voice that Mervaut recognized all too well, sent his dark gaze to the coach; for an instant he stared, incredulous, then he drew back among the throng.

Two men rode in the coach. The one, cloaked in the robes of a Benedictine, was a man of some girth and huge frame. His tonsured features were broad and heavy; his great bluish jowl conveyed an air of joviality that much belied his garb, and his small, deep eyes were wrinkled with laughter. In effect, a man

of no great strength, of some cunning, and of irrepressible good
humor—a man who loved ease and the good things of life. A
man, peasant born, who had come to high estate and who was
making the most of it without scruple. Such, in a word, was the
prior of Mont St. Michel, he who was dubbed Dom Charlatan.

Seated in the coach beside the prior, roaring with laughter,
was Cyrano.

"By the bones of the blessed St. Maur, I never heard a better
story!" cried Dom Ratran, in a shrill, laughter-faint voice. "Excellent, my dear marquis, excellent! If only I had known that
rascal Boisrobert in his younger days, eh, eh? Well, they have
some of my own particular wine at this scoundrelly tavern, so
let us see what we can do about a meal while we await the ebb
tide. Your horse will be taken care of; we have no horses except
mine own at the Mont, nor room for them. What a providen-
tial meeting was ours! And you know Effiat, eh? Good! Why
the deuce he should be here, I don't know—just when I was
comfortably settled at Brion for the summer, too!"

"I'll warrant you were," and Cyrano winked broadly. "Faith,
I'd like to visit your manor of Brion, over a few fast days, at
least! But what have we here—more travelers?"

The coach had rumbled into the inn courtyard, and Cyrano,
alighting, surveyed the two coaches whose horses were being
baited. The horsemen and lackeys filled the place; voices rose
high; Dom Ratran came to earth, shook his girth, slapped
Cyrano on the shoulder, and sent a stream of commands at the
inn host and hostlers. Gemmed rings sparkled on his fingers
in the sunlight, and from a golden chain about his neck was
suspended a huge cross of amethyst.

Upon this bustling scene intruded two figures: Marianne de
Gisy, leaning upon the arm of the Marquis de Salignan. Dom
Ratran turned in astonishment at their approach, and was more
astonished to see Cyrano sweep off his hat and go to one knee
before Marianne, who smilingly extended her hand.

"I knew you would not be far behind!" she exclaimed. "There
was no—accident?"

"None, Madonna," said Cyrano, his eyes hungry upon her face. For him, everything around was swept away in an instant. "Ah! Now let the sun shine out anew for Cyrano! Now let the winds blow, and the singing heart be glad again, since your eyes are looking into mine."

SALIGNAN CAME forward and stood beside Marianne, his hard and piercing eyes surveying Cyrano. Marianne turned to him.

"Ah, the friend of whom I was speaking, the Marquis de Bergerac! My dear Cyrano, let me present an older friend, the Marquis de Salignan."

The two men bowed; and thus brought back to reality, Cyrano bethought him of the prior, and gestured Dom Ratran forward with a flourish of his long arm.

"A miracle, Dom Ratran, a very miracle! Here is the lady of whom I told you, and while to your unworthy eyes she may appear mere woman, I assure you on the faith of a gentleman that she is the daughter of the sun and the sister to the moon, and that the soul looking from her eyes is a breath of heaven! Mademoiselle de Gisy, allow me the honor of presenting Dom Ratran, prior of the abbey whither we both journey."

It must be confessed that Dom Charlatan, not being accustomed to the society of ladies or to courtly speeches, bore himself rather awkwardly; from which he was relieved by presentation to Salignan, who very dryly and curtly addressed him.

"I believe that we have business together, Dom Ratran, since I am ordered to assume immediate charge of the temporal defenses of your spiritual domain. However, that may wait until our arrival. Meantime—"

"Meantime, you are my guests!" exclaimed Dom Ratran with gusto. The innkeeper had appeared at one side, making a sign which the prior well understood. "You are our new royal commander, my dear marquis? Excellent! M. d'Effiat is now at the Mont, I understand. The late commandant departed last night, being summoned hastily to court. Come, come, we shall have rare times in those old walls, I promise you; no hospice rooms, but quarters in the abbey itself, and a table together in my own chambers. I have a special dispensation from the vows of silence, it may interest you to know, for that refectory is a deadly place to put down a meal, with Dom Hyacinth droning out his readings from the lectern! Well, my friends, enter and let us see whether the passing pilgrims have left anything to eat that is worthy our attention."

Spouting words, as it were, beaming upon Salignan and the others, the prior shepherded his guests toward the appointed table, then bethought himself of a welcome to Salignan, and took the marquis most warmly by the arm with a simple and naïve cordiality which was rather disarming. Indeed, the fat prior was no dissembler, and one could see readily that he was not given to intrigue or plot—unless, it might be, in the matter of a sturgeon, or a fat buck misappropriated from the abbey preserves.

Cyrano, with Marianne upon his arm, swaggered into the tavern, and was seated betwixt her and the prior, with Salignan opposite. And, at once, he found unexplainable enmity in the straight, level eyes of the old soldier. It broke upon him almost with a shock, but there was no mistake. Cyrano was quick to sense such things, and he accepted this singular hostility with a shrug and a smile and an arrogant eye.

"You are, *monsieur,* from Gascony?" asked Salignan, after certain talk had passed.

"Faith, *monsieur,* service in the guards would presuppose such a thing!" and Cyrano laughed and touched his scarred throat. "The siege of Arras came near to sending me into the service of heaven instead, so I took a hint and became a good Parisian."

"*Diantre!* I had thought all Parisians were shop-keeping rascals," and Salignan gave the device on Cyrano's cloak a slow look. "Odd, *monsieur.* Seven stars—would it be impertinent to ask that you supplement my faint knowledge of heraldry?"

"Aye, by all means!" exclaimed Dom Ratran, and leaned over

to dig his elbow into the ribs of Cyrano. "I asked the same thing, and he flung ribaldry into my tonsured features, the sacrilegious rogue! Come, Bergerac, what mean the stars?"

"WHY," SAID Cyrano coolly, "like St. Paul of blessed memory, they mean all things to all men! Should I say they were granted an ancestor by the holy St. Louis, for seven Saracens slain in Egypt? Bah! Then they were of small merit to me! No, my dear marquis, they signify, if you like, certain memories of recent years."

And with swift finger he touched the scars at his throat, on his face, the while he spoke:

"This is for the siege of Arras, then—the scurvy wound that knocked me back under the walls and left me for dead! I always detested bullets. And this is for M. de Morsan's rapier, which taught me not to slip in gutter filth. Third, a very pretty meeting of four behind the Palais Cardinal, when two gentlemen went straight to Paradise. Fourth, here on the cheek, for a stroll toward the Pomme-de-Pin and two bravos who were buried by the archers of the watch next morning. Fifth, a slight nick, an excellent lesson to guard the eye; it came from a big German on my first campaign. Poor fellow, he neglected to guard the heart, which was more important! Sixth, an ignoble fair in fencing, when Vautier lost his temper and used a dagger from behind—alas, that my rapier plunged into his throat! He was a gallant gentleman when sober and in his right mind."

Cyrano gestured in finality and emptied his goblet. Salignan, who was watching him closely, frowned a little. Marianne spoke out, her eyes a little startled.

"But that is only six, and there are seven stars! Come—the seventh?"

"Ah! That is for the wound that has not yet been inflicted!" exclaimed Cyrano, with a bursting laugh. Salignan leaned forward.

"Is this a matter for jest, *monsieur?*" he demanded coldly. Cyrano gave him a cool look.

"Why not? Everything's a matter for jest! That's the way of Cyrano—jest with all things, hide the devil under a mask of laughter! We who take ourselves seriously—what do we get out of life that's worth while?"

"H-m!" said Salignan. "I think, *monsieur*, that you take shelter behind a laugh."

Cyrano shrugged. "At all events, I don't take shelter behind a lie. And a laugh can always turn serious, while it is sometimes difficult to reverse the operation. Well, I have talked enough. Dom Ratran, carry on the conversation, I beg of you, while I give my attention to the excellent food and wine before us!"

The fat prior laughed heartily, and Cyrano suited action to words, refusing to open his mouth again except to fill it with baked sturgeon from the bay, or the coquilles for which Mont St. Michel was so famous, or the admirable pasty of quail and meadow-larks which was the particular pride of their host.

If he talked no more, however, his mind was extremely busy. That agile brain, continually flying off at tangents and hiding its shrewdness behind a laugh, as Salignan perceived, had by this time analyzed the situation; and to be frank about it, Cyrano was in no little alarm.

"This cursed Salignan is an enemy; why, I don't know," he thought. "And there's deep peril in his enmity. The prior's friend, but ineffectual enough to give any help. H-m! That rascal, Mervaut, is in the offing, too. Effiat's at Mont St. Michel, and much depends on how he swings. Ergo, reach him first! But how?"

The answer came almost on the instant. Two pilgrims and a guide came into the tavern, and the guide told his charges that they had another half hour before the sands could be safely traversed. Hearing this, Cyrano pushed back his chair and rose.

"My friends," he said, twisting his mustache with his best military gesture, "I regret to tell you—ah! One word in your ear, Dom Ratran; an excellent jest!" And leaning down, he put his lips to the ear of the prior and breathed six low words.

"Hold them here—give me time!"

Dom Ratran blinked, then chuckled heartily and nodded assent, as at some joke. Cyrano smiled, and met the inquiring gaze of Marianne. He bowed to her.

"I regret that, since I carry dispatches, I cannot pause to keep you company longer," he pursued, with an air of grandeur. "It will not be safe for coaches to cross the sands for some little time; but I am compelled to go ahead—my dispatches take precedence of comfort, alas!"

"Yes, yes," put in Dom Ratran. "We must wait for an hour, then all is safe. And you, my friend, are a fool not to wait also."

Cyrano shrugged. "Bah! Fools make the world move. *Au revoir,* my friends—to our meeting at the Mont this afternoon!"

And he swung away, swaggering out to the courtyard, where he beckoned a groom.

"My horse," he said, taking a gold piece from his pocket. "And this gold écu—a trifle thin, but still gold—goes to you if you find me a guide within two minutes who'll venture to take me to the Mont at once. Another like it to him."

"Good!" said the groom promptly. "I shall guide you myself. It is only a matter of avoiding the channel of the Couesnon, and there is no fog. In two minutes I shall fetch your horse, *monsieur!*"

ONE OF the two minutes passed; and then Cyrano, feeling a touch on his arm, turned to find Salignan at his side, regarding him with bitter, piercing eyes.

"Your pardon, M. de Bergerac," said the real marquis. "I must inform you that in taking over command of Mont St. Michel for his majesty, I have been invested with full powers. I must, therefore, ask you to turn over to me the dispatches you carry."

"Eh?" said Cyrano, taken aback. "And if I refuse, *monsieur?*"

"Then you shall be arrested here this moment. Whether you be Marquis de Bergerac, as I somewhat doubt, or plain M. de Bergerac, I fear that the seventh wound which you anticipate may come to pass in this place, which were a pity."

In the features of the soldier, Cyrano read an implacable determination. He could not tell whether Salignan were a friend of Effiat or no; yet this was no moment for hesitation. He must stake everything upon one cast of the dice.

"Very well, *monsieur*," he assented amiably. "Certainly I am not the man to invoke the anger of his majesty! At least, however, you will grant me the courtesy of breaking the seal of this dispatch with my own hand."

The Marquis de Salignan bowed slightly, his eyes very sharp.

Cyrano took out the paper he had received from Père Carré. It had reposed, untouched, through his misadventures, within an inner pocket. Coolly he broke the seal and opened the paper, glanced at it with widening eyes, and then extended it to Salignan, a sudden laugh of exultation breaking on his lips.

"Here, *monsieur;* you have made one error," he said, his voice ringing. "I did not say I carried dispatches to deliver—I only said they were being carried! This is the dispatch. Evidently you are welcome to peruse it now, since in fullness of time it must be intended for your eyes, after the blank has been filled in."

Salignan took the paper, looked at it, then lifted astonished gaze to Cyrano.

"Eh, *monsieur,* an order of arrest in blank?"

"Signed by his majesty, countersigned by his eminence," and Cyrano twirled his mustache with an amused air. "And if you will observe the broken seal, *monsieur,* you may recognize it as that of Père Carré, whom you may know."

Salignan returned the paper.

"May I ask, *monsieur,*" the royal commandant inquired calmly, "for whom this is intended?"

"That I do not know, as yet," said Cyrano. "I have my suspicions, *monsieur;* Father Time holds many things in his pack, and we should not try to hurry him."

Salignan knew that the man who carried this order of arrest must come from Père Carré, unless the paper had been fraudulently obtained. In any event the holder of the royal signature was to be respected. The marquis bowed slightly.

"Very well, *monsieur*," he said in a cold voice. "We shall meet again, no doubt, later in the day."

"And for several days thereafter, I trust," said Cyrano, laughing.

He was still laughing as he swung up on his horse and left the courtyard with his guide.

CHAPTER VIII

—COMES TO THE MONT.

CYRANO, WITH the guide trotting before, was the first of men to leave Pontorson for the Mont that day; and the broad yellow sands, glinting wet and threaded with streams and pools, stretched out before him to the place which, so wondrous was it, was known sometimes by the simple name of The Marvel, a name more usually applied to the upper portion of the abbey.

Here, in ancient days, two islets had lain among the waters. The farther one, Tombelaine, had been the seat of the English forces during their long siege of the abbey. Except for the fortifications, Tombelaine showed only like a whale-back arising from the sand. It was at the other that Cyrano stared with all his eyes.

Now, where had been an islet, a great pile of masonry was reared toward heaven, flanked by green trees—stout, squat towers and walls about the lower part, leading sharply upward in a maze of buildings, ending with the abbey far above, whose flying buttresses and high towers seemed not the work of human hands. There was something unreal, fairylike, about this high abbey, whose fortifications had resisted all assaults of enemies across the centuries.

Those massive walls seemed part of the rock itself; the flowing, upward-running lines gave a singular effect, when viewed from this side, as though the entire place had been carved out of the solid stone.

From Pontorson, in its remarkably clear-cut outline against an immense horizon of sea and sky, it was a huge gray mass; but as Cyrano, superbly equipped to appreciate this marvel to the utmost, drew closer to the Mont, its aspect changed insensibly, its grayness became a blend of hues and nuances.

There was a glint of steel, too, from the walls and towers. No soldiers were on guard here; the defense force which Salignan was to command was drawn from mainland peasants, serfs of the abbey fiefs that stretched along the shore, but these were guard sufficient both for Mont St. Michel and for Tombelaine. The latter place had an ancient chapel, but was uninhabited. It was to St. Michel's mount that pilgrims came, and it was here that one found the ancient history of both France and England intermingled. No longer were garrisons placed on Tombelaine, and its defending walls stood bare and empty. Its cells and barracks served only for the occasional retreat of monks from the abbey.

Before the solitary grandeur of this place, Cyrano remained silent and wondering; for the moment his volatile and sardonic nature was crushed down. This high abbey seemed to rule men, rather than to be ruled by them. Built across the centuries to resist not man alone, but also fire and earthquake, cut off from the mainland by the water and by sudden fogs which often made the sands impassable at low tide, the Mont gave a very definite impression of solidity, of impervious aloofness, quite apart from its religious character.

Now, as they drew near the sole entrance, the guide came to the stirrup of Cyrano and pointed ahead.

"There, past that gate, *m'sieur*, lies the Court of the Lion. One must give up all arms there. Not even a sword or dagger is allowed. Visitors are expected, one sees; what a devil of a stir must be going on up above, eh? And not a pilgrim these three weeks. That's because of the war. Wait until peace comes, and you'll see the Boulevard crowded all the way up!"

CYRANO WAS not interested in pilgrims. Outside this gate, carelessly dumped on either hand, were two ancient cannon or bombards. The drawbridge was up, but the tiny postern to the left stood open, a little group of guards around it. And suddenly Cyrano realized that he could no longer see anything of what led upward. Squat and small as these walls and towers had seemed from a distance, at close view they loomed tremendous and formidable.

"Your horse, *m'sieur,*" said the guide as Cyrano, coming to the sloping cobbled approach to the gate, was forced to dismount. "The stable can accommodate only the horses of the prior, and all others must go back to the inn. I will take care of it, be assured."

Perforce, Cyrano dismounted, and perceived a gentleman coming through the group of soldiers; a rustic gentleman, shabby and sour-visaged, yet with the sword of his estate.

"Welcome, *monsieur,*" said the other. "I am M. d'Ouville, major of the garrison. If you will honor me with your name, and with whatever weapons you may carry, it will be my privilege to place myself at your service."

Cyrano bowed, and removed his baldric, as the guide took his horse and started back to Pontorson.

"M. d'Effiat is here, I believe," Cyrano said. "Will you have the kindness to let him know that M. le Marquis de Bergerac seeks the honor of an interview with him?"

The major bowed. "I believe, *monsieur,* that your approach was noted. A messenger has just come, commanding that you be brought to the presence of M. d'Effiat immediately. You are acquainted with our Mont? No? Then, if you will permit me to point out a few of its beauties as we ascend—"

Cyrano was only too glad, for at the moment he sorely distrusted his own tongue, and was in wary mood. His pistols had gone with his horse; his sword and dagger were deposited at the gate, and he accompanied Major d'Ouville past the Court of the Lion, so-called because of the beast sculptured above the inner gate, into that of the Boulevard, a larger courtyard whose massive gateway, with portcullis lifted, gave access to the single steep street of the little town.

Not yet, however, was Cyrano to mount these ancient stones. Ouville paused in the open gateway, pointing out various objects, then gestured toward the buildings surmounting the gate and walls and tower beyond.

"M. d'Effiat is here. This morning he is going over the reports and accounts of the late royal commandant, whose quarters are here. If you will please to follow me—"

Being so pleased, Cyrano found himself mounting to the upper part of the gate building, had a glimpse of pleasant-terraced gardens, and so came into a long room where Effiat and two black-clad Benedictines sat at a table heaped with papers, books, quill-racks, inkstands; and very glad indeed was M. d'Effiat of the interruption. He rose at once, and returned Cyrano's bow with a half-smile on his pointed features.

"Ah, M. de Bergerac! Welcome indeed. Dom Le Roy, I leave these matters in your hands; I must have a word with M. de Bergerac. Come, Bergerac, we may take a turn in the gardens, or shall we have a glass of wine?"

"When business presses, wine waits," said Cyrano. The other gave him a sharp glance, then nodded and took his arm.

"Come, then."

Neither spoke until they were out in the sunlight, in the privacy of the little gardens that stretched along beneath the wall as far as the lofty King's Tower and gate a hundred yards farther up the hill. Then Effiat turned.

"Come, *monsieur,* what means this report I had of you?"

"To the devil with it," said Cyrano gayly. "I have a letter for you, my lord. Salignan, the new commandant here, is at Pontorson. He is an old friend of Mlle. de Gisy, whom he is bringing on here at once. That scoundrelly fellow of yours, Mervaut, is a traitor to you. The prior, Dom Ratran, is also at Pontorson, and repays cultivation. He's holding Salignan for a space over the table, until I could have a word with you."

EFFIAT WAS inexpressibly startled by this information. He caught Cyrano's arm, whirled him around, stared into his face for a moment. His own features were white.

"Salignan!" he exclaimed in a low voice. "Marquis de Salignan, eh? The devil!"

"And quite convinced of his own authority," said Cyrano dryly. He was now his assured self once more; he had reached here first with the news, which meant everything. "A difficult gentleman to deal with, I assure you."

"Hm! I know him," said Effiat, biting his lip. "But—you spoke of Mervaut! What mean you? How could he be a traitor to me?"

"Ask that of yourself, *monsieur*," said Cyrano, with a twirl of his mustache.

"*Diable!* Speak out, man. I received word from him that you had attempted to carry off the lady and that he was taking measures to bring her on here."

Cyrano shrugged. "I do not bandy words with lackeys," he said grandly. "You know M. d'Avillon, of course, the honest gentleman who carries so many messages for Monseigneur the Cardinal, and who supplies Richelieu with so much information? Well, your worthy Mervaut is a very good friend of Avillon, that's all. So much so, that he did his best to help Avillon put a knife into me, in consequence of which I lashed him well. I should have left Avillon dead, but contented myself with taking his dispatches."

"His dispatches?" An eager light swept into the face of Effiat. "What were they? Where are they?"

Cyrano twirled his mustache again.

"Ask of your lackey, *monsieur*. Thanks to his efficiency, they were regained by Avillon."

"The devil!"

Consternation and bewilderment had for the moment gripped Sieur d'Effiat. His angry eyes darted this way and that. With a species of contempt, Cyrano saw that here was a man adept at crafty plotting, but utterly helpless when faced with an emergency. In Paris, where he was a great lord, Effiat was a dangerous antagonist. Here, where he was a nominal master, indeed, yet in reality far removed from his own environment, the matter was entirely different. Cyrano, who seldom lost his assurance under any circumstances, lost in this moment his hitherto respect for the abilities of this great noble.

"Come, M. d'Effiat, let us discuss our own relations, if you please," he said quietly, yet compellingly. "I have kept my promise to you; the lady arrives here voluntarily. Therefore, our arrangement is at an end."

Effiat stared at him, brows slightly knitted. Cyrano remembered quite clearly the odd remark made by Mervaut, and was staking his entire play upon it—that remark about Effiat's needing Cyrano.

"So," he continued negligently, "shall I say farewell to you here, and go about my business in these parts, or—"

"Stay," said Effiat. "No—you say you have business in these parts?"

Cyrano shrugged. "Nothing of importance; an old friend whom I have promised to look up whenever I came into the west—one M. de Lorges. True, he is a Huguenot, so it might not be the part of prudence to be too hasty in seeking him out. And on the other hand, I recollect that I promised Mlle. de Gisy to help her ferret out certain manuscripts she hopes to find in the abbey here."

Effiat took his arm, with an air of confidence.

"Look you, Bergerac—an excellent idea! But this scoundrelly Salignan; he and I are not good friends, you comprehend? Remain here for the present, under plea of aiding Mlle. de Gisy in her search. Throw dust in the eyes of Salignan. It may be that things will turn up—things greatly to your advantage. You say that you know M. de Lorges?"

Cyrano smiled to himself. This casual air, this confidential tone, did not deceive him in the least; indeed, it merely emphasized the importance of that final query.

"NATURALLY," CYRANO responded. "Only the other night I met him and we were talking of various matters. He was on the way to his château of Ducey, where a little gathering was being held. A strange man, a strange house, *monsieur;* fatality attending each generation; The father of this gentleman all but captured our sacred Mont during the religious wars, failed disastrously, and is said to walk the shores at night with the devil himself for companion, hoping to capture some errant monk. The grandfather was executed in 1574—he, the Grand Montgommery, who had the supreme misfortune to kill Henry II in a tournament. The great-grandfather—did he not burn François I most grievously, by an accident? Fatality there, in each generation. We should ask Mlle. de Gisy to demand advices from the stars regarding this M. de Lorges."

"Enough," said Effiat, lifting his head. From the lower courtyards, invisible from this spot, ascended a great stir; voices rising, the clatter of hooves on the stones, the rumbling and creaking of coaches. "Our friends are arrived, and I must go. Remain here for a day or so; I must have a talk with you at the first opportunity. You have money? Good; then take a room at one of the taverns, for the hostelry in the abbey, devoted to pilgrims, would scarce suit the comfort or stomach of M. le Marquis de Bergerac. Did you note that lean, white-haired monk in the room above? Seek him out. Dom Le Roy is the name. He is writing volumes about the history of the abbey, and if you seek aught here to interest Mlle. de Gisy, he's your man. I will send for you when the chance offers. *Au revoir!*"

Effiat hurried away, as one of the garrison summoned him in haste.

Thus thrown on his own resources, Cyrano was more than

content. He found his way back to the street, that steep, cobbled way of inns and taverns, running in a gentle left curve up the hill, past the parish church and graveyard, to the platform and enormous sweeping stone stairs that elbowed to the entrance of the abbey above.

Few people were about. At low tide the Montois, as the inhabitants were termed, were out upon the sands below with their morning's catch of fish and those little cockles for which the place was famous. Cyrano had money, he was unhurried, and he was thirsty; there were no pilgrims to advise him, but there were tavern signs in plenty, and he was not unmindful of the popular saying: "Does one go to Mont St. Michel seeking its shrines or its wines?" Thus, when his eyes chanced upon the sign of the Licorne, he twirled his mustache and swaggered into the tavern.

"A Unicorn, a veritable Unicorn!" he murmured. "Therefore made for Cyrano. What ho, mine host! To eat, to drink, to watch the world go by—*holà!*"

The ring of a coin on a table drew the aproned host, and Cyrano installed himself in a corner by the window, while suggestions were poured into his ear. He had eaten hastily at Pontorson, and he was entirely ready to fortify himself anew with strange dishes.

"*Monsieur* may confide his appetite to me! Some *chevrettes, coques fricassées aux fines herbes* in the marvelous butter of Avranches, worthy any gourmet! A fresh salmon from the bay, perhaps, cooked in cider and *tordboyau—*"

"Bring me everything, and your best wine!" exclaimed Cyrano, who could not comprehend the local patois. "And perchance a room afterward, while I am at the Mont—"

"We have no rooms here, *monsieur,*" said the host regretfully. "Great lords like *monsieur* commonly find quarters at the Teste d'Or; I shall myself command you a room there."

"Devil take you, do it after you fetch some wine!"

SO PRESENTLY Cyrano's thirst was appeased, and he

was in proper frame of mind to watch the procession wending its way up the street past his window—a sight which every one else in the place also gathered to watch. Their comments gave Cyrano more than a hint regarding certain of the personages involved, also.

Effiat was handsome, hair freshly curled, a proper lord—but not, of course, to be mentioned in the same breath with the late abbot, the great Duc de Guise. Were not the arms and quarterings of Lorraine so numerous that not a wall in the whole abbey would hold them all, so that a simple cross of Lorraine had been carven instead? But some day, please St. Michel, the abbey would be restored to its old glory. Eh, a lady indeed, and no pilgrim, and with red hair! The blessed Archangel protect us all! And not so young, neither, as might be, and plain in the face, too—

Well, what of that? Every one knows that a man may fall in love with a pretty face and find another prettier, but let him find love in an ugly woman and he is in love for life. And the soldier who walks by her—the new commandant, eh? Looks more of a soldier than the last, and has a sharp eye to boot. A noble, too: things are picking up a bit if he brought along lackeys and valets.

And Dom Charlatan puffing up the hill—shame on his fat face! A disgrace to the Mont, that's what it is, to have such a prior; and the good fathers all know it and feel it, too—him and his horses and his coach! And not to mention the stories about the summer manor at Brion, and you could hear a few stories closer to home as well, if you went to the right quarter—

So they flowed past, noble and soldier and lady and prior, lackeys and guards, and Mervaut fetching up the rear with his red-wealed face, sharp eyes prying here and there. Cyrano grinned at him from the window, and caught the venomous glance, but Mervaut made no sign and passed on.

And, all alone, came a tall, bent figure with white hair—the monk of whom Effiat had spoken, laden down with his books and quills. Cyrano, whose meal had just arrived, hailed him from the doorway, and glad enough was Dom Le Roy to pause in his hot climb and refresh himself with a glass of wine or so; especially as he was a man of insatiable curiosity, and all his wide learning gave him no inkling of what escutcheon those seven stars might be on the flaunting cloak of Cyrano.

An old man, very wise, cynical in his own fashion, sharp-faced and tired of eye, who spent his life delving in the records of the abbey and ferreting out curious tales wherewith to engage his quill and enrich future generations. Presently Dom Le Roy was helping Cyrano with the repast as well as with the wine. As the monk's tongue loosened, his liking for this curious Marquis de Bergerac grew apace; for Cyrano, fresh from the College of Lisieux, himself a delver into curious things, had a smattering of everything from Latinity to witchcraft.

S O T H E Y talked together at length, and Dom Le Roy told of how the dead Montgommery walked at night, and made false money on Tombelaine, and harried the lands and herds of the abbey fiefs; of the felon Abbé Jolivet who had helped at the burning of Jeanne d'Arc; of the long siege during the Hundred Years' War; and finally of Dame Tiphaine, the sorcer-ess—

"Ha! Pause there," exclaimed Cyrano, starting up. "What know you of Du Guesclin's wife, good father? Is it true that she left manuscripts on the stars? It is to look into this report that I am here, as is the lady, Mlle. de Gisy, who knows more of the stars than you or I! Are these reports true?"

"Are they, indeed!" and Dom Le Roy winked across the table. "The good brethren would be scandalized if they knew the truth, but I have set it all down in my 'Curious Researches'[1]— at least, as much of it as might be read without danger to a tender conscience! And is it true that this lady—eh, eh! There's a woman for you! Well, I'm the only soul who knows about those manuscripts, and about the house she built up yonder at

---

1   *This MS is now in the Bibliothèque de Caen.*

the end of the street. It's a ruined heap of stones now. They show pilgrims another house altogether, and I suppose it does the poor souls just as much good. Come, I have the afternoon free!"

"Excellent!" exclaimed Cyrano, and rapped on the table for his score. "You shall show me about the place, my good father, and perhaps we can arrange with the prior for those manuscripts to be seen by the lady, eh?"

"Agreed, my son, agreed!" assented Dom Le Roy joyfully. "To tell you the truth, I should like to know a little more about them myself—their strange symbols, their singular use of words! And while I think of it, what do those seven stars represent upon your cloak? Is it the device of your house?"

Cyrano glanced about, then leaned forward.

"It is a penance laid upon me!" he said solemnly, while the old monk stared at him. "I was under vow during the last campaign, you comprehend. You see this scar here at my throat? I was left for dead under the walls of Arras, when we stormed the breach; and vowed that if I recovered, I would make a pilgrimage hither. Well, I recovered, and I forgot the vow; and good Father Jerome laid the penance upon me of making the pilgrimage, and upon it, of wearing a star on my coat for each time I broke the seventh commandment while on the road—you see, the worthy father knew me of old—and he had me supplied with stars, a plenty of them, in my pouch. So I started from Paris, but I was a long while on the road, and being a fragile man and even as the blessed angels themselves—you will recall the passage in Scripture, no doubt—well, there you are, in brief."

And Cyrano broke into a roar of laughter, for the shocked Dom Le Roy had taken him as seriously as any father confessor. But none the less they started up the hill arm in arm, when the score had been paid, and the old monk pointed out the house where Dame Tiphaine had lived.

Now, however, Cyrano was looking at other and quite different things, for he had recollected his real mission here. And, if he were not mistaken, Marquis de Salignan had also embarked upon a tour of inspection.

CHAPTER IX

— BECOMES A FISHERMAN.

CYRANO AND his guide had come around the great sweep of stairs at the upper end of the street. Here was where the platform and lookout tower faced toward the mainland. The climb was steep, and Dom Le Roy paused for breath.

Seeing a group of guards, armed with pikes, drawn up at one side of the platform, apparently being drilled by his friend Major d'Ouville, Cyrano approached them. As he did so, Salignan strode from the tower and, unobserved, watched Cyrano as he looked over the equipment of the men.

"So, M. de Bergerac, you are interested in our garrison?"

Cyrano turned and swept him a bow.

"Tremendously, my dear Salignan! A soldier is interested in soldiers!"

"Bah!" Salignan fairly spat out the word, and his hard-bitten features expressed all his disgust and contempt for the man facing him. "Look you, M. de Bergerac, I do not care to have you interested in the defenses of this place. You comprehend?"

In his best guardsman's style, Cyrano twirled his mustache, swept the other a slow bow of magnificent insolence, and made response in hot anger. For once, perhaps because he did not hold this soldier-marquis in great esteem, he let impulse rule his tongue.

"And do you, M. de Salignan, imagine that your likes or dislikes are of importance? Not a bit of it, I assure you. Besides, I seriously doubt whether you'll be commandant here very long. If your present attitude persists, I shall certainly be forced to show you how easily a sword-point can take a barber's part, removing choler, blood and life itself at need!"

All this was mere word-play, braggadocio, but it infuriated Salignan, who had his own reasons for suspecting every one around him.

"Look you," Salignan said, coming a step closer, and speaking with cold menace, "whether you be spy or secret agent, noble or serf, I care not. My orders are from His Majesty—and, *pardieu,* I think he has all power to act here!"

"You mistake," riposted Cyrano. "This may be a royal château, but it is also an abbey, and you are not abbot, here. If it comes to an issue of authority, have a care!"

"So!" said Salignan. "You dare to threaten me, eh? I shall not be long here. You dare to speak of killing me? Young man, I know my duty and my powers; you do not. Have a care yourself, lest you come to a surprising and unhappy point of fortune!"

Salignan turned coldly away, and Cyrano rejoined Dom Le Roy, who had heard nothing of the words exchanged. Nor did Cyrano think of it again.

They mounted the remaining steps to the Châtelet, that massive-towered portal which five men could hold against an army, and so came upon a view that astounded Cyrano. Ahead, to left and right, towered high, tremendous walls mounting into heaven. Between these walls ran up a steeper roadway than any they had yet followed, here with steps built, there with the naked rock under their feet.

"This is called the Great Inner Degree," said Dom Le Roy, pausing momentarily for wind. "Those are the abbatial buildings on the left; on the right is the church. Guillaume de Lamps, the thirty-fourth abbot, built that wide stairway ahead of us and the platform at the top of it, called the South Platform. He, too, finished the abbatial buildings and built the bridge over our heads."

Cyrano had nothing to say, for he was lost at the bottom of a great cañon which had been five hundred years in the building. At the height of the fourth story, a covered bridge connected the abbatial buildings on the left with the church on the right.

As Dom Le Roy talked on, Cyrano began to realize something of what this church really was—church built upon church, with the old Norman and pre-Norman foundations and chapels remaining underneath the whole. The very crypt where William the Conqueror and Harold of England had knelt together, was still to be seen. Not a stone in this place but was known to Dom Le Roy, who dwelt in loving detail on every aspect of its building, and knew by heart the chronicle of each successive addition to the vast pile of masonry, from the tread-mill below to the cisterns above.

CLIMBING THE stairs, they came out at length upon the South Platform, before the church, and now the coasts of Normandy and Brittany were suddenly outspread before the eyes of Cyrano—a huge sweep of coast-line, with the sea to the West. Yet, turning, he saw that the ascent was still far from finished. On the north lay the church, and beyond it the buildings which were collectively known as The Marvel.

"And France," exclaimed the enthusiastic Dom Le Roy, "has no richer inheritance of architecture from ancient days than this, my friend! You shall see for yourself."

So Cyrano saw for himself—saw marvels of history in the Hall of the Knights of St. Michael, marvels of wealth in the church, whose treasure was the richest of all France, saw marvels of architecture on every hand, and from the high West Platform looked out across the miles of glistening sands to the distant sea and the far Chausey Islands whence had come the stone for all this work here at the Mont.

These things Cyrano beheld with Dom Le Roy at his elbow; for the old monk the rule of silence did not obtain, and he poured into the ear of Cyrano an eager knowledge, an enthusiasm on every detail. And finally the library, the little room with painted ceiling where the manuscripts were stored, opened to them; but here arrived a brother who made Dom Le Roy an imperious sign, and the latter assented.

"An hour after nones to-morrow, my son," he said to Cyrano. "I am wanted now; but meet me here then, and we will take the manuscripts to her. She would not be admitted here; all this portion of the abbey is cloistered."

Cyrano departed, and was astonished to find sunset not far away. He had experienced an amazing day—one of hard riding, swift changes, action of mind and body. Yet, despite his weariness, he descended the Mont slowly, not disdaining a visit to the guardroom beside the Châtelet entrance as he left the abbey; and, ere he gained the Outer Degree and the huge steps leading down into the little town, the purpose of his visit was accomplished. Fresh from the company of the austere but garrulous Dom Le Roy, he burned with indignation at thought of Dom Charlatan.

"That such a place should be under such a rascally prior!" he reflected. "It's an outrage. Still, I should not complain. This Dom Charlatan may yet serve me well. A score or so of guards here, few arms, no cannon—hm!

"With a mere hint of inside aid, and half a company of musketeers at my back, I'd guarantee to seize the place any dark night. So Effiat has need of me, eh? We'll look into that a trifle—on the morrow."

He located the Teste d'Or, found a room awaiting him, and like a good campaigner turned in without supper and made up for lost sleep.

With morning, Cyrano boldly invaded the abbey and the quarters of Dom Ratran, who greeted him with open arms and worried brow. The excellent prior was deep in accounts, having settlements to make with Sieur d'Effiat; and he complained bitterly of the unexpectedly businesslike attitude of the titular abbot. Cyrano left him, after discovering that Marianne de Gisy occupied a chamber in the abbatial building—to the great scandal of the monks.

*"But monsieur, you forgot my
poniard," Cyrano pointed out.*

Between his accounting with the prior and the archdeacon,
who held the treasury keys, and a heated interview with M. de
Salignan, who was most vigorously taking over all dispositions
as to the defense of the Mont, Sieur d'Effiat was spending an
energetic if not exactly peaceful morning, and had no time for
amusement. Thus it was not strange that Cyrano, unhindered,
was presently escorting Marianne de Gisy about such portions
of the Mont as would not be profaned by the footsteps of a
woman.

SINCE, HOWEVER, the greater part of The Marvel
was thus cloistered, presently the two came to rest upon the
great West Platform outside the front doors of the church. The
terrace fronted upon a gulf that dropped away to the sea, hun-
dreds of feet below. Across the gardens and rabbit-warrens,
across the fount and chapel of St. Aubert at the edge of the isle,
they looked out upon the vista which opened to them—the
Chausey islets, fiefs of the abbey, lying outspread upon the
horizon; the headland of Granville, the green Norman fields

beyond the glistening sands, and southward the green Breton fields and the rising summit of Mont Dol. But to Cyrano all this was as nothing; he was alone here with Marianne, and she was smiling upon him.

"The manuscripts, then, this afternoon!" she exclaimed, when he had told her of Dom Le Roy.

"Oh, yes; and Effiat, and your quarrel with the abbey, and other things," said Cyrano. "You are a very busy lady."

"And you have not yet explained your absence," said she, her kindly eyes dwelling upon him thoughtfully. "What happened to you?"

"Hm! If I tell you the truth," said Cyrano, thinking aloud, "then I must risk a great deal; and if I lied to you, Daughter of the Sun, I should despise myself all my life thereafter. It seems to me that here before the church doors we have come to the parting of the ways, you and I."

"Eh? The parting of the ways?" she repeated, alertness in her eyes now.

"Exactly." Cyrano leaned one elbow on the parapet and considered her features, and those dark and liquid eyes of his were alight with the gambler's eagerness. "Could not you have read these things in the stars? Consider what can happen in a day, in an hour! I can read the eyes of men, at any rate. You have found in Salignan a more powerful friend than I; and this fat prior, Dom Ratran, assuredly would fall at your feet in a moment. So you are safe enough without me; and what shall I do? Destiny trembles on the turn of a word. If I lie, it may be the better part, yet we shall then assuredly come no closer together. If I tell the truth, you'll learn what is no business of yours or any woman's, and yet thereby our paths may run together. A proper gamble, Daughter of the Sun, with the remainder of life staked on the outcome."

She divined the passionate earnestness beneath his cryptic words, and laid her hand on his, and smiled a little.

"Ah, Cyrano, you are a strange man!" she said quietly. "Surely there is none other just like you, and I should not care to have our paths diverge; so gamble, my Marquis of the Seven Stars! And never do it by halves. Once you said not to ask you whence you came, until later. Well, I ask you now."

"So be it, shining lady," answered Cyrano, with a hint of pallor in his swarthy scarred cheeks. "Of your sweet sad face, of your clear eyes, of your frank and comradely spirit, I make my litany; henceforth and always we travel the highway together, or here and now we separate. So be it!"

"So be it," she echoed, and there was a shining light in her face as she watched him. "Whence come you?"

Cyrano looked into her eyes. "From uselessness," he responded in a low, clear voice. "From pretense and falsity, from the benches of cabarets and wine-shops, from the barracks of a soldier, from glittering lies, from shabby mockeries! My grandsire was a fish merchant of Paris; Savinien de Cyrano my name. As a guardsman I played the Gascon, took the name of Bergerac from an estate my father had purchased."

There in the sunlight on the platform, high between sea and sky, he stripped himself bare and laid before her the shamed and sorry Cyrano, holding back nothing—relating even the story of the slain monkey, whereby laughter had drummed him out of the guards into purgatory. And he came to the day when Effiat had found him and had hired him.

"So there's the truth for you, dear shining lady," he said. "You see what I am. And yet you would have our ways lie together? I think not."

VERY WARM and sweet was her smile, and her eyes very bright as she regarded him.

"And why should you think so, my Cyrano?" she asked.

"Why?" He made an impatient gesture. "Bah! What am I, before you? You are a Madonna placed high upon a mountaintop, shining afar in beauty and goodness; peace lies in your presence, and in the touch of your hand is a benediction. And I—what am I?"

"You are Cyrano," she said, unsmiling now. "And I am a woman, no more,"

He met her eyes for a deep unmoving moment, and a slow tinge of red crept into his cheeks, and a flash leaped in his eye.

"So be it! God bless you for those words," he said simply. "Then here's the wager on the table!"

And he told her of Père Carré, and of his own errand here, and of all he suspected; he told of Avillon and the little whip, of M. de Frontard and Sieur de Lorges—the Montgommery. Then he fell silent, for her eyes were strange.

"You did not know that I am of the religion?" said Marianne.

"So?" Cyrano shrugged, and the light died out of his face. "Well, no matter; I might have known the dream could not last. .So, dear shining lady, I lose my stake like a gentleman, and kiss your hand—"

"Not so fast," and she smiled into his eyes. "It is true that my family are all Huguenot, but I am no politician, my friend; and in this affair I seem to see more then you. Père Carré mentioned the English?"

"Not in so many words," admitted Cyrano. "I inferred—"

"And I, too, infer," said Marianne, her fair brow knitted. "Listen. Twice the Huguenots attempted to seize this place. The first time they went away, bootless. The second time, they entered one by one at night, ninety-six of them—and as each man entered, he was seized and decapitated. I have met this Sieur de Lorges, and he is no soldier. The enemies of France are concerned in this whole affair, my friend. Let us wait a little, let me try the turn of astrology in this business! If, as I think possible, English are concerned in it—then you will not find me a traitor to France."

"No?" Cyrano was frankly puzzled. "And yet my wager is lost."

"Is it lost?" she broke in, smiling again. "Have I said so? Not I."

Cyrano seized her hand. "Plain words, plain words!" he cried out passionately. "I am weary to death of pretty speeches, of fine mockeries, of deadly politeness that stabs in the back! I can play the game of intrigue with those whose life it is, but not with you; no lies with you, no deception, no trickery or pretense, dear shining lady! Let the thing lie clear-cut between us. All the future hangs on it, and the dead past can drop away from us! Plain words, then—"

"Have you given me plain words, poet?" said she, still smiling at him.

"I have not dared," he returned simply. "I love you, Daughter of the Sun; from the moment our eyes first met, I have loved you. That I should dare utter such words to you were sacrilege unless my whole heart and spirit were in them. Is that plain enough?"

His face was very white, so that the scars upon it showed darkly, as his intent eyes devoured her.

"Plain enough, Cyrano," she said, very softly. "Would you have me utter plain words also—though I might later be sorry for them?"

"I would have you regret nothing for my sake or because of me," returned Cyrano. "But you are no silly girl who does not know her own mind, dear lady."

Marianne sighed a little. "No, that is too true, I fear. Very well, then; I love you, Cyrano."

Even as he trembled under these words, scarce believing that he heard aright, there were steps, and several of the monks appeared, entering the church. From the doors hurried a lay brother, approaching the two as they stood at the parapet.

"YOUR PARDON," the messenger interrupted them, "but Prior Ratran has had me seeking you this long while. You are both bidden to his table. Sieur d'Effiat and Marquis de Salignan are awaiting your coming."

So there was no more chance for words between them in privacy, but the smile in the eyes of Marianne, and the exultant happiness in the scarred face of Cyrano, were words enough.

Cyrano, indeed, was beside himself with joy; he was uplifted to the heights, and the result of this mental intoxication was to prove serious.

Salignan was so ill-advised as to forget his courtesy in his dislike of Cyrano. To tell the truth, the old soldier had discovered a lamentable slackness in the discipline of the Mont's soldiery, and a lack of arms and equipment; even the cisterns which would supply the abbey with water in the event of a siege or drought, were uncleaned and leaky. During the meal, Salignan broached all this to Effiat, who impatiently waved him aside.

Dom Ratran, now in mood of jollity, flung a jest at Cyrano; and the harassed Salignan directed a biting observation in regard to his seven stars. Whereupon Cyrano laughed out and broke into an amazing farrago—half absurd, half serious—pouring upon the head of the furious commandant a flood of poorly digested wisdom which, none the less, held his hearers spellbound. For Cyrano had this quality, that when he spoke, his furious earnestness and intense nature made men listen.

Salignan, who considered that the extravagances of Cyrano were in mockery of him, became white with fury.

"I should like to know, *monsieur*," he intervened icily, "just who you are and what you are doing here at Mont St. Michel. Come! What is your actual errand here?"

"He is here as my escort, *monsieur*," said Marianne de Gisy.

Effiat, laughing, leaned forward. "Ah! He is here as my very good friend."

Dom Ratran, holding his sides with laughter, squeaked out his own response:

"Furthermore, he is here because I like him, I also! Bergerac, stay here as long as you like. You are not accountable to any one but me and Sieur d'Effiat. The royal commander had better not interfere with the jurisdiction of the abbey, which is jealously held in the hands of—"

The badgered Salignan had lost his temper by this time, for

it was quite true that the monks held most jealously to their privileges. He darted one angry glance around, but said nothing of having been accorded full powers here. Instead, he rose and bowed.

"In such case, gentlemen, I retire very gladly to my own quarters, now and hereafter. Mlle. de Gisy, I shall do myself the honor of visiting you later. Good day, gentlemen."

Effiat smiled thinly as the marquis departed. Marianne de Gisy frowned a little, for she liked Salignan. Cyrano twirled his mustache and met the jovial laugh of Prior Ratran, who clapped him on the shoulder.

"By St. Michel! I'm not sorry. I didn't like that rascal. I'd not be astonished if he were a rank heretic, the stern-faced rogue!"

This flicked Effiat's pride of caste on the raw. He rose, in his lazy, elegant manner, and was about to speak when there was a knock and Dom Le Roy entered the chamber. The old monk addressed himself to Prior Ratran, somewhat nervously.

"Reverend father, there—there is a dispute with the librarian. I desire to remove certain manuscripts, and as there was no signed order—"

"Ah, the manuscripts of Dame Tiphaine!" exclaimed Cyrano delightedly. "They are for Mlle. de Gisy to peruse—you will remember I spoke to you about them yesterday?"

"Certainly, certainly." Dom Ratran rose and beckoned Effiat. "Will you be good enough to come into the next room; we'll give this librarian a countersigned order that will set his precious doubts at rest! Dom Le Roy, you can give us the proper wording of it—devil take these rules and regulations! Another strip of vellum to be pasted away and filed and counter-filed!"

And with a growl, the prior led the way into the little alcove adjoining, which served as a writing room.

CYRANO, ALONE with Marianne de Gisy, swooped hawklike above her, his eyes alight.

"I have it, I have it!" he said softly. "You spoke of astrology; good! Test out your astrology on Effiat. He's a gullible fool, like all these courtiers. Test him out; speak of the English—you comprehend? You've read it in the stars, and so forth. Give him a sample of judiciary astronomy that will leave him gaping for the next fortnight."

Laughing, she lifted her face to him, and Cyrano's lips met hers for a brief instant. It was their first kiss.

Effiat came back into the room, bowing to Marianne.

"May I escort you to your chamber, *mademoiselle?* Dom Le Roy will bring the manuscripts to you there, in ten minutes, together with writing materials. M. de Bergerac, my chamber adjoins this; will you have the goodness to await me there? I desire a few words with you at once."

"My faith," mocked Cyrano to himself, as he bowed assent, "no less than I desire a few with you, my good lord!"

So Effiat escorted Marianne to her own lodging, and Dom Le Roy departed to the library. Dom Charles Ratran came back to find Cyrano filling the wine cups for a last toast.

"With all my heart," said the fat prior, lifting his flagon. "To our fair astrologer!"

"And confusion to that simpering abbot of yours," amended Cyrano. "Hark you, Dom Ratran! A word of warning. Look to yourself! This new captain of the Mont is a veritable living ramrod, devil take him. As soon as he settles down to writing a few reports, you'll all be in hot water. And as for Monsieur d'Effiat, speak him fair on all counts, but watch him narrowly. I have reason to believe that he is in close friendship with the Sieur de Lorges and other Huguenots of the vicinity."

Dom Ratran goggled at this, and swiftly signed himself.

"Thanks, my friend," he said with his odd simplicity of manner, so in contrast with his superficially crafty features. "And M. de Salignan warned me against you, also, though for no particular reason. He does not like any one, it seems."

"They're all at odds," and Cyrano laughed gayly. "So much the better for honest men, good father! And now I must leave you."

He reached Effiat's apartment, a huge and very handsomely furnished room set aside for the use of the abbot, but rarely occupied, and it was Mervaut who admitted him. The lackey said no word, and did not lift his eyes. Cyrano surveyed him and chuckled.

"So you've learned your lesson, my friend? I trust so. Where is Avillon?"

"I do not know, my lord," said Mervaut humbly, eyes on the ground. Yet a dusky flush crept into his marked features, and Cyrano knew there was hatred behind the lowered lids.

"Get out and stay out," said Cyrano testily. Mervaut left the room in silence.

Cyrano walked over to the casement and looked out across the sands to the Norman coast. The great happiness that had come to him was, for the instant, forgotten; he had of a sudden entered upon a new game. All these men around him, even Dom Ratran, were potential enemies; he stood quite alone, and now his groping hand had chanced upon a weapon.

"Why not? I am Cyrano!" he murmured in cheerful mockery of himself. "I can juggle them, if any one can—aye, lead them all in a fine morris dance! By to-morrow, Marianne will know whether Effiat is really planning treachery. A word to Dom Ratran that Effiat plans to remove him and appoint another prior; a word to Salignan that Effiat and Dom Ratran are conspiring to turn over the Mont to the Huguenots; a word to Effiat that Salignan holds full powers instead of being merely the royal captain here. And that rascal Avillon! I wish I could reach him—him, above all! Hm!"

HE STRODE to the entrance, threw open the door, and saw Mervaut standing outside.

"Hark you, Mervaut! I ask no questions, you comprehend; but I have reasons for desiring speech with Sieur d'Avillon as quickly as possible."

"You, M. le Marquis?" said Mervaut, incredulity in his face. "With Sieur d'Avillon?"

"Exactly," returned Cyrano. "He will understand, if you do not."

"I know nothing about him, my lord," said the lackey, evading his glance.

Cyrano laughed and went into the room again. From this brief dialogue he knew or guessed two things. First, Mervaut could and would get the message to Avillon. Second, Avillon had not told Mervaut that M. de Bergerac was no Gascon marquis at all, but a mere Parisian commoner. Cyrano was still chuckling, over this stroke of luck, when Effiat came into the room.

"Ah, M. de Bergerac, good! The lady has her manuscripts, and to-night we take up with the monks the matter of her disputed lands. Now, a word with you. We are friends. You are to be relied upon. You detest the cardinal—"

Cyrano lifted his hand. "One moment," he exclaimed gravely. "I gather that this is a question of intrigue; say no more! Let no word of it pass your lips in this place. I suspect your lackey, I suspect these, very walls. Tell me no details; tell me but one thing! This conspiracy—will it assure the overthrow of that damned Richelieu?"

"It will assure not only his overthrow," said Effiat, "but his disgrace and arrest."

"Excellent! Then, *monsieur,* to attain such an end, I would conspire against St. Michel himself! You may count upon me."

If there were irony in these words, Effiat quite missed it.

"Very well," he said, with a nod of satisfaction. "It's understood. As to Mervaut, you have already warned me. I'm watching the fellow, giving him false information; if he betrays it, there's no harm done, and he'll betray himself. Meanwhile, he's of use to me. So, it's agreed, *monsieur?*"

"Agreed," said Cyrano, and twirled his mustache.

A knock at the door, and Mervaut entered. There was a fisherman below, he said, who had just come across the sands from Avranches; a man from St. Malo, who declared that he had a vow to fulfill, and that part of this vow consisted in obtaining the blessing of the abbot of Mont St. Michel. Protest and expostulation had been vain. The man had insisted that his petition be taken to Sieur d'Effiat, and nothing the monks could say was of any avail.

Effiat laughed carelessly. "Bring him to me, then; much good may my blessing do him!" he said. "Wait a moment, Bergerac. Let us see what manner of fisherman this man from St. Malo may be!"

"Oh-ho!" said Cyrano, but to himself, with a low chuckle. "Something in the wind here—and now's the time for my gentle hint!" So thinking, he came close to Effiat, the while they waited. "A word in your ear, *monsieur:* look you to our friend M. de Salignan! He and I had speech yesterday, and I gather that his is no ordinary commission. I'd not be surprised if he had a troop of horse somewhere close by on the coast, awaiting a summons from him!"

Effiat started. For an instant his face blanched, then he nodded. He said no word, however, for now Mervaut was showing a bearded fisherman into the room, a hesitant, burly, sea-tanned man, who looked from Effiat to Cyrano inquiringly. Curtly ordering Mervaut to leave the room, Effiat stepped forward.

"I am Sieur d'Effiat. You may speak plainly before us both. A message?"

"To-morrow or next day the fish can be delivered, *monsieur.* Where?"

"Tombelaine," said Effiat. "Instructions will be waiting there. The second night from this."

The fisherman departed with a nod of comprehension. Effiat looked at Cyrano and smiled, in his thin way, but gave no explanation. Cyrano, however, needed none. What better place could be found for men to hide themselves than on Tombelaine?

"So," muttered Cyrano, as he also took his departure, "so we are fishermen now—fishers of men, eh? Well, I believe we have most distinguished predecessors in that occupation!"

CHAPTER X

—GOES A RIDING.

THESE TWO days Cyrano spent delving about the ancient Mont like a veritable mole, reveling in its beauty, its solid grandeur, its ways and customs. He dined in the huge refectory where Henry II of England had sat at meat, while the silent brethren listened to the drone of the reader from the lectern. He visited the library with its painted domed ceiling, and saw the manuscripts collected here in the twelfth century, and ever increased with the years until Mont St. Michel became known as the "City of Books."

With his lively curiosity, Cyrano neglected nothing, went everywhere, from the dungeons beneath the crypts to the treasury where the greatest treasure in all France was stored; and, it must be admitted, he paid due attention to the taverns and wine-shops down the single street.

He made friends with the monks, whom he respected, and he fraternized with the sullen guards, serfs from the abbey fiefs who were forced to this duty. Of Marianne he saw a little, and of Salignan he saw nothing until the second morning, when he encountered the marquis in the street of the town. Cyrano halted and saluted him.

"A moment, M. le Marquis!" he said gayly, when Salignan would have passed on. "Come, grant me but a moment and you'll not regret it!"

Salignan eyed him sourly. "Well?" he rasped.

"Not at all well, *monsieur*," said Cyrano, coming closer and lowering his voice. He spoke quietly, soberly, driving home his words. "You dislike me, heaven knows why—"

"I suspect you, *monsieur*," said Salignan.

"Very good. There are others toward whom your suspicions

might better be directed, then. Our friend Effiat, for one—how if I were to prove to you that he is in communication with certain of the Huguenot leaders?"

Salignan showed no surprise. "Then I should say that you were betraying him, *monsieur.* I know more than you think, my good Bergerac."

With which Salignan bowed coldly and went his way, leaving Cyrano somewhat discomfited and a trifle startled. How much did the man know, indeed? Four of Salignan's own servants, who looked like soldiers, had arrived and served the commandant in his quarters in the King's Tower; except for these, Salignan seemed very much alone, treating Effiat with extremely cold courtesy and Prior Ratran with open contempt and disdain.

"The devil!" cogitated Cyrano. "I am afraid of that man; evidently he believes in doing his duty; and just what is his duty here?"

Later that morning, standing in the transept of the church with Marianne de Gisy and watching the ancient stained glass windows lighted into glory by the sun, he mentioned Salignan. She turned to him quickly.

"Ah, Cyrano—have you not guessed? Years ago when I was a girl he would have married me; and I think he is of the same mind to-day. He is a very proud man, a great soldier and no courtier; Richelieu trusts him implicitly. He dislikes you, has almost hated you from the first."

"Come, then, we have answer enough!" and Cyrano laughed gayly. "He has sensed the truth, eh? Well, I'll not be angry with him, poor man! By the way, you've had no trouble with Effiat, nor any hint of what he intends toward you?"

Her eyes became troubled. "Hints enough, but nothing definite. I talked with him this morning—pretended to have drawn his horoscope, and said that an English alliance would bring him to great heights. He said nothing, but smiled to himself in his sly way—oh, I hate the man! You know we go riding this afternoon?"

"Dom Charlatan said something of it. Does Salignan go with us?"

"I think not. Major d'Ouville is going in his stead. A hunt in the abbey preserves, and we spend the night at the Brion manor. Dom Ratran offered me his coach, but I prefer to ride with you and the others."

"By all means!" exclaimed Cyrano. "When do we leave—oh, we must await the tide, eh? Very good. Marianne, there's more than riding afoot for to-night. I do not yet know just what; but our honest Effiat is up to some deviltry. I'll get to the bottom of it before the day's over."

IMMEDIATELY AFTER noon meat came word that Dom Ratran's coach was ready and that horses for the others were coming across the new-bared sands from Pontorson, so the prior and his guests descended the winding street, and were joined at the barbican gate by d'Ouville, who would have charge of the prior's usual escort. Effiat and his lackey, Dom Ratran and his equipage, Marianne and Cyrano made up the party.

Mervaut hastened forth to meet the stream of peasants with their carts and barrows, and brought in the horses. As he held Effiat's stirrup, he slipped a bit of paper into his master's hand; Cyrano detected it, and saw Effiat read the message, held in his cupped hands, an instant later. Having read, the noble smiled slightly and shredded the paper between his fingers into tiny bits; but, in doing this, his eyes lifted to the Norman coast as though he were smiling approval at some one there.

"So!" thought Cyrano, accustomed to read men's faces rather than their words. "Some one has sent you a note, has made a rendezvous, eh? No fisherman this time; who, then? Now, Cyrano, step carefully! Ice is on the cobblestones—ashes on your shoes, my Cyrano, and no mercy for any one who slips!"

Mervaut was at his side, putting the reins in his hands, murmuring a low word.

"Stop at the Pontorson inn—the first room at the head of the stairs. Avillon."

"Mervaut!" Effiat had turned, and addressed the lackey sharply. "This extra horse—"

"Is for me, *monsieur*," said Mervaut.

"You will not accompany us to-day," rejoined his master. "Dom Ratran! Perhaps one of your attendants can lead this horse back to Pontorson. Ready?"

They set off, leaving Mervaut staring and scowling there at the entrance gate, and Cyrano chuckled at the lackey's discomfiture. It so happened that M. d'Ouville, who for all his sour and shabby appearance was of the provincial nobility, was riding ahead of the coach with Marianne; thus Cyrano fell in with Effiat behind the coach, and laughed softly.

"Good, *monsieur*, good! You did well to leave that man behind. Now I have proof of his treachery."

Effiat gave him a sharp and wary glance. "Proof?"

"Yes. He told me that a man wants to see me at the Pontorson inn. No other than Sieur d'Avillon, emissary and messenger of M. the Cardinal-Duke, whom may God protect!" Cyrano whined devoutly, then broke into his gay laugh, as Effiat looked startled. "Contrive a halt there, you comprehend? Let me see this man. Ten to one he wants to bribe me, pump information out of me! Well; I'll give him plenty—and a swordthrust to boot if needs be."

Effiat was obviously disquieted. "Spies!" he muttered. "I don't like this, Bergerac. This Avillon is a viper. It were better to—"

He bit his lip, and Cyrano could well read the uneasy alarm, the half-uttered wish, in the man's heart. Effiat was weighing chances; he was not a man of swift decision, and to kill the chief emissary of the Cardinal was a matter for sober second thought.

Cyrano eyed him askance, with derision and contempt for such crafty scheming, and so broke the silence.

"Better to finish him on the spot! Aye, perhaps. Yet, consider: what if Salignan came not alone to the Mont, but has a troop of horse somewhere near by, ready to be thrown into the abbey at a moment's signal? What if this Avillon be working with Salignan, suspecting much, waiting to learn more?

"Say the word and I'll twist my dagger in Avillon's belly right gladly—but is it wise?"

"You are right, you are right," murmured Effiat. "Talk with him, then, learn what's in the wind, throw him off the scent! Aye, the stop at Pontorson will suit me well. Just the thing, indeed."

CYRANO PONDERED this. Ah, the message Effiat had received! And to-night, the "fish" would be delivered at Tombelaine! Cyrano's pulse stirred to it all—things were happening this day, of a certainty.

As they rode shoreward, he took counsel with himself. In his pocket reposed that blank *lettre de cachet;* he had but to fill in Effiat's name, call upon Salignan to arrest the noble, tell what he knew. But this smacked too rankly of spy's work to suit Cyrano's taste. Further, his evidence was by no means conclusive.

"Slowly does it!" he told himself complacently. "I've got them all by the ears now; the next thing is to make certain about these English. Then, to action!"

What he quite overlooked was that Sieur d'Avillon might cherish a very natural resentment over what had happened at their first meeting.

The yellow cliffs spread out ahead, and the road turned sharply, and they were climbing the little ascent to Pontorson, when Effiat spurred ahead and drew in beside the coach, speaking with Dom Ratran. Cyrano delayed no longer, but with a wave of his hand to Marianne, put in his spurs and drove his horse on toward the tavern.

Turning into the inn yard, he dismounted and glanced around. At one side a stone stairway ran up the inner wall, gaining the upper rooms. Cyrano noted three cavaliers talking at one side as their horses were baited, but did not pause;

mounting the stairs, he entered the corridor above and knocked on the first door. The voice of Avillon bade him enter.

Cyrano stood on the threshold, then advanced and closed the door. The room was small. Avillon sat at a table, writing, staring up at his visitor with quick recognition and a half-snarling smile. His wide-boned face with its cleft chin and steady eyes was weary; his clothes evidenced hard riding of late.

"Good morning, M. de Bergerac," he said, without rising. "I am indeed honored."

"Naturally, you are," assented Cyrano, with a deep bow, and fastened his mocking gaze upon Avillon. "It is a pity you did not take more direct measures to obtain your whip, *monsieur,* you might have saved us both some inconvenience. However—"

"However, you desire to see me, and I desire to see you," said Avillon. "Come! Place to a guest! Your errand with me?"

"Is a simple one. By this time you have undoubtedly assured yourself that I come from Père Carré indeed," said Cyrano, dropping his mocking air. "Well, then; do we work together or against each other?"

Avillon smiled slightly. "I know nothing about you, my dear M. de Bergerac," he said.

"Excellent!" returned Cyrano blandly. "Then we quite understand one another."

He paused, for a singular expression had come into the face of Avillon, whose eyes were directed at the reliquary given Cyrano by Père Carré. This golden star on its thin gold chain had escaped at his throat and hung against his royal purple velvet, lending richness to his appearance.

"You appear to be replete with stars, *monsieur,*" said Avillon slowly. "May I inquire whence came this sample of the goldsmith's art? It seems familiar to me."

"This reliquary? Oh, it was a token of esteem from our good Père Carré," and Cyrano twisted his mustache complacently, more than a little pleased by the impression he was making. "You recognize it? Perhaps you know that it contains a fragment of feather from the wing of St. Michel himself. A very appropriate gift, under the circumstances."

"So it would seem," replied Avillon dryly. "There is something I desire to ask you, *monsieur*. On the occasion of our first meeting—you recall the two Egyptians? Well, then, when you were so astute as to take my whip, did you also take anything from them? In the way of a memento, perchance."

Cyrano probed that wide and powerful face for the meaning behind these words. There must be a meaning, and a weighty one, he knew on the instant. The very fact of Avillon's presenting such a question in this manner, showed its importance.

THEN, FOR the first time, Cyrano recollected the leather scapulary which the Egyptian woman had torn from her neck and thrust into the hand of Marianne. He had never thought about it since, but of a sudden the memory broke sharply on his mind. And, instantly, Cyrano lost his swagger and became an ingenuous and guileless young man.

"Ah, *monsieur*, I did not think it worth while to search those Egyptians," he responded, with a shrug. "As to your whip, that was largely accident, for it served me well as a weapon. Also, it was a pretty toy. What might it be that so interests you? The Egyptians carried treasure, then?"

Avillon looked at him for a moment, then snarled.

"The saints preserve us from meddling fools such as you! Ah, well, what is done, is done!" And, suddenly as he had snarled, Avillon forced a smile, put on a mantle of affability, and held out a hand. "Come—I was wrong to despise you. I perceive that you are a gentleman of more worth than I had thought. Père Carré gave you that reliquary, eh? Have you any mind to part with it, *monsieur?*"

Cyrano looked rather stupid at this.

"But why would you want it?" he asked.

"As a matter of religious sentiment, of course," was the negligent response.

"Alas, *monsieur*, I regret that I cannot accommodate you,"

said Cyrano, with a sigh. "Unhappily, I myself have a certain amount of the same feeling—"

"Ah!" Avillon started as though in recollection. "I had all but forgotten. Among other things, I received a letter yesterday addressed to you, *monsieur*. Where did I put those dispatches? Here they are; and yours—

He produced a folded and sealed paper. Cyrano took it, and a sudden premonition seized upon him; the seal was that of Père Hugo Carré. Avillon was watching him, half smiling, as he broke the seal and opened the paper.

The letter was a curt instruction: to return immediately to Paris and report to the Dominican in Rue St. Jacques.

For a long moment Cyrano stared at the writing, his brain racing at top speed. For this, of course, he had to thank Avillon and his own imprudent words on the road near Palaiseau. Avillon was in charge of this intrigue and would brook no interference; at his word, Cyrano had been called in like a dog brought to heel.

The thought burned. Cyrano knew that he himself, and he alone, held all the threads of this affair in his own hand. He was not minded to serve as a spy and make report; no! Action was one thing, betrayal another. Now, all in a moment, was gone the glorious sense of free authority, the feeling that he was directing destiny and playing with puppet-men; this buoyant magnificence was suddenly stripped away, and again he was the drunken poet of the taverns.

And what of Marianne de Gisy?

"Thank you, *monsieur*," said Cyrano quietly, as he folded the letter. A fire was burning in the hearth; Cyrano dropped the paper into the flames and turned, met the gaze of Avillon. "You are, perhaps, aware that within a few hours certain Englishmen will be landed upon the soil of France?"

"Eh?" Avillon's face suddenly lighted up. "English? Is this true, *monsieur?*"

Cyrano looked at him and laughed, scornfully. Give up now, when he alone held mastery of the situation? Never!

"As to that, *monsieur,* you will know soon," he said, and strode to the door. Avillon sprang erect, called sharply to him, but Cyrano left the room without response.

O N T H E stairs, he paused, looked down into the courtyard. Outside in the street, Dom Ratran's coach had halted, with the horses; men were carrying out flagons of wine. In the courtyard, however, stood Effiat, talking with the three cavaliers whom Cyrano had observed; they were glancing up, had seen him, and Effiat looked up at him. Cyrano made an imperative gesture, repeated it. The four men exchanged a look and a word, then Effiat led the way to the stairs.

Cyrano knew now who they were. The note had told Effiat to meet them here; undoubtedly they were Huguenots, emissaries from Sieur de Lorges. And watching them, Cyrano laughed to himself.

"Well?" exclaimed Effiat sharply, joining Cyrano.

"Well enough, *monsieur,*" said Cyrano gayly, so that the three others could hear. "I think that your destiny sits in that first room yonder. Is it true that within a day there will be a party of English landed near by?"

A low oath burst from Effiat; the three cavaliers exchanged a look of consternation and dismay. Cyrano smiled ironically. True, then!

"If this Sieur d'Avillon goes on to the Mont," he pursued, "he will certainly interview M. de Salignan, who will as certainly summon a few score men and throw them into the place. I am not aware, gentlemen, just how such action would coincide with your private desires—"

"Ha, Effiat!" said one of the cavaliers in a low voice. "Do you want to see us all follow the road my uncle went, to the scaffold?"

Effiat reached out and plucked from its sheath the large poniard at Cyrano's belt; a tide of passion suffused his features, and without a word he pushed Cyrano savagely to one side and strode past him. The other three followed, hands at swords; steel rasped on scabbard as they plunged into the corridor.

Cyrano stood there for a space,, looking down at the courtyard. He knew these great nobles, these crafty and indecisive men, slow to impulse, so well served as seldom to serve themselves; put blade in hand, sudden fury in heart, and tragedy came swiftly. A smile of sardonic delight touched his lips.

"And I, Savinien de Cyrano, the gutter bravo, the hireling— at my bidding he goes to do his own killing! I like this. Decidedly, it has a savor! I am indeed become Marquis de Bergerac when an Effiat does my work for me!"

EFFIAT REAPPEARED suddenly. Murder was in his white face, and his gray eyes were blazing and scintillating sparks of light; he was breathing hard. He paused, looked down at his hands, and with his crimson cloak rubbed at a red smear on his right hand.

"Come," he said abruptly, and gestured toward the courtyard. "Let us be off. They are destroying his papers."

"But, *monsieur,* you forgot my poniard!" complained Cyrano with a grimace. "And now I have no weapon at all, but the pistols at my saddle. Decidedly, M. l'Abbé, you must give me dispensation—release me from my vow not to carry sword!"

Effiat looked straitly at him for an instant, and caught his humor. In this glance the two men came to closer understanding than ever before. A savage little laugh came to Effiat's lips.

"I release you, and Dom Ratran will verify it," said he ironically. "Get a sword when and where you can—but in God's love let's be off! You and I must ride hard this day if we're to meet M. de Lorges."

He was descending the stairs hastily as he spoke. Cyrano followed, blinking, taking his time. Meet Sieur de Lorges, eh? Then he had been right. A meeting with the Huguenot leaders. And up there in the room papers were being burned while a dead man lay sprawled across the table with a poniard sunk in his throat.

"Ah, M. d'Avillon!" murmured Cyrano, glancing up behind him at the corridor. "You have turned many an ugly trick in your day; but the sorriest of them all, for yourself, was when you made Père Carré recall me. I am glad I didn't kill you myself. Not that you'd burden my conscience particularly—but it's good to be able to tell the truth occasionally. And when I tell Salignan who killed you—ha! *Au revoir,* Sieur d'Avillon; I'll see you on the other side the Styx in due time."

When Cyrano came out to the coach he found Effiat speaking with the prior, while Marianne and M. d'Ouville sipped stirrup-cups and listened.

"These gentlemen informed me that the Royal Commissioners are at Avranches, so it were best for me to ride on there at once and abandon hunting for to-day; but I need not spoil our party. Do you ride on to Brion, my friends. I will join you there some time to-night. Perhaps M. de Bergerac would care to ride to Avranches with me?"

"With all my heart!" exclaimed Cyrano, only too eager. He met the eyes of Marianne and smiled reassurance. Dom Ratran was all for sending an escort with Effiat, but this the latter refused point-blank.

While they were talking the three Huguenot cavaliers rode out of the inn yard and took their departure, spurring hard. It would probably be some little time ere the fate of Avillon was discovered.

So Effiat put Marianne into her saddle, then Cyrano came to her and touched his lips to her hand and looked up into her eyes.

"The Egyptian's scapulary—you have it?" he murmured. Her eyes widened.

"Yes; but not here."

"No matter. *Au revoir!* Until to-night, Dom Ratran!"

Two minutes later Cyrano and Effiat clattered away together on the road to Avranches. But Avranches was not their destination.

CHAPTER XI

—RIDES WITH STRANGE MEN.

EFFIAT AND Cyrano rode on the road to Avranches; Dom Ratran, with the rest of the party, passed through Pontorson for his manor of Brion. Almost immediately on their departure from the inn, the tavern and the little town were flung into turmoil. A shrieking chambermaid brought every one in the place crowding into Avillon's chamber.

The room was in utmost confusion. Avillon, who had dragged himself to the doorway, lay in a pool of blood, conscious, his eyes open. One hand grasped the little braided whip with the gold disk in the handle. The innkeeper rushed in, cursed the pack of them for staring fools, ordered a surgeon summoned from the hospital, and lifted the head of Avillon in his arms.

"Ah!" he exclaimed, seeing the silver haft of a large poniard protruding from the side of the dying man. Avillon pushed the whip into his hand.

"Take this—take this—Salignan!" murmured Avillon. The death sweat was on his face, his eyes were distended: "Tell him—"

A long shiver and Sieur d'Avillon was dead.

Thus it chanced that, long ere the tide came sweeping in again across the wide leagues of sand, an hostler from the inn sought out the Marquis de Salignan with word of what had happened at Pontorson. None knew why or by whose hand Avillon had been slain, nor indeed did any know his identity; but Salignan knew it. He looked at the two articles given him— the cleaned poniard, and the braided whip. He knew that whip, as many men knew it; but its secret was quite unknown to him. So he laid it aside and forgot it.

The poniard, also, he knew very well; and here entered a

singular toil of destiny. Cyrano had bought this poniard in a booth of the Pont Neuf, quite careless of the arms adorning the silver hilt. As it chanced, these arms had belonged to one Count de St. Méloir, a gentleman killed at the siege of Arras, and with whom Salignan was very familiar, since their estates were adjoining. Thus, at first meeting Cyrano, he had instantly recognized the dagger; and now, knowing that this weapon had taken the life of Avillon, Marquis de Salignan smiled grimly to himself and laid his plans.

If Salignan did not know the secret of the little whip, however there was another at the Mont who did; and this was the lackey Mervaut.

MEANWHILE CYRANO and Effiat were riding, not for Avranches, but for Ducey, the seat of the Montgommery. When they left the highway, Effiat pulled up and turned his horse to face Cyrano.

"*Monsieur,*" he said with a determined air, "it is time we had a word regarding the work ahead. I take it that you are with us. I propose, then, to place Mont St. Michel in the hands of Sieur de Lorges."

"Who will present the remarkable spectacle of a Huguenot being the abbot of a Benedictine monastery, eh?" and Cyrano burst out laughing heartily. Effiat frowned.

"This is no fit subject for jest, my dear Bergerac. No sacrilege will be committed; the abbey remains unharmed; as a fortress it will be placed in Huguenot hands. Let us have a thorough understanding here and now. Does this offend your sense of the fitness of things?"

Cyrano shrugged. "M. d'Effiat, my sense of propriety does not extend to religious matters; I am, thank Heaven, no theologian! As to politics, they bore me. Your noble act of renunciation has my fullest approval, and my sword shall back it up. Are you satisfied?"

Effiat met the gay, mocking eyes, the light smile, and he nodded; but his narrow eyes regarded Cyrano fixedly.

"Entirely. There is another slight matter which I should like to discuss with you—touching Mlle. de Gisy."

Effiat paused, thoughtfully, and in this pause he was very close to death. Cyrano, however, reconsidered; his pistols were empty, and he had no weapon whatever. Besides, it was not yet time for Effiat to die. So, being unable to say what he wished, Cyrano twirled his mustache and said the first thing that came into his head.

"My dear Effiat, really you should not discuss this matter with me at all, but with M. le Marquis de Salignan."

A cowardly thing, shifting the issue thus, yet necessary. Having spoken, Cyrano's laughter died out. Upon him settled that old terrible sense of futility, that realization of his origin, of his real self, of his very life. At every turn he was balked. His heart hungered to kill Effiat here and now because of Marianne; but the issue presented, he was forced to evade it. He was a mockery, a shadow, a bit of scum caught helpless in the drift of the deeper currents of society. In this world where brains meant nothing, where birth, blood, caste, meant everything, he was a lost man. The very fates conspired against him. And so, despising himself, he threw the name of Salignan into the game—and won his play.

Effiat started as though stung. For an instant his eyes widened; he was recalling little incidents, words, gestures that had passed. A slow pallor crept into his face, and his hand wandered toward the poniard at his girdle.

"Ah!" he said. "Ah! Come, then."

And catching up his reins he drove in spurs like a madman; Cyrano followed him. It was only a little past noon when these things transpired, since the midday meal at the Mont had been suited to the turn of the tide.

As they rode, three highly important matters occupied the mind of Cyrano. First, a weapon. His fine brass pistols were unloaded, as the salt air would ruin a load within a few hours, and he had no powder. Cyrano was no fool; if he had forsworn wearing a sword he had not forsworn using one, and it was for a sword that his fingers itched now. He had no intention of allowing false pride to interfere with self-preservation.

Second, the scapulary—if such it really were—given by the dying Egyptian woman to Marianne. In this bit of leather sewn on a cord, Cyrano now saw, might lie the reason for Avillon's having instigated the murder of those two wanderers. But what could be within this scrap of leather to justify two deaths?

And third—the reliquary at his own neck. Moved by curiosity, Cyrano had once or twice examined this flat star of gold, but had found no indication that it opened or contained anything. Being what he was, he found himself skeptical of relics in general, and had no belief whatever in the authenticity of this particular relic. The star had on one side the device of the Company of Jesus—which, Cyrano shrewdly reflected, was reason enough for the Dominican Père Carré to lose no sleep over parting with the Jesuit relic. Avillon's thinly disguised interest in the star now piqued Cyrano's curiosity afresh, but for the moment he had no chance to gratify it.

"Time enough!" he told himself cheerfully. "At present, larger things are afoot. This rascally conspiracy—h-m! Salignan won't believe anything I say, there's no time to write Père Carré, Avillon is out of the way; only Cyrano remains. Well, why not? France is usually saved by those whom she despises."

THE AFTERNOON was wearing well on when Effiat and Cyrano, passing through the little burg of Ducey, came to the château of the Montgommery; nor were they the first travelers to come this day to the imposing structure of bricks and granite, with its tall Corinthian columns. Built in 1624 by Gabriel II, this château, with its lands adjoined the barony of Ardevon, the chief mainland fief of Mont St. Michel; and in his lighter moments the present Sieur de Lorges was wont to sweep through Ardevon with his retainers and his huge packs of dogs, laying waste the fields of the peasants and giving no heed to life or property.

In the pleasant gardens of the château, Sieur de Lorges was talking with his guests. Here in his own house the man's savage and intolerant pride was laid aside and he showed something of that gracious courtesy and knightly manner which had made his grandsire, the "Grand Montgommery," famous as the pattern of chivalry.

With him were a few men; not many, but of importance. The coldly proud M. de Frontard, the only soldier of them all; two Huguenot leaders from the south, who spoke for the men of La Rochelle and the fragments of the Huguenot state shattered by Richelieu; and a bluff Norman seaman who had brought with him two strangers. Others were close at hand, for Sieur de Lorges lived in state, and many gentlemen were in the house or about the gardens, but they did not attend this conference of the leaders.

The two strangers who had arrived during the afternoon were the focus of attention. Both were Englishmen, both spoke French fluently; both were merry gentlemen, booted and spurred and armed, blithely staking life and fortune on the mad invasion of all France with a scant three-score men.

It was to this assemblage that a groom announced the arrival of Sieur d'Effiat and the Marquis de Bergerac. Sieur de Lorges received them most graciously, looked at Bergerac and bowed to him without apparent recognition, and presented them to his guests.

Cyrano met the eye of Frontard, who came to him with an ironic smile.

"Well, *monsieur!*" said the Huguenot. "It seems that you must forego the promise which you made as to our next meeting!"

Cyrano laughed. "One can always defer a thing, *monsieur!* Especially if the wine be good and the time inopportune. But—"

Effiat took his arm and presented him to the two Englishmen. And he now learned of what value was his name and rank to M. d'Effiat.

"Gentlemen, allow me to present M. le Marquis de Bergerac," said the latter, with all the impressive manner of a great noble. "You will find, in conferring with him and with M. de Frontard here, all necessary advice and furtherance as to your military problems. Your names?"

M. de Lorges intervened and presented the Englishmen. One Sir John Ottery, was a bluff and hearty gentleman, something of a courtier, who had traveled widely; the other, Messire Courtney; a young blade gay with flaunting ribbons, was of high family and had furnished the means for the expedition in hand. Neither of them answered to Cyrano's conception of Puritans; as a matter of fact, they represented the portion of the Puritan party drawn from the old landed gentry and not the more zealous Roundhead element later to come into control of affairs. That they were much impressed with Cyrano's title and appearance, was obvious.

As for Cyrano, to him they represented Englishmen upon the soil of France, that is to say, enemies. He did not, however, voice his private thoughts, but made himself extremely agreeable. He observed that Courtney wore a very handsome rapier— a Milan blade, Cyrano told himself.

"NOW, GENTLEMEN," said Sieur de Lorges, when wine was served, "let us proceed at once to the business which has brought us here. We all know the nature of this business, I take it."

Frontard, who must have been hugely astonished at the appearance of Cyrano in company with Effiat, eyed the high-nosed marquis, but held his peace. Effiat, by no means forgetting that he was dealing with Huguenots and Englishmen, took up the word.

"*Messieurs*," he said a trifle stiffly, "this is a curious alliance; so much the better. I speak for the court. You may not be aware that we propose to overthrow Richelieu and secure the Duc d' Orleans as regent. The news of the king's death may come at any moment. Our party is large; the queen herself is with us. Definite action is to be taken in the south by my cousin Cinq-

Mars; the Duc de Bouillon will lead an army on Paris, augmented with Spanish veterans from Flanders. At the same time, the Huguenots here in the west will rise. Our friends from England have brought the nucleus of an army. We propose to seize Mont St. Michel with their help and place it in Huguenot hands. Am I correct, M. de Lorges?"

Montgommery, who saw himself the new great leader of the Huguenot party, reestablishing its strength, assented with some pomposity.

"You are, M. d'Effiat," he said. "It is understood that we do not wish to interfere with your feudal rights; Mont St. Michel remains your appanage and shall be unconditionally restored to you later. It shall remain under your command until I return from the south—I leave to-night with these other gentlemen, to raise the promised army. I trust that I may take them word that the Mont is in our hands?"

"You may," said Effiat, and looked to the Englishmen. "Gentlemen, your force—"

"Disembarks to-night," said Sir John Ottery. "The place, I know not. It was to be named by you, *monsieur*."

"I saw the messenger," said Effiat. "Your men will land on Tombelaine, which is empty. There they can lie hid until, let us say, to-morrow night. I will then arrange matters with them. M. de Bergerac and M. de Frontard, with you two gentlemen, might ride to Beauvoir or another of the coast villages to-night, and pass to Tombelaine with a guide."

"Excellent!" approved Cyrano loudly, and twirled his mustache. "And to-morrow night at low tide we'll come to the Mont. We must enter the abbey, however, not the lower town—once the alarm is given, that accursed Salignan can defend the upper works with his four men against an army!"

"Very good," said Effiat. "Come to the Fount of St. Aubert, ascend the stairs that lead to the abbey, look for a lantern above. Where that lantern is, you'll find men with ropes—a rope ladder might be better. The rest is simple."

M. de Lorges stroked his handsome face reflectively. Perhaps he was thinking that his late sire had projected this identical scheme, with the result that nearly five-score graves lay under the walls of that same spot. The rest had been all too simple, indeed.

"Agreed, *monsieur*," said Cyrano with his grandest air, and the others nodded assent.

Having now disposed of the essential details that wiped Cyrano and the two Englishmen from further consideration, Effiat turned to Sieur de Lorges and spoke of the broader elements of the conspiracy, to which Cyrano listened with all his ears. Effiat did not go into the details of his cousin's scheme, however.

"The main point between us, *monsieur*," said Lorges reflectively, "and the one which I must report on to the gentlemen at La Rochelle, is the question of religion. It was my understanding that certain guarantees were to be made over the signatures of the Duc de Bouillon and Monsieur le Duc d'Orleans; these guarantees were to satisfy the Huguenots."

Effiat started. "But, *monsieur*, you must have long since received these guarantees! I had letters from Sedan before I left Paris, stating that they were already on the way to you, sent by a sure hand! And a letter from my cousin at Tarascon confirmed this—the duke had signed the guarantees, in return for a promise of your support!"

THERE WAS a brief startled silence. So obvious was the sincerity of Effiat that none questioned it. The only alternative was an ominous one.

"Can these guarantees have fallen into the hand of Richelieu?" said Lorges, troubled.

"No matter," and for once Effiat rose to emergency. He held out his hand to the Huguenot chieftain, and in his whole manner was a certain nobility, a grandeur, that was deeply impressive, even to Cyrano. "*Monsieur*," Effiat said gravely, "before these gentlemen I pledge you my word of honor regarding the guarantees to your coreligionists. Further, I shall place Mont St. Michel absolutely in your hands, as a pledge of these guarantees."

Sieur de Lorges, moved by emotion, came swiftly and embraced him.

"M. d'Effiat," he said, with the lofty, almost kingly air that he could so well assume, "we are gentlemen. I accept your word, I refuse the pledge you offer. As you say, it does not matter, even were the worst known to Richelieu himself. To-morrow night the Mont passes into our hands. Within two days I shall be raising ten thousand men; within a week I shall be back here with a regiment of light horse. Until then you can easily hold the Mont against any force that may be sent hither."

Now; in all that had been said, Cyrano not only gained a fairly exact notion of what conspiracy was afoot, but he had been utterly astounded by its magnitude and extent. That Cinq-Mars was to move in the south, probably to imprison or kill Richelieu, was certain. Bouillon was to lead an army from Sedan on Paris, with Spanish backing. The rebel Duc de Guise, now exiled in Italy, would probably move from that quarter also, upon Savoy. Cinq-Mars might be foiled, Bouillon might be defeated, Guise might be repulsed—but here in the west was the deadliest danger of all.

And it was unsuspected. Cyrano knew as much, having heard Père Carré mention it as a bare possibility. A spy or two, a new commander at the Mont—and no other provision made against it! The Huguenots were ready to rise. News that help had come to them from England would put the whole Huguenot population in the field; the Montgommery would have at his back a greater array than any Henry of Navarre had led on Paris. And, with the impregnable fortress of Mont St. Michel in their hands, the Huguenots would sweep across all the west of France like a devouring flame.

"Good!" said Cyrano to himself, as he looked around. "Now the matter is simplified, and my conscience is at rest. I am no longer dealing with gentlemen and with Frenchmen; I am dealing with enemies and with traitors. And they are dealing with—Cyrano!"

He turned to Frontard.

"*Monsieur,*" he said, "I gather that you and I are to accompany these English gentlemen to Tombelaine?"

"Exactly," returned Frontard, with a slight frown of anxiety as he glanced at the lowering sun. "If they are to be landed there some time to-night, I believe that we should be on our way; it were best to be on the island when they arrive. We, of course, must reach there at low tide, across the sands. They will come by boat—is it not so, *monsieur?*"

Sir John Ottery nodded.

"Yes. We have arranged with two shipmen of St. Malo, who will transfer our men into swift luggers and bring them to the appointed spot. Our own ships could not come too far into the bay, it appears."

"Then," suggested Cyrano, "let's be moving. We'll need a guide?"

Frontard waved his hand. "I know every inch of the coast, and the sands as well," he said confidently. "We follow the Selune river here to Pontaubault—five leagues in all to our destination."

"Five leagues—*mordious!*" Cyrano sprang to his feet. "And we'll dine at Pontaubault, then? Excellent!" He turned to Effiat. "I believe you rejoin our little party at Brion to-night?"

"Yes, *monsieur,*" said Effiat, "and we return to the Mont some time to-morrow."

"Then, I advise you, look to that rascal Salignan, for there is danger in him! M. de Lorges, will you have the kindness to bid one of your men load the pistols at my saddle? I have no powder, and with things as they are, I should like very well to have a weapon in case of need."

S O I T came to pass that the four men rode from Ducey

together, and Cyrano, being very grave and even sad at heart, was in his most uproarious good humor. He broke into swaggering tales of the wars, and Sir John Ottery, who had not long since been soldiering against the O'Neill in Ireland, told of the stark fighting there, to all of which young Courtney listened with wide eyes. All three of them were very curious about Cyrano, since Frontard knew no more of him than did the rest, and had been thunderstruck to see him appear with Effiat.

Presently, riding with Courtney behind the others, Cyrano fell to talk of spies and secret agents, and told the ugly story of Mlle. de Lafayette, that sad girl whom the king loved, and mentioned Avillon.

"Ah!" said Courtney. "Sieur d'Avillon? I heard of him in London—he was there some months ago and came near to being hung as a Papist spy."

Cyrano gestured toward the pair in front. "Careful, my friend! Not so loud. M. de Frontard is a near relative of his, and has been working with him of late."

"What?" Courtney turned horrified eyes upon him. "Is this truth, *monsieur*? Impossible!"

"Not a bit of it. Listen! I myself lately left this Avillon for dead in the road, and carried off his dispatches. Well, what happened?"

He recounted the story of the little whip, and by what ruse Frontard had returned it to Sieur d'Avillon. To this Courtney listened in quivering hot passion, then caught Cyrano by the arm, impulsively.

"If this be true, we are in danger from that man!" he exclaimed earnestly. "How can it be possible?"

Cyrano shrugged. "Probably few knew of the relationship, my friend. It is very likely, indeed, that Frontard expects to betray us. Why not? Avillon is close by, or was. This very afternoon I left him at Pontorson on our way here."

"You—left him?" echoed Courtney, staring wide-eyed. "You recognized the arch-spy, and left him?"

Cyrano twirled his mustache and smiled. "Aye," he responded. "With my dagger sunk into him and his papers burned. Avillon is dead, my friend; but Frontard does not know it."

The young Englishman stared from him to the two riders ahead in the sunset.

"The devil! Are we in danger, think you? Will this Frontard betray us?"

"Oh, we take our chance of that! What matter, after all?" said Cyrano carelessly. "Man is born to die, soon or late—"

"But not until he can no longer fight off his destiny!" exclaimed Courtney. "Will you of your kindness ride on ahead for a space with this Frontard, and let me follow with Sir John Ottery?'"

Of his kindness, Cyrano assented gladly, and chuckled to himself as he took place in the lead at Frontard's stirrup. The Huguenot soldier, still mystified by Cyrano's personality and knowing of no Marquis de Bergerac, voiced his frank curiosity, but Cyrano turned him off with swaggering evasions. Then, as the others had dropped behind out of hearing, Cyrano looked at Frontard, half frowningly.

"*Monsieur*," Cyrano said gravely, "what mean you by antagonizing our English friends?"

"Eh?" returned Frontard, astonished. "Those gallant gentlemen? I have not—"

"Bah!" broke in Cyrano. "Something you have said. They are insulted, I tell you. There is ill feeling. They have heard that Avillon was killed to-day—"

"What? Are you mad?" exclaimed the Huguenot. There had been no word spoken at Ducey regarding the episode at the Pontorson inn.

"No," said Cyrano. "Avillon was at Pontorson. M. d'Effiat poniarded him." He briefly, and not too accurately, recounted the incident.

"And no word said to me of it?" commented Frontard gloomingly. "When they all knew that we were related? I do not like this, *monsieur!*"

"I am telling of it, am I not?" said Cyrano.

After this they rode on in silence toward the deepening west, and the face of Frontard was dark with unpleasant thoughts. The two Englishmen behind were talking together as they rode, but in low voices.

In this fashion they came to Pontaubault, after darkness had fallen, and dismounted at the inn. There was no moon. The glint of stars was reflected from the dark waters; the tide was in.

Cyrano stamped into the inn and ordered dinner for four. They had a good two hours to await the ebb tide.

CHAPTER XII

— OBTAINS A SWORD.

M. DE BERGERAC viewed his three companions with cheerful eye, as they sat over their wine and waited for the big hearth-spit to turn their dinner to the proper brownness. Frontard, he perceived, was gloomy, hesitant, eying the two Englishmen furtively. Sir John Ottery was much disturbed in spirit. Young Courtney applied himself deeply to the wine. Cyrano did most of the talking, but despite his jests and laughter, a somber mood was upon them all.

Sir John had been gazing with no little interest at Cyrano's velvet cloak, now somewhat travel-stained and at the golden reliquary star which hung about his neck.

"I trust you will pardon my question," said the Englishman, "and permit me to inquire as to the meaning of those stars upon your cloak? That is to say, if they have a meaning, as I think they must have."

Cyrano's ironic, gusty laughter broke upon the room.

"Oh, meaning enough, if only to hide a sword-rent in the

velvet!" he responded. "Seven stars, *monsieur*—know you not their names, indeed? The angels of the seven planets, let us say: Semeliel, Nogael, Cochabiel, Levaniel, Sabathiel, Zedechiel, and Madimiel! But since we are touching upon events political, then there must be a deeper reading of the riddle. How many electors of the Holy Roman Empire are there?"

"Electors?" Sir John frowned. "Why, seven, of course."

"Exactly!" Cyrano leaned forward, fastening his somber gaze, at once sad and burning, upon the eyes of the Englishman. "Know you the thesis of Carlo Fabri the Italian upon this topic, *monsieur?* A fascinating thing, I assure you: and, since each of the electors possesses a certain guardian angel, what more appropriate than that this suit, a gift from the King of Bohemia, should bear the names of these angels—when properly interpreted? Here, then, is the star of Michel, who watches over the Archbishop of Mayence, Grand Chancellor of Germany; this represents Gabriel, angel of the Archbishop of Treves; here we have Raphael, protector of the Archbishop of Cologne, Grand Chancellor of Italy; here Uriel, guardian of the Palatine of the Rhine; here Scealtiel, who hovers above the Duke of Saxony; here Jehudiel, who holds the Marquis of Brandenburg in his keeping—and last, Ferechiel, angel of the grateful King of Bohemia! There's the riddle for you in plain reading, *messieurs.*"

"And the golden star?" asked Frontard coldly. "If I mistake not, it bears the insignia of the Jesuits."

"Ah, yes!" said Cyrano. "That was a gift to me, *monsieur;* it bears a fragment of pennon fallen from the wing of St. Michel himself! So, at least, I was told; but M. d'Avillon was so eager to have it from me to-day that I suspect it may contain something more worldly and practical."

AT THE name of Avillon there was a peculiar silence. It was broken by Courtney, who turned to Frontard, his cheeks flushed.

"Is it true, *monsieur,* that you are a friend and close relative of that arch-spy and assassin?" he demanded in an aggressive voice.

*"Dinner? What sort of man are you,
to talk of dinner—after this?"*

"Your tone is peculiar," Frontard returned.

"No less peculiar," retorted Courtney hotly, "than that you, presented to us as an aid and a leader of the Huguenots, should be on terms of intimacy with such a man!"

Frontard became very pale. "Young man," he said in a low voice, "do you realize that you are uttering insults?"

"Which you do not deny." Courtney laughed harshly, and flung off the anxiously restraining hand of Sir John. "Unhand me! You, *monsieur,* have not denied these insults, as you term them. Think you that we will easily let ourselves be betrayed?"

Frontard came to his feet. "Betrayed!" he echoed.

With the agility of a cat, young Courtney sprang up and his hand struck across the face of Frontard.

"So it is true!" he cried in a passionate voice. "Out with your sword, traitor that you are!"

Now indeed Sir John rose and came between the two, but Cyrano sat motionless, watching. Courtney, his blade rasping out, thrust his friend aside; then Frontard, still coldly calm, turned to the older Englishman.

"I do not accept blows—and a blow can be wiped out in only one way, *monsieur*. Will you have the goodness to stand aside?"

The host and the inn servants, crowded about the hearth, dared not interfere. Cyrano rose to his feet and spoke, impressively.

"Gentlemen, this is an affair of honor, and no tavern brawl. A cresset is burning in the courtyard. Let us adjourn thither. M. de Frontard, I shall be honored to serve as your second in this matter, and I doubt not that Sir John will thus serve his friend."

"Come, then!" cried Courtney heatedly, and Frontard bowed. Sir John Ottery followed them outside, perforce. At the doorway, Cyrano halted him and spoke, low-voiced.

"Can the boy use sword?"

"He is no veteran," said the Englishman gloomily. "Yet he has learned the Italian method fairly well."

"Good." Cyrano joined the two others, who, swords bared, stood in the ruddy light of the high cresset. "*Monsieur,*" he said to Frontard, "we are all engaged in an enterprise which will not brook internecine strife. Forget this matter, I beg of you."

"Let this Englishman apologise first, and perhaps I will spare him."

"Be damned to you!" cried Courtney passionately. Frontard bowed, but Cyrano caught his arm.

"Wait. He is young, headstrong, unused to arms! You need not harm him—"

Frontard looked Cyrano in the eyes for a cold and deliberate moment.

"*Monsieur,*" he said, "you are offensive."

Cyrano stepped back and bowed. "Proceed, Destiny!" he cried out.

The two blades crossed. Heated with wine, spurred by more

heated youth, Courtney launched an attack which was rash, impulsive, ineffective. Frontard smiled disdainfully as he stood, cold and impassive, feeling out the wrist of his adversary. A low groan broke from Sir John.

"The boy is lost! Bergerac, there is murder in that man's face."

Cyrano pressed his arm. "Peace, my lord. If he falls, I will avenge him, on the faith of a gentleman!"

Before the words had left his lips, Frontard suddenly moved; his arm shot out; his rapier drove nearly to the hilt through the breast of Courtney. The young Englishman threw his arms wide, dropped his weapon, and was dead before he collapsed on the stones.

THERE WAS a moment of paralyzed silence; then Cyrano moved. He stepped forward and picked up the fallen weapon of Courtney, and turned to Frontard. Sir John plunged to his knees above the body of his friend, then rose, hot words on his lips, hand on his sword; but the words remained unspoken, the sword undrawn.

The black-red, murky flames of the cresset struck full upon the two men facing one another, and this moment of silence held a dramatic tension which Cyrano, assuredly, did not despise. He had dropped his cloak and stood tall, long-armed, ominous, smiling at Frontard in a terrible manner. Before the eyes of all, a man had just been slain—yet in the eyes of all who saw, the fact was dwarfed by the appearance of this man who was standing, silent and unmoving, before the slayer. And now, upon this silence, came the low, throaty voice of Cyrano in composed accents.

"M. de Frontard, you need not have killed this young man."

Frontard, held motionless in astonishment, relaxed his pose.

"*Monsieur*," Frontard said coldly, "I labor under the conviction that an open insult is past all apology and can have but one honorable issue."

Very courteously, Cyrano saluted him with the untarnished blade, and bowed low.

"And I, *monsieur,* share your conviction," he responded. "Since we are discussing such matters, I must recall to your attention the promise which I made you at your château—that upon the occasion of our next meeting, I should kill you."

The calm assurance of these words, the lofty air of the young man who uttered them, produced a singular effect. The inn-folk, clustered about the doorway, crossed themselves and gaped anew. Sir John Ottery shivered, as though an invisible hand had touched his neck. Frontard drew himself up sternly.

"*Monsieur,* are you serious?" he demanded.

"I am never serious!" retorted Cyrano, shaking back his long hair and showing all his teeth in a silent laugh. "Least of all, when about to kill a traitor. *En garde!*"

And, as he spoke, he engaged the rapier of Frontard.

NOW WAS witnessed a very different sort of bout from the preceding one. Like Courtney, Cyrano attacked, it is true; but his attack was that of a master; his lithe body held a surety of movement and his arm a level strength which Courtney had lacked. His rapier seemed but an extension of his arm, so slightly did it move, and he smiled at Frontard as though engaged in a friendly bout; but at the third pass desperation came into Frontard's eyes and he took a backward step. Cyrano laughed shortly.

"What, *monsieur?* You, a soldier, cannot square your shoulders in the face of death? For shame! Men who betray their king and country should have more heart—ah! Now, *monsieur,* now!"

And, even as he spoke, Cyrano's attack became sharper, his thrusts more dazzling in their rapidity. Into his face came that expression of savagery, of merciless determination, which his foes of other days had known. Frontard was purely on the defensive, parried frantically, uttered a choking cry.

A gush of blood came from the lips of Frontard. That long, beautifully balanced sliver of Milan steel passed through his heart and was jerked out again, red, as he toppled over and fell face down on the stones.

Cyrano stood looking down at him for a moment, then taking a long breath, he looked up, found Sir John Ottery staring at him.

"Good God!" exclaimed the awed Englishman. "Do you know what you have done?"

"All too well, *monsieur.*" With these words, Cyrano stepped to the body of Courtney and unbuckled the young man's baldric. He swung it over his shoulder and thrust the still wet rapier into the empty sheath. "I have acquired a weapon and avenged your friend."

"And now, what?" demanded Sir John. Cyrano gave him a look of surprise and fingered his mustache.

"Dinner, of course!"

The other made a gesture of abhorrence. "Dinner! What sort of man are you, to talk of dinner—after this?"

"*Monsieur,*" said Cyrano with a singular gravity, "I am like other men; a dastard, a hero, a helpless mixture of the best and the worst, of God and Devil! Like other men, I have a stomach and must needs fill it. Go inside, I beg of you, and swallow a bottle of wine, and make up your mind to food. We have work ahead."

Sir John glanced at the bodies on the stones.

"And—and these? "he said, hesitant. "We cannot leave them here."

"Trust all to me," said Cyrano.

So compelling was his manner that the Englishman, after one shocked look around, turned, and walked drearily into the tavern. When he had departed, Cyrano bent his gaze upon the two dead men at his feet, then lowered his head and signed himself, and his eyes closed for a moment; his features were old and drawn and very sad.

"Rest in peace" he murmured. "There was no other way; I do what I can. Forgive me, rash young man, you who now comprehend everything. Forgive me, honest soldier, you who have now realized the truth. It is your misfortune that poor Cyrano

fights not for himself nor for filthy money, but for the king and
country whom you assail. Rest in peace!"

HE OPENED his eyes, saw one of the hostlers gaping at
him, and beckoned.

"Wrap all the pistols at our saddles in cloths," he said, "to
protect them against the damp. I shall want flint and steel, a
filled lantern, and a small bundle of dry brush and fagots ready
for lighting; wrap these and tie them at one of the saddles. Then
place each of these two men upon his own horse and tie the
bodies securely in place."

"Eh, eh?" The staring hostler took a backward step. "But,
monsieur, they are dead!"

"Naturally," said Cyrano, and laughed. "If they were alive,
there were no need to tie them in place! These gentlemen must
finish their journey, you comprehend? Shall we need a guide to
cross from here to the Mont, when the tide is out?"

"No, *monsieur;* with horses you are safe enough, and there
will be a moon later," said the hostler. "The quicksands here
endanger a man afoot, but a horse pulls out of them at once."

Cyrano gave the man a coin, and passed into the tavern.

With gloomy satisfaction he observed that Sir John Ottery
was applying himself to the bottle; and in this Cyrano followed
suit. Their dinner was already on the table, and he forced the
English knight to make semblance of eating.

"There is work ahead," said Cyrano, as he drained his third
bottle, "and the saints forbid that we should either of us go to
Hades on an empty stomach."

"I doubt it not," returned Sir John gloomily, and Cyrano
transfixed him with a gaze that was half mournful, half sardonic. "You have arranged about the bodies?"

"Yes. They ride with us."

Sir John compressed his lips and refilled his flagon. All the
cheerful gayety had been stricken out of the Englishman, as
though he had some prescience of the destiny awaiting him on
that lonely islet amid the floods.

When their meal was finished, Cyrano paid the score, discovered that his funds were low, and shrugged, Frontard and the Englishmen were well supplied, and this, he reflected, was after all war. For what he had done, and for what he was about to do, he felt profound regret; but regret does not win campaigns.

In the courtyard again, he and Sir John Ottery mounted into the saddle, took the reins of the lead horses, with their grisly burdens, and moved out into the night, following the road leading down to the shore. Cyrano had not neglected to bring along a brace of bottles, and since the tide was not yet out, this precaution stood them in good stead as they waited on the beach under the cliffs, and watched the starlit waters gradually recede and change into glistening sands.

Neither man spoke. Cyrano had certain things to say, but the proper time and place had not come to say them; and Sir John seemed weighed down and oppressed by dark thoughts, like a man driven deeper with each instant into the toils of destiny, and helpless to escape or evade the snare.

"The waters are retreating," said Cyrano suddenly, and hurled an empty bottle to crash upon the cliff. Sir John turned to him and spoke in a quiet voice.

"*Monsieur,* perhaps these unfortunate events have unduly affected me, but I feel a conviction that this affair will not hold a happy issue for me. I have one request to make: that, if I fall, I be not left unburied."

"Sir John, I promise you decent interment," said Cyrano in a mournful tone that held more of prophecy than of promise. "And I'll say an *Ave* for the repose of your soul."

"I did not know you were a Catholic," exclaimed the Englishman.

"There is a great deal you do not know," returned Cyrano. "You are a gentleman whom I could love and cherish dearly, *monsieur,* had our paths crossed in another fashion; as it is, we must each fulfill our destiny."

"Your words are singularly ominous," murmured Sir John, staring hard at him. Cyrano shrugged and turned to his horse.

"Why not? I am not happy at what has passed, I assure you. Ready?"

THEY STRUCK out across the wet sands toward the vague blots that marked the islets. The moon, nearly full, was just rising above Avranches and the Norman cliffs.

Out across the miles of sand, now firm and steady, now sucking with invisible fingers. A slow-moving advance, with a dim twinkle of light from the Mont, ever bulking higher against the stars, to guide them. Presently the moonlight was bringing their goal into plainer sight—Tombelaine, larger in extent than the Mont, but lying low and close to the sand, a shaggy mass of rock encircled with a few defenses, dark, empty.

And now they came upon a river amid the sand—a river, where an hour previously had been the open sweep of ocean waves. Cyrano halted and stared at it in utter astonishment, for the peculiar nature of these sands was unknown to him—their rivers, or rather their prolongation of the brooks that came down to the shore, their sudden fogs, their rushing sweep of incoming tide that had caught many a man unawares. Sir John, either in no mood to take the heed of the curiosities of nature, or disdaining this winding trickle of water in the wet sand, urged his horse at it.

Cyrano was following, when he heard a sudden startled cry from the Englishman. The two horses were plunging madly in a quicksand. To relieve his own beast, Sir John Ottery dismounted and started for the shore, waist-deep in water. An instant later he was drawn downward, but caught the tail of his lead horse, that which the dead Frontard bestrode. Beast and man were pulled down, the horse of Sir John dragging itself free.

Horrified, Cyrano saw the Englishman vanish, then come head and shoulders above the water, hauling himself clear by dint of pulling down the poor beast with its terrible burden.

The horse's head came up, and across the dark sands echoed one shrill and horrible scream—then Cyrano had acted.

Catching his cloak by one corner, he urged his own horse as close to the sinking animal as he dared, and shouted to the Englishman. He drove in his spurs. His horse bounded ahead, and Cyrano swung out the cloak. Sir John caught it, just as the unhappy animal that had sustained him, went under. A moment after, Cyrano had drawn him clear of the quicksands and was retrieving the two other horses. That bearing the dead Frontard had vanished forever.

"My friend—I owe you my life!" gasped Sir John, when Cyrano led up his horse. "That was well done, well done! I owe you thanks—"

"You owe me nothing," said Cyrano, looking down at him with a dour and frowning eye. "I saved you because I had need of you, *monsieur.* Come, mount and let us get on! There is work awaiting us, and whether it be devil's work or not, I cannot tell! Mount."

He rode on, leading the other horse on which rode the body of Courtney; and after an astonished moment, Sir John mounted and followed.

Tombelaine was growing clearer before them, now showing itself an enormous mass of rocks which seemed to burst upward through the sand and offer no point of access to the island. Nor was it difficult to see, as one drew under those shaggy masses of rock, why the English had been able to fortify and hold this island for years, during the old wars. Here and there could be seen half-ruined walls and towers; then, as the two cavaliers drew around the islet to the north, a tiny sand-cove was revealed, a recess in the rocks.

"At last! "said Sir John Ottery in a voice of relief.

"At last," echoed Cyrano, but in gloomy and ominous tones, as he bent a strange regard upon his companion.

AMID THE rocks could be discerned the outlines of buildings; the ancient chapel of Notre Dame, with its cells for the monks, now all dark and deserted. This was the landing-place, the spot at which the English must disembark, hidden from Mont St. Michel, a half-league distant, by the island of Tombelaine itself.

"Even the horses seem glad to reach here alive," said Sir John, as he dismounted.

"Yes," said Cyrano, "for they do not know what is to take place here."

He dismounted in turn, and let his horse go on to the strip of sand, studded with black and dripping fragments of rock, which made the shore of the cove. The animal which bore the drooped dead body of Courtney, followed the other two.

"You mean to bury him—here?" asked Sir John Ottery.

"Yes," said Cyrano, and drew his sword. "I shall keep the promise which I made you, *monsieur.*"

"Eh?" The Englishman turned to him, took a step backward. "Your words are singular, M. de Bergerac! And so is your look. What mean you?"

Cyrano threw down his cloak on the wet sand and faced Sir John.

"I mean, *monsieur,*" he said calmly, "to expound to you, here and now, the meaning of those seven stars upon my cloak. You see our three horses; at each saddle is a brace of loaded pistols. Those pistols will, therefore, cause the death of six Englishmen. You, *monsieur,* make up the number seven. That is all."

"Are you mad?" exclaimed Sir John, staring at him.

"Yes," said Cyrano, in a somber and savage voice. "Yes, *monsieur,* that is undoubtedly the case. You have been deceived. I am not here to help you; I have brought you here to kill you, if needs be. Think you that because spoiled courtiers like Effiat and disloyal Huguenots like Sieur de Lorges—the Montgommery—would gladly see Englishmen land upon the soil of France, there are not loyal Frenchmen to defend that soil? A mistake, *monsieur.*"

Sir John Ottery studied him for a moment, as he stood there in the moonlight, then spoke.

"So! This explains it, eh? Yet you saved my life back there."

Cyrano bowed ironically.

"We are gentlemen, *monsieur*. Also I saved your life because I had need of your body here. I intend to kill you, to my deep regret—"

A short and angry laugh broke from the other. "I believe you are mad, indeed! If you intend to kill me, why not use your pistols and be done with it?"

Cyrano shrugged. "Am I an assassin? Besides, there is an alternative. Give me your word that when your English come you will go aboard their craft, give up your undertaking, and leave the shore of France—and I will be satisfied."

"I cannot do that," murmured the astonished Englishman.

Cyrano bowed again.

"Then, *monsieur—en garde!*"

"Eh? You mean that I must fight you? That if you lose—"

"I cannot lose. *En garde!*"

"So be it, then!" exclaimed Sir John. His cloak fell to the sand, his blade leaped out in the moonlight. "I salute you, *monsieur;* it is a pleasure to cross swords with so true a gentleman!"

An ironic smile played about the lips of Cyrano as the rapiers met and clung together. He did not speak again.

A STRANGE meeting was this, in the limpid moonlight beneath the massy black rocks. Sir John was a finished master of fence, and almost at the first pass his point touched the velvet above Cyrano's heart, but without breaking the skin.

"An inch farther, *monsieur,* and you'd have won your game!" and Cyrano laughed gayly. Then, as he fenced for position, his foot slid in the wet sand and he went to one knee. Sir John drew back and waited.

"Thank you, *monsieur,*" said Cyrano simply, and the steel slithered again.

Moment by moment heat grew upon the two men, person-
alities faded away. All that hung before their eyes was the issue
of life or death as the slender blades drove in and out, with
lunge and parry and riposte. In the moonlight, the features of
the Englishman showed grimly earnest; the dark face of Cyrano
was tense and cold, but his eyes blazed forth like glittering stars.

And now, for a little, neither man moved position; as though
their bodies were stationary things, as though their blades citing
magnetized together, they stood almost motionless, wrist
playing against wrist, feet sinking ankle-keep in the sand. Of
a sudden, Cyrano disengaged and drove in a deadly thrust. Sir
John parried it desperately, but lost balance; unable to extricate
his feet from the sand, he staggered, and Cyrano's blade tore
the rapier from his hand. With a quick spring, Cyrano leaped
backward and saluted.

"Courtesy for courtesy, *monsieur!*"

Sir John, panting, retrieved his sword, saluted, and the blades
crossed anew. But now sweat stood upon each man's face, and
their breath came in short gasps. Blood sprang abruptly on the
neck of Cyrano.

"*Touché!*" he exclaimed, and laughed a little. "A good thrust,
monsieur—but now beware—of this riposte in—tierce—"

He attacked, and before the savage fury of this attack Sir
John was driven backward a pace or two. All the dazzling speed,
all the concentrated intensity, which had made Guardsman
Cyrano the most dreaded duelist in Paris, suddenly appeared
before the eyes of the Englishman; desperately he parried,
evaded, strove anew to meet wrist with wrist—but strength was
failing him now.

"The riposte, *monsieur*—the riposte!" cried out Cyrano. "In
God's name guard yourself!"

His whole body uncoiled like a steel spring, and at the end
of this steel spring was the rapier, darting like a silver snake in
the moonlight. For one terrible instant Sir John stood as though
paralyzed. Cyrano leaped back.

Then the arms of the Englishman fell, and his rapier dropped on the sand, and a slow smile crept into his weary, drawn features.

"Well fought—well lost." His gasping words ended in a rush of black blood, and he quietly collapsed.

Cyrano flung down the rapier, came forward, dropped to one knee; his hand rested upon the heart of the Englishman for a moment, then lifted, dark in the moonlight. He crossed himself, and raised his face to the sky, silent with emotion.

And strangely, the scarred face framed in sweat-dank hair was at this moment singularly beautiful—for beauty is not a physical thing, but an expression of the spirit. Then the dark and liquid eyes of Cyrano closed, and upon his cheeks, on either side of that keen hawk-nose, sparkled a tear. Again, more slowly, he signed himself, and his head drooped and his voice came thick and husky:

"*Ave Maria—pleni gratia—*"

CHAPTER XIII

— BECOMES A GUEST.

TWO DARK, unlighted shapes drew in across the face of the waters, now but thinly lit by the moon; for a scud of cloud had crept across the heavens, and morning was not far away. The two shadowy blots were apparently heading for Avranches, until they tacked in the light wind and stood back for Tombelaine.

In the rocky cove at the northern side of this island appeared a feeble glimmer of light—a lantern set there to guide their landing. The tide was nearly at flood, and a waste of waters surrounded the two islands in the night.

Slowly the two bluff-bowed St. Malo luggers drew in, the wind freshening by degrees. A rift in the clouds displayed the dark Tombelaine clearly. With a creak of sheaves the canvas fluttered down and anchors plunged. The lantern in the little cove showed no one to meet them, no voice cried a greeting. The rear of the cove, studded with huge rocks, ended in a grotto. Men called from the ships, called to Sir John, but there was no reply.

"Send in a boat," commanded the voice of a St. Malo man. "Take a sounding or two. No use letting ourselves go ashore on these cursed sands!"

A skiff was dropped into the water, and amid a low-voiced discussion a number of men got into her, and the oars dipped. They could see a tall figure ashore now; he was lighting a cresset placed on a high rock, as though to illumine the sands. Half a dozen Englishmen were in the skiff, with two oarsmen, and they called again to Sir John.

"He is here," responded the man on shore, in French. Then, as the cresset caught and blazed up, he withdrew from their sight.

The boat came into the little cove, whose sandy nose was well lighted now by the cresset. Her keel grounded. The men leaped outboard, pulled her up, advanced a few paces; one of them called Sir John again, another called Courtney. These men were the leaders of the English force.

"There he is!" called one of them. A sitting figure, on a slab of rock, had come into their vision. They pressed toward it. At the next instant a terrible cry broke from them.

Courtney lay half behind a jutting rock, in a curiously awkward position; beside him sat Sir John Ottery. But both were dead.

The half dozen Englishmen crowded around the two bodies, then looked up as a mocking laugh and a voice came reverberating with uncanny effect from the grotto.

"You're betrayed, Englishmen!" it cried. "Fire, my friends! No quarter!"

And a pistol roared, sending a bullet into the breast of the

nearest man. A second and a third pistol spoke; two more Englishmen fell. Cries of dismay burst from them all. The two
seamen were shoving at the boat, in panic. The three remaining
Englishmen ran to aid them. Another and another pistol
vomited smoke and flame, and to the reëchoing crashes a fourth
man fell. The fifth spun about, clapped hand to his side, fell
over the gunnel of the boat, and sat up again.

Now into the full light of the cresset darted the tall figure
of Cyrano, the last loaded pistol in his hand. From the two
luggers came a pandemonium of cries, oaths, orders; the anchors
were being jerked up, the canvas was lifting; panic was upon all
those men. Cyrano laughed and leveled his pistol at the boat,
whose oars were plunging frantically at the water.

"Take this message back to your friends, Englishmen!" he
cried, and pressed the trigger.

The one unhurt man cried out and fell backward into the lap
of his wounded companion. Cyrano stood there, shaking his
fist, laughing wildly. Then came a ragged volley of shots from
the luggers. Bullets struck all around him; one of them cut the
plume from his hat. He swept off the beaver and bowed ironically.

"Poor shooting, *messieurs!*" he shouted mockingly. "A pleasant
journey home!"

Then he was gone from sight. In all haste the boat came
alongside the nearer lugger, which was already turning. The
brown canvas rattled up, caught, filled. The two shadowy shapes
drew away, heading out into the bay.

One man had repulsed sixty.

F O R A N hour Cyrano was extremely busy, working by
lantern light in the loose sand above high-water mark. He had
only swords and poniards for tools, and his bare hands; but
these sufficed. When he had finished, dawn was at hand and
the tide was going out. He dropped to his knees, said an Ave
and a Paternoster, and then rose wearily, for he had not slept
all this night.

"An ill job well done," he reflected aloud, watching the swiftly departing water, the swiftly growing waste of wet sand. "And now, to get back to the Mont with my tidings for Salignan! Then to arrest Effiat when he returns. Thus it is all ended like any honest theatrical episode; and the Marquis de Bergerac is ended, likewise, his little day drawn to its close, his little game played out and won. What lies in the future, with Marianne— who can say?"

It seemed indeed to Cyrano in this moment that his masquerade was ended, his game won and finished; but he forgot that his destiny had ever been an awkward jade, an ironic and cantankerous jade, decorating him with laurel wreaths in the same moment she smote him across the cheek.

He rested a little; he was tired in body, more tired and sad in mind, for gallant gentlemen had died that night by his hand. He had Père Carré's purse intact, and had taken no little gold from English pockets; but wealth gave him no pleasure. It was in a gloomy and bitter frame of mind that he finally led out the three horses, mounted his own, and started in the dawn light across the sands toward the high-looming mass of the Mont, half a league distant.

Evidently, he reflected, those pistol shots had passed unobserved in the night, unheard. The astonishing spectacle of a cavalier and two empty saddles coming from Tombelaine before sunrise created no alarm or confusion that he could see. He was forced to skirt the Mont in order to reach the gate below the town, and as he passed along beneath the walls he saw wains on their way thither, and men far above at the great wheel which would pull up nets of produce and supplies for the abbey, straight up to the opening in the side of the Great Inner Degree.

He saw a horseman, too, spurring hard from Pontorson and reaching the entrance far ahead of him, but thought little of it. When at length he had rounded the angle of the island and was drawing into the gate, he saw this same cavalier emerge, speak with the guards, and turn toward him. Reaching the paved entrance, Cyrano dismounted, and the cavalier came up to him.

He was weary with hard riding; his horse, at one side, was exhausted.

"*Monsieur*," he said, "I perceive that you have extra horses. Mine is spent. I must have one of yours, in the king's name."

"With all my heart," said Cyrano.

Upon the instant, with a brief word of thanks, the cavalier climbed into one of the empty saddles, struck in his spurs, and departed in the direction of Pontorson. Cyrano turned, to find at his elbow two of Salignan's soldierly lackeys.

"M. de Bergerac," said one of them, "M. le Commandant wishes your presence immediately. Will you have the goodness to accompany us?"

Cyrano shrugged and assented, smiling to himself at the news he would have for Salignan.

MEANWHILE, IN his large room in the King's Tower, in the lower town, M. de Salignan sat at a table. He was hastily dressed; two candelabra lighted the room, for the sun was not yet up. With astonishment and a fierce excitement in his eyes, he read anew the brief dispatch which had just arrived from the south of France.

MONSIEUR:

The conspiracy is at an end. Cinq-Mars and de Thou are in our hands; ere this reaches you, Orleans and Bouillon will be arrested. Seize M. d'Effiat; send him to Tours. We need all possible evidence; therefore, spare no effort to obtain and forward to us any documents bearing on the case. May God preserve you!

MAZARIN.

"So!" A thin, cruel smile touched the lips of Salignan. One of his lackeys entered and saluted stiffly. "Well?"

"*Monsieur*, the prisoner is here."

Salignan gestured. The door opened, and into the room came Effiat's lackey Mervaut, between two guards. He was not, however, frightened. Instead, he regarded Salignan with sullen effrontery.

"You are a prisoner, Mervaut," said Salignan curtly. "Before you go to a cell, tell me what you know of your master's movements in—"

"Pardon, *monsieur*," said Mervaut, one hand slipping to his pocket. "Will you have the goodness to look at this paper?"

He gave a folded paper to a guard, who laid it before Salignan.

The latter read it, and looked up, startled.

"From Avillon! Then you have been betraying your master, you rogue? You've been a spy, have you?"

"If you call it so, *monsieur*," said Mervaut composedly. "One man serves the king in the uniform of a soldier; another, in that of a lackey."

Salignan sniffed. "Have you any further information you should impart?"

"Nothing, *monsieur*."

"Very well; you are free." Salignan signed to the guards, who stepped back. "Do not leave the Mont without my permission. What do you know of M. le Marquis de Bergerac?"

A malicious smile touched Mervaut's lips, and was gone.

"Little, *monsieur*, but I do not believe he is a marquis. I have heard tales of one M. Savinien de Cyrano, called Bergerac, who is a gutter bravo of Paris. I believe this to be the same man."

Salignan started. "Ah! He is, I understand, an accomplice of M. d'Effiat?"

"His chief aid, *monsieur*."

"Very well. You may go."

Mervaut bowed. On a chair by the door was Avillon's little whip, where it had been carelessly thrown. In passing, Mervaut quietly, openly, stooped and picked it up and took it with him; in so unconcealed and natural a manner was the thing done, it passed unobserved.

Another lackey-soldier entered and saluted.

"M. de Bergerac, M. le Commandant!"

SALIGNAN GESTURED, and Cyrano swaggered into the room. He tendered Salignan a deep bow, to which the other smiled ironically, and returned curt words.

"M. de Cyrano, called de Bergerac, you are under arrest."

"I, *monsieur?*" Cyrano smiled scornfully, despite the manner in which he was addressed. He attempted no denial of his real personality. "That is but natural."

"Eh?" Salignan's brows lifted, "Natural?"

"Of course. That, after saving France, I should be arrested?"

"Oh! You have saved France, *monsieur?*"

"Assuredly. Last night I killed M. de Frontard, a Huguenot leader; certain Englishmen; and drove off two ships filled with English who were landing on Tombelaine. This place was to have been turned over to them to-night by M. d'Effiat—"

Salignan threw back his head and broke into an amused laugh.

"Come, come, M. de Bergerac! You should have assumed the name and title of Roland, or of Bertrand du Guesclin, at the least! You have, of course, proofs of your prowess?"

Cyrano was so dumfounded at this reception of his news, that he could only stand and stare, a dull flush rising into his face. Proofs! In any case, he had none to hand.

"You gutter bravo!" snapped Salignan, suddenly in heated anger. He took the silver-hilted poniard from a drawer and threw it on the table before Cyrano's astonished gaze. "You vile assassin! You slew Sieur d'Avillon yesterday with this weapon— this poniard which bears the arms of my good friend the Comte de St. Méloir, and which you have had the audacity to wear, doubtless to bolster up your assumed title. Dare you deny it?"

"Eh?" Cyrano was overwhelmed by all this. "But I did not kill him—it was Effiat."

"With your poniard? Liar!" Salignan gestured, and a man

stepped forward from either side, seizing the arms of Cyrano; next instant, his wrists were drawn behind his back and bound. He attempted no struggle. A sort of paralysis was upon him, and utter despair.

"*Monsieur,*" he exclaimed in a choked voice, "I have told you that Père Carré—"

"Be silent!" snapped Salignan. "You have told lies enough, my fine rascal. Where you got the blank order of arrest, I know not; but I shall make use of it. Guard, give me the papers from his pocket."

One of the guards searched him, found the *lettre de cachet,* and handed it to Salignan. Cyrano had no further papers. Salignan ordered his other effects left untouched, despising the money which loaded his pockets, and bent a stern eye upon him.

"Sirrah, you go into a cell as a murderer, and for having falsely assumed the title of a nobleman. You, indeed, acting as the escort of a noble lady! And you've filled her ears with your fine stories. Bah!"

A mortal pallor had overspread the features of Cyrano.

"*Monsieur,*" he said, "if you will listen to me, I can afford you proof of what I have said. What was done last night, was done for France, as my duty, not of my own will."

"Oh, insufferable rogue! Where learned your tongue this prating of duty?" cried out Salignan. "On the contrary, rascal, I am an officer of the king, with special powers to act here; and I am doing my duty."

"Will you not let me warn you, *monsieur*—"

"Be silent! I'll listen to no more of your lies. Men, place him in that barred chamber down below here. Raoul, remain as guard at his door."

Cyrano drew himself up with a certain strange and impressive dignity.

"*Monsieur,*" he said quietly, "paradise is full of fools who have done their duty. Me, I prefer—"

Salignan leaped to his feet and struck him across the face. "Take him away!"

WHEN THE men had gone with their captive to the lower prison-room of the tower, however, Salignan dropped into his chair again, frowning.

"That was a coward's blow," he muttered unhappily. "Why did I let the fellow's prating so goad me? But he dared aspire to Marianne! Well, no matter."

He looked again at the dispatch from Mazarin, with its order to send Effiat to Tours as a prisoner. Then he picked up the *lettre de cachet*.

"Excellent! This fits in admirably," he murmured. "When Effiat arrives, I fill in his name, in his presence. Hm! Perhaps there was some truth in this rascal's story about the English; is that why Effiat went to the mainland? And that name—M. de Frontard! Yes, there is a Huguenot gentleman of that name; I recall, he was in the light cavalry of M. de Nemours. The same man, perhaps! Well, once affairs are settled, I can get the truth out of the rogue Cyrano; a touch of the rack will wring him dry. And meantime, no harm in using his story when Effiat comes. Now, as to dispositions—"

He looked up at the lackey who guarded his door.

"The tide is out? Good. Take horse, ride with all speed to Avranches. There, as you know, M. de Montluc is waiting. Tell him that he may dismiss the two companies of horse as all danger is over; they may return to Caen. I shall want, however, a traveling coach and an escort of six musketeers. They must be here—let me see! When does this accursed tide change? When can they arrive? It should be some time to-night."

"They cannot come across the sands, *monsieur*," said the lackey. "They must come by road to Pontorson and then hither. About midnight, or perhaps a little before. I can ascertain the exact time from one of the fishermen."

"No. Never mind. That is close enough," said Salignan. "This coach and escort will take a prisoner to Tours. It will be commanded by M. de Montluc in person, for the prisoner is of importance. That is all. Repeat my message."

The man, who was in reality a soldier and not a lackey, repeated his commander's message, and then departed. M. de Salignan looked at the dispatch again, and laid it on the table. He placed the order of arrest on it, and upon them both laid the silver-hilted poniard, to serve as weight.

Another of his four lackeys had appeared at the door, and Salignan beckoned him.

"This Major d'Ouville of the garrison is a faithful man, is he not?"

"*Monsieur,* he is an old veteran of La Rochelle, where he was badly wounded and disabled for active service," was the response. Evidently, the four lackeys of M. de Salignan had not been neglecting their business. "Since then he has been posted here. He is a very loyal gentleman."

"Good. When think you the party of Dom Ratran will return?"

"Probably not until the tide goes out after dinner, *monsieur;* this afternoon."

"Keep watch. When you see the party returning, go out and meet them. Take M. d'Ouville aside and give him these orders from me. At the gate, he is to take charge of the guard on the instant. He is to bring M. d'Effiat to me direct—without weapons."

"*Monsieur,* we have been instructed to disregard the rule as to weapons, in the case of M. d'Effiat. He is, as you know, the abbot here."

Salignan looked coldly astonished. "Am I mistaken in thinking that you are a soldier?"

The lackey saluted stiffly. "The orders of M. le Commandant shall be obeyed. If M. d'Effiat refuses to give up his sword?"

"Arrest him. If he resists arrest, kill him. But he will not refuse."

"Very good, *monsieur.*"

"Further, M. d'Ouville will request the prior, Dom Ratran, and Mlle. de Gisy to ascend to the abbatial quarters and to remain there until I have finished with M. d'Effiat and can do myself the honor of waiting upon them. That is all.

"Repeat the instructions."

The lackey repeated them, then departed. The third lackey took his place, at the door.

M. de Salignan smiled to himself and pinched out the candles, for by this time the sun was up. One of his four lackeys had departed for Avranches; three remained here. As he had said, there was no need for the two companies of horse awaiting his orders at Avranches. The situation was in hand.

CHAPTER XIV

— REMAINS BEHIND BARS.

IT WAS mid afternoon when the coach of Dom Ratran, attended by its escort, with Effiat, Ouville and Marianne de Gisy riding in the van, left Pontorson. Having mistaken the hour of the tide, they were late—so late, indeed, that Dom Ratran would have remained on the mainland but for Effiat, who was determined to gain the Mont ere night.

Dom Ratran knew well enough the dangers of these sands, where the flood tide came in so swiftly as to catch many a hapless person unawares; therefore he commanded his grooms to use whip and spur, and the party approached the Mont at a gallop. Ouville, seeing one of the commandant's four lackeys come forth to meet him, drew rein. There was no time to waste, for the tide was already coming in. Hence, the lackey mounted behind Ouville and repeated in his ear the instructions, as they drew in at the gate of the Mont.

In this manner it came to pass that, as Effiat dismounted, the major advanced to him and demanded his sword, with word

that M. de Salignan desired his presence immediately. Effiat
was furious; Dom Ratran, alighting from his coach, intervened
with equal anger, but M. d'Ouville was firm.

"Is this to say that I am under arrest?" exclaimed Effiat, white
with fury. "Why, it is incredible! The effrontery—"

"Not at all, *monsieur,*" returned the hapless major. "There was
no word of arrest. I was instructed to bring you to the presence
of M. de Salignan, and to request Dom Ratran and Mlle. de
Gisy to await M. de Salignan in the upper building."

Effiat glanced around. Mervaut was not in sight. He was
quite alone, and a number of the guards were drawn up with
muskets, at the inner gate, with two of Salignan's lackeys directing them. This fact alarmed and warned Effiat, who wanted at
all costs to gain time and avoid any trouble until night fell;
therefore, he turned composedly to Ouville, and bowed as he
removed his baldric.

"Very well, I go with you," he said proudly, and quieted the
noisy protests of the prior.

To the latter he added, in a low voice: "Wait here if possible.
I may have need of you."

Dom Ratran, who did not love the commandant, nodded
comprehension.

As he followed to the quarters of the commandant, Effiat
was more than on the alert; he was in a state of high tension.
He realized that something had occurred; the most natural
supposition was that the English had landed on Tombelaine
and had been discovered. Yet this was not possible, for there
was no general excitement at the Mont. Nor had any soldiers
arrived during his absence. He had, then, only Salignan and the
latter's four trooper-lackeys with whom to deal. This fact steadied him.

When he was ushered into Salignan's presence, the latter
rose at the table and bowed.

"M. d'Ouville," he said, "will you have the goodness to wait
in the outer room while I have a private word with M. d'Effiat?"

And, to the guard: "Remain outside the door until I summon you."

Effiat advanced to the table, bowed, and waited until they were left alone. His rapid glance took in the papers beneath the poniard, then came to rest on the face of Salignan, who resumed his seat.

"WILL YOU be seated, *monsieur?*" said Salignan. Effiat refused mutely. "Very well. I have asked you here in order to inform you that M. de Cinq-Mars and his associates are under arrest. Their conspiracy has been exposed and broken."

Effiat, stunned as he must have been, merely shrugged negligently.

"I have heard nothing of it," he returned. "It is many weeks since I have seen my cousin."

"Indeed!" murmured Salignan, with a slow smile. He was dealing now with a great noble, a gentleman of his own caste and rank; the words and actions of both men were, for the moment, governed by the conventions demanded by that caste. "Since you spent the night at the manor of Brion, *monsieur,* you must be unaware of the very curious incidents which have transpired on our adjacent island."

"Naturally, *monsieur,*" said Effiat calmly, but a sudden pallor drove into his cheeks. "May I inquire what all this has to do with me?"

Salignan inclined his head. "But you are the abbot of Mont St. Michel, my dear Effiat! It is only courteous of me to acquaint you with events—and with the loyal devotion of the man whom we have known here as M. le Marquis de Bergerac."

At this thrust, Effiat's eyes widened. He had anticipated some reference to the killing of Sieur d'Avillon; but these words filled him with genuine astonishment.

"Eh, *monsieur?* I'm afraid I don't comprehend your meaning."

Salignan at once thrust home his point, to determine whether there was any truth in the story told by Cyrano.

"It appears, *monsieur,* that this Marquis de Bergerac—who is now in an adjoining room—is no marquis whatever, nor is he a de Bergerac. He is, on the contrary, an agent of Cardinal de Richelieu, and has frustrated a plot to seize this place on this very night—a plot of these rascally Huguenots, aided and abetted by certain Englishmen."

The thrust went home with deadly effect. Effiat maintained his composure, but all color was drained from his face.

"You astonish me, *monsieur!*" he exclaimed, with affected interest whose effort was all too obvious. "Is it possible that you are jesting?"

"Upon such a subject? You wrong me, my dear Effiat!" returned Salignan dryly, now sure of his ground. "This honest fellow, who has posed before us all as a marquis, has proved himself a very Hercules. Alone and unaided, he repulsed two small ships filled with English, who were about to land on Tombelaine. He has killed several of their leaders, and also one M. de Frontard, a Huguenot gentleman, and has provided us with a great amount of the most invaluable information."

Effiat perceived that he was a lost man. The mention of Frontard's name alone proved that Salignan knew everything. But the exclusion of all others from the room, also proved that Salignan had as yet shared his knowledge with none.

Effiat drew himself up a trifle, and fastened a steady regard upon Salignan.

"Well, *monsieur?*" he said coolly. "Let us abandon evasion. You have something further to say to me?"

"I regret, *monsieur,*" returned Salignan courteously, "to inform you that you are under arrest. I have instructions to arrest you and send you to Tours."

Effiat bowed slightly. "You will, perhaps, permit me to see your authority to arrest the abbot of this place?"

"If you so desire." Salignan touched the papers held down by the poniard. "Here is my authority to arrest you, under the hand of Mazarin. Here is a blank *lettre de cachet,* which M. de

Bergerac furnished me, and which I shall fill in with your name. I have ordered a coach and escort to be here about midnight to-night."

EFFIAT WAS thinking swiftly. He lowered his eyes suddenly and pretended to study his nails.

"This is most regrettable, *monsieur*," he said in a quiet voice, and, taking a step closer to the table, looked at Salignan. "I am, of course, in your hands; yet, to have it known among the monks and people here that their abbot is under arrest—you can readily comprehend my position, *monsieur*. Not to mention Mlle. de Gisy."

Salignan made a brusque gesture and leaned back in his chair.

"Very good, Effiat!" he observed. "I comprehend perfectly. As yet, your name has not been mentioned. The coach and escort come for a prisoner, that is all. Give me the word of a gentleman that you will attempt no evasion, will remain in your quarters above until I send for you to-night, and not a soul will know of this. Your departure will not become known until to-morrow. There will be no scandal."

A flash of unholy joy illumined the eyes of Effiat. He knew now that his conjecture was true—that Salignan alone was aware of events.

"But, *monsieur*," Effiat objected, "this M. de Bergerac! We cannot trust such a man."

"We can very well trust him," broke in Salignan dryly, "since I have confined him in the prison-chamber below us, for his own safekeeping, until I can obtain the proper statement signed by him. One other condition, *monsieur:* you will permit me to look personally through your quarters for any documents that may be there, and that you may now have upon you."

"Certainly, *monsieur*," said Effiat.

He put his hand to his pocket and drew out a sealed paper. Stepping forward, he laid this upon the desk before Salignan, who reached out for it.

Swift as light, the hand of Effiat closed upon the silver-hilted poniard, and in the same motion he drove the blade into the throat of Salignan. Then he leaped back.

A horrible convulsion seized upon Salignan. The silver hilt was driven home beneath his chin, the steel point emerged behind his neck. He clawed at the hilt with both hands, gripped it, and with a frightful effort tore the weapon free. From the wound escaped a rushing crimson tide. Distended eyes fastened upon Effiat. He attempted to cry out, but vainly. In the very act, a tremor seized upon him, his head jerked forward, and his body slowly slid out of the chair and was a mere lump of clay upon the floor.

Effiat, with a panting breath of excitement, darted to the desk, scrutinized the papers there, then straightened up and glanced swiftly around.

"Saved!" he muttered. "Bergerac confined—Salignan dead— the game in my own hands! If I can make sure of those four lackeys of his, good! Then, no hurry. Details, details—and fast horses north to Trouville, a boat, safety in England. Yes, yes, all is possible with a little finesse."

He perceived that his sole salvation lay outside the frontier of France; and if he made haste slowly, he had every chance of getting there.

He read over the dispatch from Mazarin, grimly enough. So they had netted Cinq-Mars after all! Richelieu might be dying, but in dying he would once more send the greatest nobles in France to the scaffold. And the *lettre de cachet*—Effiat smiled thoughtfully as he read over its phrases. Salignan had filled in the address, to the royal provost at Tours, but had not filled in any name. Effiat pocketed the paper and went to the door. He opened it and stepped into the adjoining room, where Ouville and the lackey-guard waited.

"M. D'OUVILLE," he said, "M. de Salignan desires to speak with you." He turned to the guard. "Will you summon the prior, Dom Ratran, at once? M. de Salignan wishes his presence."

The guard hesitated, then saluted and strode out. Effiat held open the door. As the major entered the larger room, a choked cry burst from him; he stared at the body of Salignan, then whirled on Effiat, hand going to sword.

"What's this? What's this? *Monsieur*—"

Effiat regarded him with cold hauteur, and extended the *lettre de cachet.*

"This, *monsieur*, is the result of treachery. M. de Salignan learned that I was about to arrest him and send him to Tours, by order of His Majesty.

"He attempted to kill me; instead, I killed him. You are now in command of the garrison here, and I call upon you to lend me every assistance. Ah, here is Dom Ratran!"

Effiat strode to the door and threw it open before the guard could enter. The fat prior came into the room; Effiat closed and locked the door. Seeing the body of Salignan, Dom Ratran was seized with a sort of paralysis for an instant, then he crossed himself jerkily. Before he could speak, Effiat took the situation in hand; his calm dignity, his haughty manner and perfect assurance made an enormous impression upon the petty noble and the simple-minded friar.

"Dom Ratran, I have just been telling M. d'Ouville of my instructions to arrest M. de Salignan and send him to Tours. He and his four men, who are soldiers disguised as lackeys, had planned to place Mont St. Michel in the hands of the Sieur de Lorges and the Huguenots."

Ouville stiffened, his eyes wide. An exclamation of horror broke from Dom Ratran.

"Yesterday, in passing through Pontorson," pursued Effiat calmly, "I met certain agents of M. de Richelieu at the inn, and was apprised of this plot. I took measures against it at once. Just before we reached the Mont to-day, M. de Salignan learned of what I had done. He had no time to flee; instead, he attempted to silence me—with the result that you see. Dom

Ratran and you, M. d'Ouville, are loyal gentlemen. I call upon you to aid me in every way possible."

"But certainly, certainly!" said the prior, in some agitation. "This is terrible news!"

Ouville bowed to Sieur d'Effiat.

"*Monsieur,* I have fought the Huguenots all my life," he observed, "and you will certainly not find me lacking at this crisis. Your orders?"

"Take men of the garrison and arrest all four of M. de Salignan's lackeys," said Effiat, a trace of joy in his face as he perceived the credulity of his hearers. "Have them placed in the dungeon of the abbey and allow them to communicate with no one until Dom Ratran and I have examined them severally. Find my lackey Mervaut and have him sent here to me."

"But, *monsieur,* what of our good friend Bergerac?" demanded Dom Ratran. "I have just heard that he returned here this morning and was placed under arrest by M. de Salignan!"

"Alas, gentlemen," returned Effiat gloomily, with a gesture of helplessness. "You know the Marquis de Bergerac is my friend; I supposed him loyal, and when I rode to Avranches yesterday to crush this conspiracy, I confided in him, counting upon his aid. To my amazement, he parted from me last night; I supposed him lost. In reality, he made his way hither to warn Salignan. Of this, Salignan knew nothing, but at once flung M. de Bergerac into a cell, for reasons which I know not.

"Since I have found that M. de Bergerac was implicated in this plot, we had best leave him where he is. To-morrow the three of us will hold an examination and reduce this whole affair to writing, in a report to His Majesty.

"That is to say, if such a program meets with your approval."

"Of course, of course," approved Dom Ratran heartily. M. d'Ouville bowed in assent. Neither of them found anything incongruous or absurd in the very imperfect story told by Effiat, for they were filled with alarm and astonishment to the exclusion of all critical faculties.

M. d'Ouville saluted and left the room to carry out his orders.

"DOM RATRAN, say nothing to Mlle. de Gisy of these matters," said Effiat, bending a stern and gloomy look upon the prior. "You were not aware that she is of the Religion?"

The prior looked at him with eyes widening in startled comprehension.

"A Huguenot? But, *monsieur*, no, no! You cannot mean—"

Effiat made a curt gesture. "*Monsieur*, such an implication grieves me, as you may well guess; but in a matter of this grave import we can neglect nothing, we can spare no one, not even our own feelings. Escort the lady to her own quarters, I beg of you, and say no word of what has happened. I shall interview her later, and if necessary we can interrogate her to-morrow. Meantime, kindly have the body of M. de Salignan disposed of at once."

"A Huguenot!" murmured the prior, and signed himself. "That sweet lady! And I had never dreamed that she could be a heretic!"

"She may yet prove more than that," said Effiat ominously. There was a sparkling glint in his narrow eyes. "How, think you, could a gentleman like Salignan suddenly become a traitor to his king, unless he were bewitched? But enough: we shall see later."

Dom Ratran waddled off, mumbling to himself like a man stricken. As he departed, Mervaut passed him and came into the room. He stopped stock-still, looked at the body of Salignan, and his eyes rose to the coldly smiling gaze of Effiat. Terror was in his face.

"*Monsieur!*" he exclaimed.

"My good Mervaut, will you kindly close the door?" said Effiat with deadly politeness. "Thank you. Perhaps you already know that your friend the Sieur d'Avillon is dead?"

The scarred features of Mervaut were pallid.

"Yes, *monsieur*," he muttered. "But—but he was not my friend!"

"No lies, fellow!" cut in Effiat coldly. "You were in league with him. I know it well enough. In fact—"

Mervaut, in pitiable terror, flung himself upon his knees and held out his hands.

"Master, have mercy! I'll confess everything, everything!" he cried. "That man Avillon came to me in Paris. He knew that I had escaped from the galleys some years ago; he threatened to have me denounced, seized, returned to Marseilles, unless I aided him. He did not ask very much at first. He never asked very much; merely that I report on your movements. It could not hurt you, and I was afraid, master! You do not know the life of the galleys—the beatings, the hunger, the pains!"

"Stop whining," intervened Effiat with cold disdain. "Mervaut, you have served me well; you can still serve me. Let us see! If your tale is true, you bear the evidence of it upon your body. Strip."

Still kneeling, Mervaut eagerly stripped off his shirt to the waist. His broad back was scarred by whips. Upon his shoulder was branded the *fleur-de-lis*—proof positive that he had served in the galleys, at least.

"Good. Rise," said Effiat, and frowned a little. The sullen Mervaut rose and clad himself again. "Now, my man, there's none to whom you can betray me; Avillon is dead, Salignan is dead; Bergerac, that emissary of Satan, is in a cell. But you, my good fellow, have been denounced as implicated in this Huguenot plot to seize Mont St. Michel. Silence!" he rasped, as the astounded Mervaut opened his mouth. "Not a word out of you! I'll have you seized and put to the question and broken on the wheel, if you try any more tricks! For your own sake, you must get outside of France, with me. To-night at midnight, or a little after, whenever the tide is out, go to the mainland. To-morrow morning return here at low tide, the next tide, understand? Bring our horses from the Pontorson inn. I'll give you a written order for them when you serve my dinner—I'll remain here for the night. You understand?"

*"So you love this spy, this bravo of
the gutter?" Effiat sneered.*

"Yes, master, of course," muttered Mervaut, staring. "Then
we depart in the morning?"

"We depart," and Effiat smiled thinly, "and we do not cease
to depart until we land in England! Now go. Fetch my things
here and bring all my papers. All, you understand!"

MERVAUT DEPARTED. A monk, followed by four
gaping servants, entered to take charge of Salignan's body. It
was being removed to the parish church, higher up the street,
pending decision as to its disposal.

They had just left when Major d'Ouville entered.

"*Monsieur,*" he reported, "three of those lackeys have been
arrested and sent to the abbey prisons. The fourth is not here.
It seems that he departed for the mainland."

"Ah!" murmured Effiat. "To get the coach, no doubt, M.
d'Ouville! At low tide to-night, about midnight, I understand,

this lackey will return. With him will be a coach and escort of soldiers. I shall depend upon you to have the lackey quietly seized and placed with his comrades; the commander of the escort will be brought to me at once. This is most important."

Ouville assented. A few questions, and Effiat learned that the cell of Cyrano was situated directly below them, with a soldier of the garrison on guard.

These varied matters had taken some time. The afternoon was waning when Cyrano looked up from his morose contemplation of the floor, and found a cloaked visitor outside the iron grille which served him as door. His prison chamber had no window, and nothing in the way of comforts except a broken bench; its only use was as a place of detention for soldiers of the garrison when drunk or guilty of some slight infraction of the rules. Beyond the open grille of the door was visible the corridor which divided this lower portion of the tower.

"Well, *monsieur!*"

At the voice of Effiat, the prisoner started to his feet, incredulous. He knew nothing of what had happened; he could not comprehend why Effiat should be standing here in a position and voice of authority, after his own interview with Salignan.

"So, my dear Bergerac, you are no marquis at all, eh? And you have been very heroic in repulsing these English and Huguenots, eh? You have no words of greeting for me, *monsieur?*"

Cyrano was dumb. Those mocking words revealed a great deal to him, and left him unable to speak or move for the moment. Perceiving his utter consternation, Effiat burst into a contemptuous laugh.

"Spy, betrayer, accursed agent!" he exclaimed. "Murderer of honest men! So you in turn have been betrayed, exposed, shown for what you are, eh? What have you to say?"

Cyrano recovered. "There is nothing to say, *monsieur,*" he responded in a low voice. "You sought to betray France; I saved her. The matter is very simple."

"Aye, simple treachery toward a friend who trusted you!" said Effiat furiously. "Infamous dog that you are! Were you a gentleman, I'd give you what you deserved; but the saints forbid that an Effiat should soil his hand with the blood of a nameless gutter rat like you. Lie here and rot, for all I care. Saved France, indeed! Save your own neck now if you can, my fine savior of France!"

And, with a mirthless laugh, the visitor departed. Cyrano sank down upon the bench.

"This is a devilish turn of events, in truth!" he murmured hopelessly. His own laugh, bitter with irony, broke upon the silence. "Ho, good St. Michel! Now come and help poor Cyrano, who holds at his neck the blessed fragment of your gleaming feather!

"Turn it into a sword of flame, open his prison doors, set him upon a good horse, and I swear that I'll set seven candles of golden wax before your shrine! A safe vow, that!"

And his sardonic laughter echoed into silence.

CHAPTER XV

— SAYS FAREWELL TO HIS LADY.

IT WAS close upon midnight, and Effiat, who had been sleeping most of the evening, now sat before the table in the tower room. A wine-bottle was at his elbow, and he was busily sorting out papers, destroying some, laying others aside. The door opened, and Mervaut stepped into the room.

"Well?" said Effiat, glancing up. "I suppose the fat prior was asleep?"

"He was, *monsieur*," returned the lackey. "He answered that he would waken the lady and would himself escort her hither at once. She has several times requested speech with M. de

Bergerac or M. de Salignan, but Prior Dom Ratran has told her nothing."

Effiat laughed thinly. "Very good. Mount the street again and meet them. Inform them that M. de Salignan has met his death, assassinated by the hand of M. de Bergerac, who is now under arrest for the deed. And, Mervaut?"

"Yes, master?"

"You have inquired as to low tide?"

"In another hour, *monsieur.*"

"Good. See to it that you get across to Pontorson at once about those horses. Here is the order for them."

Mervaut bowed, took the folded paper handed him, and retired.

Effiat ordered the guard at the door to bring fresh candles for the two candelabra, and went on with his work. Presently he set fire to the mass of papers deposited on the hearth, and with a cynical smile watched them mount in flames. He turned, as the door opened, and bowed profoundly at sight of Dom Ratran escorting Marienne de Gisy into the room.

"Good evening, my friends, good evening!" he exclaimed. "You wear strangely alarmed faces—has something disturbed you?"

Dom Ratran grimaced. Marianne, her face pale, came forward to Effiat.

"*Monsieur!*" she said sharply. "It cannot be true that M. de Salignan has been basely murdered by M. de Bergerac!"

Effiat shrugged. "Who, it turns out, is no marquis at all but a bravo of Paris," he returned. "Unfortunately, it is quite true."

She searched his face for a long moment, her features slowly hardening.

"*Monsieur,*" she said quietly, "I desire to be allowed speech with M. de Bergerac."

It was Effiat's turn to scrutinize her, narrow-eyed. Then he bowed.

"With all my heart, *mademoiselle;* I shall myself escort you. Dom Ratran, will you have the goodness to remain here while I take Mlle. de Gisy below?"

Dom Ratran looked at the wine-bottle and assented quickly. Effiat picked up one of the candelabra and went to the door, and turned.

"Come, *mademoiselle!*"

She obeyed in silence. They passed the guard outside the door and came to the turn of the stairs leading below; then, as Effiat proffered his arm, she detained him quickly.

"One moment, *monsieur.* Shall I tell you what the stars have told me?"

They regarded each other—a strange gaze, for in his eyes was no love, but rather a cold pride and hot anger, and in hers lay a singular menace. He inclined his head, half mockingly, as he made response.

"My dear Marianne, the stars do not interest me; I neither respect nor fear them."

"But these are matters regarding your past—and your future."

EFFIAT'S LIPS curved in a slow smile. "So the stars have told you? Or this charming fellow, Bergerac? Perhaps those stars upon his cloak spoke with tongues, eh?" He laughed lightly and pressed her hand with his arm. "No, no! I know the future already, and shall tell it to you when we return above; as for the past, it is dead. Come, then!"

They continued in silence, and Effiat's light fell upon the iron grille that served Cyrano for door.

"Visitors for M. le Marquis de Bergerac!" cried Effiat. But Cyrano had heard them, and was already clutching at the grille. Marianne turned to Effiat.

"*Monsieur*—a word in private, if you please?"

Effiat bowed, smilingly. "I regret that we deal here with a prisoner of state, so I must listen while you speak."

With a gesture of impatience, she caught at the grille suddenly, put her face to it, and touched her lips to those of Cyrano.

"They tell me lies of you," she exclaimed in a hot, passionate voice. "Very well! Trust me, Cyrano—I'll do what I can. Say nothing in front of him—he wants to trap you! Leave all to me. Farewell for the present."

She turned from the grille and the white face behind it. Effiat laughed a little.

"What? After such tenderness. Well, well, I've learned all I sought to know, so let us mount again. Leave all to her, my good Cyrano!"

"Oh, scoundrel!" broke out the voice of Cyrano from the darkness, in a terrible wailing cry, as his hands shook unavailingly at the iron. "I'll have payment of you!"

Effiat made no response, and the light he bore presently flickered away and was gone. In the darkness of his cell, Cyrano clutched a small object that Marianne had thrust into his hand. Feeling, he realized what it was—the scapulary of the Egyptian woman. He burst into a low and bitter laugh and pocketed it.

Above, Effiat showed Marianne again into the large room and paused at the door.

"Dom Ratran, will you be good enough to allow us a moment in private! The guard will fetch you more of that wine, if it's to your taste."

The prior, laughing, came into the antechamber and motioned to the guard.

"Aye, by all means. The night air is devilish damp! There's midnight sounding now."

The clang of a bell came from the abbey above, faintly. Effiat came into the room, closed the door, and set the candelabra on the table. Marianne was regarding him with a tense and fixed expression, and broke the silence, her voice low and rich.

"So, traitor! I know your villainous plot! I know of the English—I know all!"

"I do not think you do," and Effiat smiled faintly. "But since you so affirm, let it be conceded. So you love this wastrel, this spy, this bravo of the gutters? I feared as much. It is no great compliment you pay me! I leave here in the morning for England, and I had hoped you might go with me."

"Preferably with your lackey," she returned, with such biting scorn that Effiat's cheek paled.

"So!" he observed, his eye steely. "I presume that I might persuade you to purchase his life; it is usually done in romances, I understand. However, complaisant love so bought does not appeal to me.

"Also, I cannot burden myself with an unwilling woman, having myself to think of first. Therefore, I'll let you purchase your own life, if you so desire. Give your word to go with me willingly, and it's accepted. Otherwise, your fate is certain."

Marianne's laugh was biting, edged with acid.

"Proud fool!" she said disdainfully. "Go with you, indeed? Would you murder me, then?"

Effiat regarded her steadily, so that she paled a little under his eyes.

"I shall certainly make sure of you," he responded. "Yes or no?"

Marianne de Gisy's eyes flashed scornfully.

"No," she rejoined curtly. He bowed and turned to the door, and opened it.

DOM RATRAN was in the act of emptying a flagon, and Effiat smiled as he beckoned. Clutching bottle and flagon, the fat prior came into the room and sank into a chair.

"This is admirable wine," Dom Ratran observed. "I know it well; it comes from the Licorne—they have a whole cask of it left, too. Well, well, you wish me to hear something?"

"Yes," said Effiat. "You recall, Dom Ratran, that this lady has been studying certain manuscripts dealing with the stars?"

"Of course," said the prior, pouring more wine. Marianne watched him half fearfully, and he jovially crossed his fingers, his paunch shaking. "Careful, careful, fair witch! Cast not the evil eye upon me!"

His laughter died out, however, at Effiat's next words.

"This lady, Dom Ratran, is under arrest." Effiat leaned over the table and dipping quill in ink, scrawled her name on the *lettre de cachet*. "Here is the royal warrant for her arrest. She is charged with witchcraft, and with deluding our poor friend, M. de Salignan. Under her spells, he forgot his duty and plotted with the Huguenots to deliver this place into her hands. Sit down, write! Shortly a coach and escort will arrive here. She will be taken to Tours. Sit down, write! Write out the indictment!"

"Liar!" cried out Marianne, her face blanching. "You know, traitor that you are, it is you who conspired to betray this place!"

Effiat nodded to the prior, significantly.

"You hear her? Raving. The devil is speaking in her. Come! There's no time to waste."

Dom Ratran, who was a bit befuddled, crossed himself and dragged his chair to the table. Effiat laid paper before him; he took a quill and began to write as the other dictated. It was an accusation of witchcraft, of dealings with Satan, of offenses innumerable.

Marianne listened with incredulity, drawn back against the wall, her eyes staring; she could not believe what she heard. When he had finished, Dom Ratran signed the paper, then seized his flagon and drained it at a long gulp. Effiat was signing in turn, when the guard entered and saluted.

"M. d'Ouville sends word that a coach and escort are approaching."

"Good," said Effiat. "Remain on guard here; this lady is under arrest. See that she does not leave this room. Remain, Dom Ratran. I return immediately."

He departed. Dom Ratran regarded Marianne, shook his head owlishly, poured another flagon of wine, and quaffed it with appreciation. Then, suddenly, tears springing to her eyes, Marianne came toward him.

"Dom Ratran, you cannot believe in this farce—you cannot

be a party to it!" she exclaimed, her voice broken. "You know that man is a liar, a traitor, a murderer—"

The good prior hastily crossed himself, emptied his flagon.

"Get thee behind me, Satan!" he cried lustily. "Ha! So that stopped you, did it? No, no, you can't cast any spells over me, my fair one!" His head rolled, as he leered at her in maudlin sagacity. "A Huguenot, eh? And studying the stars, reading old manuscripts. Ha! But you're powerless against the blessed St. Michel—you're on holy ground in this place, and St. Michel himself must ha' laid bare this plot! I'll have it entered in the book of miracles. Ho, guard—where's that new supply of wine, eh?"

The guard opened a bottle from the hamper he had fetched.

Marianne shrank back, terror and hopeless despair in her face, as she perceived the futility of any appeal to this drunken man. Now, for the first time, realization of her situation seemed to come upon her.

PRESENTLY EFFIAT stood in the doorway, and beside him a cavalier, booted and spurred, who bowed to the prior and the lady.

"Dom Ratran," said Effiat, "this is M. de Montluc. Allow me to present the captain of your escort, Mlle. de Gisy. This is the lady, *monsieur*, whose arts contrived the death of poor M. de Salignan. I have the murderer under lock and key. I warn you, do not allow her any liberty, do not let your men speak with her, be careful of every word you exchange with her! Here is the royal order for her arrest, and here is the accusation against her. You will deliver her to the king's provost at Tours."

Montluc bowed and stowed away the documents. "And we are to leave at once?"

"You will escort her to the coach and place her there under guard," said Effiat. "Dom Ratran, will you write an order admitting M. de Montluc to the abbey? Stay, I'll write it myself, and you can sign it."

He leaned over the table, writing, and shoved paper and quill at Dom Ratran, who scrawled his name. A low cry broke from Marianne.

"This is base infamy!"

She checked herself as she met the cold and uncompromising regard of Salignan's officer, Montluc. Effiat gave the latter the order.

"The soldier at the door, here, will guide you to this lady's chambers at the abbey," he said. "I request you to make search there. You will bring whatever of her effects she may desire: also, what manuscripts you may find—manuscripts dealing with witchcraft and the stars and other magical subjects. That is all. *Mademoiselle*, will you have the goodness to accompany M. de Montluc, and obviate the use of force?"

Marianne, perceiving no escape, no help, drew herself up proudly.

"Very well," she said. "You are very clever—but you will be punished for this infamy, and for your other infamies!"

Effiat, with a slightly mocking smile, tendered her a profound bow as she took the arm of M. de Montluc, whose attitude was respectful but determined. The guard at the door, on Effiat's command, took the lantern in the antechamber and preceded them.

The door closed. Effiat threw back his head in a silent, hearty laugh, a rare thing for him. Then he crossed to the table, seized the flagon, filled it, and drained it at a draft. He set it down again before Dom Ratran, who blinked at him.

"Don't understand," said the fat prior, with a hiccup. "Charming lady, witch or not! You're a fool. Too charming altogether to be sent away in old coach. No treatment for lady, M. d'Effiat! No gentleman would treat lady like that."

Effiat, his eyes glowing with hot sparks, laughed softly.

"I'm not sending her away, my dear prior!" he rejoined. "Listen! What happens? She is placed in the coach. Montluc goes to the abbey to get her effects and the manuscripts which will assuredly prove her a witch. I go to her in the coach, find her convinced of her fate; she agrees to forego her witchcraft and be a very charming woman, in my company. Excellent! I bring Montluc back here, countermand the orders, give Bergerac to him instead. You see? He will be quite satisfied to take the murderer of poor M. de Salignan, instead of a charming witch, to Tours. He'll not return from the abbey for a good twenty minutes. No hurry, no hurry! Do you get the plan now?"

Dom Ratran shook his head and poured more wine.

"Not at all, not at all," he muttered. "Personally I'm glad that rascal Salignan is gone. I never liked that man! Bergerac, now—there's another sort for you. Upon my word, I believe the rogue could drink me under the table! Mean to try it some time—pity he isn't here with us, eh?"

Effiat perceived that at the present moment all speech was, to Dom Ratran, no more than a murmur of meaningless sound. A knock, and M. d'Ouville entered the room.

"*Monsieur!* The escort is being refreshed. M. de Montluc has just placed Mlle. de Gisy in the coach—he showed me the order. There is no mistake?"

"None, my good major, none," Effiat assured him with great affability. The perplexed Ouville saluted, with a helpless air.

"There is no guard at your door here, *monsieur.*"

"Bah! He's acting as guide to Montluc, who goes to the abbey. If I were you, my good Ouville, I'd make a round of the towers at once, and be sure all sentinels are awake and watchful. These accursed heretics may yet make some effort upon us, and now that the tide is out, they could cross the sands readily."

Ouville bowed and took his departure. Effiat smiled to himself.

CHAPTER XVI

—MAKES USE OF HIS HANDS.

M. DE BERGERAC had no knowledge of the precise lies told about his doings by Sieur d'Effiat, but he knew that for some reason Effiat was in full control of the Mont, and would have no mercy upon him. That interview with Marianne had left him crushed and hopeless. He sat on his broken bench in the dark, hands gripped, impotent to think or plan or act.

From this morose despair, a slight sound roused him.

He looked around. All was darkness; yet from this darkness came the soft scrape of a foot on the stone where he sat.

"Marianne!" he cried in a low voice.

"S-sh!" came response. "Quiet, in the name of the saints!"

Cyrano relaxed. Not Marianne's voice, but that of a man. Who, then? Perhaps she had sent some one. He left his bench and came to the door, waiting there. The steps came closer, he caught the hot breath of a man close at hand.

"Well?" Cyrano demanded softly. "Who are you?"

"It is I, *monsieur*—Mervaut."

Cyrano was for an instant stupefied.

"What?" he said. "You have come to kill me in the dark, then?"

"No, *monsieur*, no!" The man's voice was eager, tense, surcharged. "You do not know what has happened. My master has killed M. de Salignan, and blames you for the deed. He is planning to leave here in the morning and fly to England. A great conspiracy has been discovered—M. de Cinq-Mars, the Prince of Sedan, even *monsieur*, the king's brother, are arrested."

"So!" exclaimed Cyrano. "Salignan dead—Lord love us all! And I cooped up here, after saving all France! After—"

"Peace, *monsieur,* peace!" intervened Mervaut. So desperately urgent was his tone that it silenced Cyrano. "Listen to me. There is little time to lose! Midnight has sounded, the tide is out; we must do something now or be lost!"

Do something—we! Cyrano caught his breath sharply, came wide awake.

"Speak, then," he said curtly.

Mervaut's words came in a swift flood.

"M. d'Effiat has fooled them all—but I have fooled him likewise! Listen, *monsieur.* Two years ago I was released from the galleys. I encountered Sieur d'Avillon, who took me into his service. No one knew this. I obtained much information for him. A year ago he had me placed with M. d'Effiat as lackey, and since then I have been reporting as much as possible to M. d'Avillon. You comprehend, *monsieur,* I was working for M. d'Avillon alone, and no one else was aware of it!

"Now M. d'Effiat threatens to denounce me as an accomplice in the whole plot unless I go with him and help him. I know this man, *monsieur.* He is a great noble. People will believe what he says about a lackey, a former galley-slave; my word is of no value. He will take me with him, make use of me, and whenever it pleases him—probably on the way to England—will destroy me. At the present moment he needs my help, you comprehend? I am supposed to be on my way to Pontorson now, to return with horses in the morning. You understand?"

"Only too well," said Cyrano grimly. "You're caught in your own net, are you?"

"Not yet, *monsieur!*" was the eager response. "I know you are an emissary of Cardinal de Richelieu's spy, Père Carré, for M. d'Avillon mentioned it. M. d'Effiat has learned that you killed his friends and ruined his plot with the English and Huguenots. Now, I have a note from M. d'Avillon stating that I am in his employ, but this will not avail me if M. d'Effiat seeks to have me destroyed; he will tell some lie about it; and M. d'Avillon is dead, which is the main thing."

CYRANO'S READY brain caught at all this and he, in turn, felt a thrill of eagerness.

"Well, well, what does all this aim at?" he made response. "I care not a *denier* about you or what happens to you."

"But I do, *monsieur*—I care a great deal!" came Mervaut's voice. "That is why I've come here; to make a bargain with you. There's no key to this door; it's fastened by bolts. I can draw those bolts, you comprehend? Also, I have here M. d'Avillon's little whip—you recall the whip, *monsieur?* It was brought to M. de Salignan, but he did not know it had any secret. There are papers in the butt. I cannot read, so I know not what they are. If you say the word, *monsieur,* we can go to Paris together, take this whip to Père Carré—"

"No, no. Wait!" Cyrano gripped at the iron grille, his agile brain leaping ahead and ahead, darting at possibilities. "I cannot leave here. You shall take the whip, go to Paris alone; I'll give you money. Where is M. d'Effiat now?"

It so chanced that Mervaut knew nothing about the coach ordered by Salignan, or of Effiat's plans regarding Marianne de Gisy and that coach.

"He is in the room above, *monsieur,*" he responded. "He was destroying papers, but sent me to summon Mlle. de Gisy and Prior Ratran. Why, I do not know."

"Have you writing materials?" demanded Cyrano quickly.

"None, *monsieur.*"

"Then you will take a verbal message from me to Père Carré, together with a token that will prove it came from me. Agreed?"

"Gladly, *monsieur!*" exclaimed Mervaut, delightedly. "But I dare not linger long here—I must get a rope, slip over the walls, and reach Pontorson afoot. When the tide comes in, it is fast and terrible, and time is passing."

"Very well. Open the door."

"Upon your word of honor, *monsieur?*"

"Upon my word of honor, Mervaut."

The iron bars at top and bottom of the grille, which fitted

into slots of the stone, squeaked as Mervaut carefully thrust them back.

Cyrano was all eagerness. He perceived here not only the chance for freedom, for action, for everything, but also the chance to send word to Père Carré of what he himself had done. Then, as the grille opened, he remembered something.

"Mervaut!" He groped, caught the man's arm. "You recollect this golden star about my neck, this reliquary? M. d'Avillon wanted it. Do you know why?"

"Yes, *monsieur*. M. d'Avillon was extremely devout, and had a great fondness for relics, of which he possessed a number. He sent me word to obtain this for him if possible—"

Cyrano burst into a laugh, which he checked instantly, and thrust the golden star and chain into the hands of Mervaut.

"And I thought it might contain something of importance to me!" he murmured ironically. "Here, take it to Père Carré; it will prove to him that you came from me, you understand? And here's money, the very purse Père Carré himself gave me, intact. I've plenty more."

"Thank you, *monsieur*, thank you!" said Mervaut, eagerly gripping the purse. "And the message?"

"Tell him all you know of events here. Add that I went with M. d'Effiat, met the Sieur de Lorges and other Huguenot leaders and two Englishmen. Later, I killed M. de Frontard and several of the Englishmen, who lie buried just above high water mark, in the little cove on the north side of Tombelaine Island. I drove off two small ships filled with English, who were about to land there. Tell Père Carré that the danger is over, and I'll give him details upon my return to Paris. Stay—this scapulary goes to him, also."

"Scapulary!" repeated Mervaut, as Cyrano thrust the little thing into his hand. "Where got you it, *monsieur?*"

"From those Egyptians in the road near Palaiseau—"

"By the saints! I know what is in it, then!" came the eager

words. "A message from Sedan to Sieur de Lorges, the Huguenot chief. M. d'Avillon was most eager to get it."

"Ha!" exclaimed Cyrano. "The guarantees to the Huguenot
leaders! Good. Take it with you. Have you a weapon?"

"My sword, *monsieur.*"

"Give it to me. The blade alone. Now begone, in the devil's
name!"

There was a scrape of feet. Mervaut needed no urging to be
away from here.

LACKEYS CARRIED excellent rapiers at this period,
the last vestige of ancient squiredom left to them, and it soon
to become outlawed. Mervaut was no exception. For a long
moment Cyrano stood testing the blade for its feel and balance,
then bent it once or twice in his hands and laughed.

"Ha, St. Michel!" he cried out softly. "You have won the
wager—the seven tapers of golden wax are yours, upon the faith
of a gentleman! Now, Hercule Alexandre Savinien de Cyrano,
be worthy your heroic names! You have but to play a bold hand
with these monks, and all is well. Bold heart, bold hand, bold
sword—and behold, the shining lady upon the far mountain-top
beckons you nearer, and her dear eyes hold a blessing for you!"

And, with a sweeping salute of his rapier. Cyrano laughed
again and felt for the stairs with groping feet. He found them,
indeed, unlighted; but he did not know that the guard at the
door above had taken the lantern wherewith to light M. de
Montluc in his search of Marianne de Gisy's quarters for
documents of witchcraft.

Treading cautiously, unaware what would greet him, Cyrano
mounted, turned at the landing, and found a beam of light
coming from the door of the commandant's room. The antechamber was empty, and no guard was here. Cyrano advanced,
then checked himself on hearing Effiat's voice.

"Well, my good and excellent prior, it is time I went about
my little business at the gate. What, no response? Come, come!
Surely a miserable half dozen of wine has not left you in such

case, honest Dom Charlatan? And two or three bottles as yet undrunk, too—I'll warrant you it would be another story if our friend Bergerac sat in your place, eh? That rogue would certainly put you under the table, and three more like you!"

"Heaven send the prophecy true!" murmured Cyrano with a grin, as he softly advanced to the partly open door.

At the table he could see Dom Ratran, most clearly and obviously drunk, yet with his eyes still open and an occasional mumble on his lips. Effiat had just risen and was donning his baldric and cloak, and reaching out for his hat, which lay upon a chair. He was wearing his very handsome suit of scarlet and seed-pearls; the cloak was voluminous, in the Spanish manner, and was fastened with a golden clasp at the throat.

"Well, fill up your fat winesack, swine!" said Effiat in contempt, to the heedless figure. "Swill and sweat, sleep your fill, and waken on the morrow to a harsh reckoning, simple fool that you are!"

Cyrano stepped into the room and closed the door. .

"Better to waken to a harsh reckoning, than not to waken at all," he observed. "How say you, my Lord Effiat? I trust you take my meaning?"

Effiat stared at him speechless, as though he were a ghost. Indeed, Cyrano looked not unlike an apparition; he was unshaved, had not eaten all this day, and his lordly and bestarred purple velvet was sadly torn, stained and daubed, after his last night's work. But the dark liquid eyes blazing in his face spoke their own message, as did the naked rapier in his hand.

"*Peste!*" exclaimed Effiat lazily, recovering from his stupefaction. "Back to your cell, fellow; do your crowing on the dunghill, my fancy cock of Paris. You've been let out, eh? Then you'll be sent back quickly enough!"

Cyrano laughed that great gay laugh of his, so bitter with ironic mockery.

"Have done, my good Effiat, have done!" he observed, taking a step forward. "The blood of Cyrano shall not sully your hand, eh? Well said, and a true word there—truer than most of yours! But I assure you that I have no such scruples. And, being both hungry and thirsty, perceiving good cheese and wine there on the table, I promise to make short shrift of you. *En garde,* liar!"

At his threatening advance, Effiat gripped his sword, then paused.

"Have a care, alley cat!" he exclaimed angrily. "One call from me and you—"

Cyrano bowed mockingly.

"Call, my good lord, call and be damned! And I promise you that at the third pass I'll spoil your throat for calling. *En garde,* liar and coward!"

Dom Ratran stirred at the table. His voice suddenly came in drunken Latin mumblings.

EFFIAT'S BLADE swept clear of the scabbard, a thin laugh on his lips. He knew himself unexcelled among the nobles of the court with the rapier, and had no fear whatever of the wild and savage eyes of the man facing him.

"At the third pass, eh?" he mocked. "Good! A marvelous prophecy to come from—"

"From Cyrano? Bah! Little you know me," and Cyrano's laugh blared anew as the blades flamed out, met, crossed with a little clang of steel. "No, no, I mean to have that pretty suit of yours, unsullied and unspoiled, to replace my own sorry garb. Ah! One, my lord, one! Watch your step, I warn you—balance is not right."

A malicious smile touched the alert, watchful eyes of Effiat. Cyrano leaped back, blood running down his sword-hand; the other point had ripped his forearm. Then, swift as a cat, he was in again, had engaged, was laughing wildly as he drove home a deadly riposte that Effiat barely parried.

"Two!" Cyrano cried, a ring of exultation in his voice. Both men had measured each other, and now Effiat lost his smile altogether. "Call for help quickly, my good Effiat! *Mordious,* but you'll need it in another moment—"

Dust rose from the floor under their stamping feet, the blades clicked and hung engaged in air, they glared into each other's eyes. Feint and parry, lunge and riposte. Effiat was attacking his opponent with a vicious determination.

"Now for it, now!" panted Cyrano suddenly. "Beware of it, Effiat—the riposte that I had from the King of Hungary himself—a delicate little thing, ha! Like the kiss of a butterfly, like the sweep of a humming bird—three! *Three*—and you have it!"

Cyrano's long body uncoiled, his rapier drove in and out, so swift as to leave the lunge almost unseen. Effiat's rapier clattered on the floor. Both hands clutching at his throat, Effiat stood swaying on his feet for an instant, then Cyrano leaped forward and caught him as he was falling.

"Careful, careful of the suit!" exclaimed Cyrano, but Effiat was past hearing him. The rapier had pierced his throat.

Laughing, Cyrano laid him across a chair, face down, unfastened cloak and doublet, flung them aside, then straightened up. He regarded the dead man with sardonic mockery.

"Two inches of steel, and so flickers away conspiracy and nobility forever!" he observed. "Why, it's but a simple thing after all, the simplest of prescriptions; and here our good Richelieu must needs revert to headsman's ax and prisons! Assuredly, I must have a word with him on the subject. A twist of the wrist, a tongue of steel, and all life's perplexities are cast aside! Mine, for example, in the matter of clothes. The Mont receives a new abbot, whose noble family feels the effects of twenty thousand livres per year; his children marry into princely families—all thanks to two inches of Cyrano's steel! Eh, Dom Ratran?"

Staggering, laughing crazily, Cyrano swung about to the table. The fat prior looked up at him with eyes that saw not, as he made shift to bandage his arm. Dom Ratran mumbled unintelligibly, so that Cyrano burst into laughter, which he choked down with a mouthful of cheese. He emptied a bottle into the big silver flagon, and after an approving taste, drained it at a draft.

"Not so bad, not so bad!" he declared, then came to a sudden pause, listening.

The one window of the room gave toward Pontorson. Looking from it, Cyrano beheld a red flare of torches near the gate, heard orders, caught the ring of hooves and wheels on the stones; he could see nothing, because of the angle of vision. Evidently, a coach was departing.

"Well, let it depart and be damned to it!" he exclaimed, swept by a fierce exultation. The reverse of fortune uplifted him, and so, mayhap, did the wine. "A coach had no business here, in any event."

H E S E A T E D himself on the table, swung his long legs, clapped Dom Ratran heartily on the back. Then he devoted himself to the cheese and wine, with all the eagerness of an appetite starved for a full twenty-four hours.

When his hunger and thirst were appeased—that is to say, when the cheese had vanished and the last bottle of wine was empty—he turned to the limp-hanging figure of Effiat and carelessly stripped it. After he had discarded his own rags, he tried the seed-pearl suit, and found that it fitted well enough. The cloak he threw about his shoulders, then donned the beaver with its flowing plume.

"*Peste!* Not a mirror wherein to behold my new glory!" he exclaimed. "Baldric and sword to complete it—so! A trifle longer in the arms than he, but that's a small matter; leave the cuff open. Ha! Now ruffle it, my good Bergerac!"

He swaggered across the room, paused to pocket the gold and silver from his own ragged pockets, then came back and halted before Dom Ratran. He had recollected something.

"Come, shameless!" he cried stentoriously, tweaking the good friar's nose. "What of my lady, eh? She was here, came with you. Where now? At the abbey? Where did this rascal dispose her? Answer, you misbegotten lump of fat!"

Dom Ratran goggled at him and mumbled scraps of Latin, Cyrano shook him, shook him so rudely that prior and chair went over together with a tremendous crash. Kicking him twice in his pronounced corpulence, Cyrano pulled him to his feet and shook him again.

"Out with it! Mlle. de Gisy—where is she? Give tongue, you drunken sot! If she's up above, then I'll walk you up to the abbey and get entrance. Where is she?"

Poor Dom Ratran blinked.

"Not so rough, *monsieur*—good M. d'Effiat!" he complained in his shrill voice. "She—she is a witch, aye! But I've not talked with her, not a word! She's down in the coach now, and it's time you were stopping M. de Montluc. Do not take her to Tours, indeed! You gave him the papers—"

"What's that? What's that?" cried Cyrano, his eyes widening. Suddenly he buffeted the prior across his fat jowl, twice—stinging, full-arm blows. "The coach! Was she in that coach? Wake up, fool! Speak!"

"Aye, 'twas you gave him the papers of arrest yourself, M. d'Effiat," mumbled the unhappy prior. "Why ask me? You said it was but to cozen her—that you'd take her from the coach at the last minute and replace her with that rascal Bergerac."

Cyrano staggered back a pace, staring wide-eyed at the prior, who went mumbling on and finally slumped down to the floor. The coach—the coach he had heard departing—and she in it! Could this be the truth, or some drunken maundering? It was his hand, then, that had halted Effiat? This was the "little business at the gate" Effiat had mentioned! And all the while he had been eating and drinking here, preening himself—

THE DOOR swung open suddenly. M. d'Ouville came into the room and saw, as he thought, Effiat standing there.

"Well, *monsieur*, the coach departed just in time!" he observed. "They say the tide will be in now."

Cyrano whirled upon him, rapier scraping out. So fearful was the contorted face of Cyrano, so awful was the agony of those blazing eyes, that they, rather than the sword-point at his throat, held Ouville silent, petrified.

"Is it true?" cried Cyrano in a dreadful voice. "Is it true that they took her away, took her to be tried as a witch? Speak!"

"True, of course." stammered Ouville, shrinking as the point touched his throat. "With an escort of musketeers."

"Oh, just God!" The unutterable anguish in Cyrano's voice was frightful to hear. A spasm twisted his features as he realized the full truth. "Effiat meant to stop her—and I killed him, and stayed here like a fool while they took her. What have I done, what have I done? Out of the way, fool!"

He wakened suddenly, dashed the major aside, and was gone from the place like a madman.

The peasant guards about the postern gate were about to close it, when the lighted cressets fell upon a terrible figure bounding down the incline toward them, sword in hand. Well they knew that scarlet velvet, that Spanish cloak; with cries of fright they fell away, so that Effiat, as they thought him, went leaping past them and through the postern, and out upon the stones beyond, running like a man crazed. Then they wakened, indeed, and shouted after him that the tide had not long ere the flood.

He paused not, heard them not. They could see that tall figure leaping and running across the moonlit sands until it merged and was gone. Then Major d'Ouville came and ordered them in pursuit, but not a man would go, for they knew too well the danger. And sure enough, it was not long ere the dry sands became seeping and glistening with water, and what had been sand soon became little running wavelets rippling away for miles under the high moon.

In the morning men went forth, but found no trace of him who had fled, so that his fate was written down as uncertain— until word arrived from Pontorson that M. le Marquis de Bergerac had staggered into the inn during the night, had fallen and lain for two hours like a man dead, and afterward had called for his horse and had gone spurring away like a madman.

But this was long after the coach and its escort had swept along the road to Tours.

CHAPTER XVII

—INTERVIEWS A SICK MAN.

JUNE HAD passed. Cardinal de Richelieu, unable to endure motion because of the ulcers eating at his decaying body, was on his way by barge up the Rhone to Lyons, there to witness the trial and execution of M. de Thou and Cinq-Mars. The king's brother, the Duc d'Orleans, was exiled to Venice. The Duc de Bouillon was saved from death by handing over his principality of Sedan to be incorporated in the realm of France. Punishment, prison, exile, struck to right and left, high and low, on every hand. Richelieu had pushed Spain back beyond the Pyrenees forever, had triumphed as never before against his personal enemies; and he was dying.

Louis XIII, somewhat recovered of his rheumatism and able to travel, was on his way to Paris with certain gentlemen of the court. Cardinal Mazarin accompanied him, among others. And on the way the journey was broken at the Château of Perronne, near the tiny hamlet of that name, where the king spent a day or two hunting.

Upon an evening, the king was in high spirits. The hunt had been excellent that day, he was feeling better in body, and the flatteries of his gentlemen had put him into the best of humors. After dinner he was closeted with Père Syrmond, his father confessor, when the secretary of state, M. de Noyers, came into the room and closed the door.

"Your pardon, sire; the curé of the village is here, asking for Père Syrmond. It seems a matter of some importance."

"Let him enter, let him enter," exclaimed Louis XIII.

Père Syrmond gestured assent, and the village curé was

brought into the room. He kissed the king's hand, in no little awe, then turned to the Jesuit.

"Perhaps I do wrong," he said, in some agitation. "But there is a madman in the village tavern. He has been here since yesterday, very drunk. Apparently he is a great gentleman, and he talks continually of endeavoring to meet his majesty. He—he tells a mad story of having been imprisoned at Tours; that he is now seeking justice at the hands of his majesty; he mentions the names of one M. d'Effiat and M. le Marquis de Salignan, and says that he has killed Englishmen and has saved all France—"

The name of Effiat produced a startled silence. True, the king had abandoned Cinq-Mars to the vengeance of Richelieu, evincing an astonishing bitterness and animosity toward his former favorite; but no one knew just what feelings might lie in the royal heart.

"Perhaps," intervened Père Syrmond smoothly, "it would be best to let this matter be investigated by Monseigneur de Mazarin."

"Your pardon, good father, I think otherwise," interrupted the king, and turned to the curé. "You do not know who this man is, or whence he comes?"

"No, your majesty. I believe that he comes from Mont St. Michel. He said as much, speaking of having traveled to Tours to find your majesty's provost there, and being flung into prison and then put out of the city. His name I do not know. He does not know your majesty is here."

"Strange!" The king frowned. "Mont St. Michel—and M. d'Effiat the abbot there! And his talk of Englishmen. Hm! Do you know, gentlemen, I am minded to hear this man's tale. It will amuse me. And perhaps," he added dryly, "it will give me information on certain points."

M. de Noyers spoke anxiously. "Sire, consider the danger! A drunken madman—"

Opposition ever had the effect of setting Louis XIII more firmly in his designs.

"Silence!" he said, with an emphatic gesture. "If the man be mad, let him be watched by two or three gentlemen. If he be drunk, then he will assuredly tell the truth. M. de Noyers, kindly go and bring him hither. Let him think I am a gentleman who may bring him to the king, you comprehend? Ply him with more wine. Come! We shall have a merry hour, I foresee."

So it was done.

THE KING sat at table, pretending to dice with three of his gentlemen; Père Syrmond and two others were close at hand. M. de Noyers and Cyrano came into the room arm in arm, and the former led his comrade to waiting chairs at the table's foot, safely distant from the king. Wine was served, and seized upon eagerly by Cyrano.

But what a Cyrano was here? Unshaved for a fortnight, his handsome seed-pearled suit half in rags, the marks of drink stamped into his face, his eyes dulled and bleared, bloodshot, set in black hollows; and his brain in wild tumult. He nodded solemnly at the king.

"Gentlemen—all good friends—damnation to Effiat and a health to the Marquis de—de Bergerac!" he hiccuped, and drank. One of the gentlemen, gaping, touched the king's arm.

"Sire—by the saints, that is the famous suit sewn with seed-pearls for which Effiat paid nine thousand crowns! I know it well; my own tailor showed it to me in the making."

"*Monsieur,*" said the king sharply, shaking off the gentleman, "you use the name of Effiat. Do you know that Sieur d'Effiat is by this time arrested?"

Cyrano blinked at him, wiped his lips, broke into a roaring laugh.

"Arrested? Then by Lucifer himself, for I sent the rogue to Hades! Aye together with Frontard and the Englishmen! Effiat murdered poor Salignan—whom, God knows, I loved not at all—and—*holà!* More wine here, somebody! Devil take me if

I'm not growing sober, I, who saved the western bulwark of France from the English. As good Père Carré himself said to me—"

There were startled glances. Père Syrmond quietly left the room.

The king plied Cyrano with questions, keen enough at all points; Louis's jaded eyes were sparkling, he was enjoying himself to the full. And Cyrano, drunk, poured forth a wild tale, needing little urging. He spoke of one thing and another, told of how he had reached Tours; of how the provost held Marianne there under accusation of witchcraft; of how he himself had been kicked out of the city after a day in jail. At mention of Marianne, however, the king looked at M. de Noyers, his eyes narrowing.

"You recall the name Gisy? Aye, I've heard of her interest in the stars. Her father served me well. Come! Let's have more of this. M. de Bergerac, why seek you the king? Know you not he's a sick man, some say dying, and that the Cardinal de Richelieu rules France?"

"Bah!" cried Cyrano lustily. "The king is the king; he was born so, and he'll die so, God rest him! And Richelieu is Richelieu—and will die so."

Louis XIII burst into sudden hearty laughter. Cyrano glared at him.

"Devil take you!" he hiccuped. "No one else can save my shining lady. Those accursed fools at Tours—"

The king looked at his gentlemen.

"Take him out. Duck him in the horse-trough, do what you like to him—but bring him back here in ten minutes, sober. Leave him with M. de Noyers."

Cyrano caught the words and arose, furious. Half laughing, half in anger, those around flung themselves upon him; for a moment he resisted madly, then weakness and dissipation had their way, and he collapsed. Presently the room was emptied, and the king looked across the table at his secretary of state.

"DE NOYERS," he said, "this is a wild and incredible tale, yet it holds the ring of truth. This M. de Bergerac—you observed his features? Is he not the man with a nose who killed a monkey, a year or so ago? I recall something of it—there was great jesting about it, eh?"

Père Syrmond came into the room, bowed to the king, and sat down.

"Sire," he said gravely, "I have just been speaking with the gentleman who arrived here this evening, bringing dispatches from Paris, for Cardinal Mazarin. He tells me a strange story— but M. de Mazarin is himself without, seeking entrance. Ah, here he is now."

Mazarin entered, sleekly, and there were documents in his hand.

"Your majesty, I have news!" the Italian exclaimed. "It appears that M. d'Effiat, the abbot of Mont St. Michel, made some attempt to place that fortress in heretic hands. M. de Salignan was killed, and M. d'Effiat himself paid with his life for the attempt—"

Disconcerted, Mazarin became silent, for the king was smiling thinly at him.

"I have that news already, my dear Mazarin," said the king silkily. "For once, it seems, the Louvre is better served than the Palais Cardinal! But come, M. de Noyers—we must assure ourselves that no word of this is noised abroad. It would not do to have it known that the English made any attempt upon our coasts."

Mazarin sank into a chair, at a gesture from the king, and listened amazedly to what was said. Then Père Syrmond leaned forward and made a suggestion.

"Sire, this man is drunk; he is not mad at all. His loyalty is of itself obvious. Why not let him bear a letter to M. de Seguier, the chancellor, commanding that Mlle. de Gisy be set free? Surely he deserves this slight reward."

"Good!" exclaimed Louis approvingly. "Bring me writing

materials, M. de Noyers—quickly! And look to that fellow; they may kill him in the effort to sober him. No, no, gentlemen! I believe that I am still the King of France, am I not? Let me handle this affair in my own way, if you please! Père Syrmond, I believe you are sending Père Andreas to Paris ahead of us, to-morrow?"

The Jesuit inclined his head. M. de Noyers brought paper and writing materials, and the king seized them eagerly. Then he looked up at the Jesuit with a sly glance.

"I shall lay the onus of this on your shoulders, my father; our good M. de Seguier does not always approve of my impulses toward clemency! Our drunken Roland may travel to Paris with your Père Andreas, then; and the Company of Jesus may well stand the blame for this pardon. According to the Huguenots, they have blame enough for other things!"

Chuckling, the king began to write in his peculiar running scrawl. Those about the table glanced one at another, without comment. Louis was clearly in the grip of one of those caprices usually foreign to his callous nature, when he desired to be known as "Louis the Just." And at such times, the less talking any one did, the better.

The king was sanding the paper when the door opened and two gentlemen came into the room with Cyrano between them.

M. de Bergerac had suffered. He was drenched, his long hair hanging dank about his face, and this face was extremely pale. The wild, almost feverish light, which had burned in his dark eyes was now gone, and he had been informed where he was. He looked at the king for a moment, then bowed profoundly.

"Well, monsieur!" said the king sharply. "I understand that you were sent by Père Carré on a mission to Mont St. Michel?"

SOMETHING LIKE a hollow groan broke from Cyrano. He had no recollection whatever of what he had said, or anything that had passed in this room; he was nauseated and weak. Yet, as his gaze swept around, he caught sight of Mazarin sitting at one side. He straightened a trifle.

"Yes, your majesty—at the request, I believe, of M. de Mazarin."

"Exactly," intervened the Italian suavely. The king gave him one sharp glance, then brought his attention back to Cyrano.

"I understand, also, that you desired speech with me?"

"Your majesty, I—yes, I desired to petition—" Cyrano, his assurance gone for once, wet his lips. Louis finished his sentence.

"In behalf of Mlle. de Gisy, perhaps? Come, *monsieur!* You need not look astonished. I know a great deal—more, perhaps, than most people think I know. For example, I have heard rumors of a descent of certain Englishmen on our coasts—most unfortunate rumors, since we do not desire any trouble with England just now. Perhaps you can inform me as to their truth?"

The pallor of Cyrano deepened. The hint here was quite plain; if he denied this report, he lost his only chance of appeal on the score of services rendered. He hesitated, then bowed.

"If it please your majesty," Cyrano said in a firm voice, "these rumors are untrue."

Louis regarded him with a species of amazement, then glanced around.

"Gentlemen," he observed, "you see before you a man who has the divine gift of understanding! It is a rare talent; I commend it to you. M. de Bergerac, you have, it appears, done me certain service. Touching the affair of Mlle. de Gisy, that is out of my hands. What other reward do you desire of me?"

A dreadful misery leaped into the eyes of Cyrano at these words.

"None other, sire," he said in a low voice. "I did not sell my services to the enemies of France; I do not sell it to my king. I ask only to be allowed to die in peace."

He bowed, turned, and staggered slightly.

"Wait!" cried out the king sharply, and extended the paper. "Give him this, some one. Read this letter, M. de Bergerac! Read it aloud, if you please. That is, if you can read—"

Cyrano took the paper, with the shadow of his old sardonic laugh. Holding it to the light, he read the words written there, in a voice that gained strength, passing from faltering accents to incredulous and wonder-filled tones that blared trumpetlike through the room in their delight and overwhelming joy:

"M. LE CHANCELIER:

"I have very willingly granted my confessor, Père Syrmond— for reasons which he has explained to me—a pardon in favor of a woman detained at Tours as a prisoner, of whom a father of the same Company will speak to you in giving you the present letter. Consequently, you will make no objection to placing your seal to the letters which will be presented to you, to that effect. May God have you in His holy keeping, M. le Chancelier!

"Written at Peronne this 5th day of July, 1642.

LOUIS."

"Sire!" Cyrano took a step forward, came to his knee, and looked up. So transfigured was his face, so lit with joy and gratitude and a great happiness as he thought of the "shining lady" so soon to be his, that it brought to the lips of Louis a lingering smile of gratification. "Sire! I—I cannot say—"

Louis held out his hand, and Cyrano pressed it to his lips.

"There is nothing to say, M. de Bergerac. For the rest, I think Père Syrmond will inform you. Go, *monsieur;* you will find M. de Seguier at Fontainebleau, and you may yourself bear the letters under his seal to Tours, to release Mlle. de Gisy. And may God go with you! Come, gentlemen."

They left the chamber—left Cyrano standing there by the table, leaning upon it with trembling hands, Père Syrmond at his elbow; and tears were glistening upon his cheeks.

H. BEDFORD-JONES

B EDFORD-JONES IS a Canadian by birth, but not by profession, having removed to the United States at the age of one year. For over twenty years he has been more or less profitably engaged in writing and traveling. As he has seldom resided in one place longer than a year or so and is a person of retiring habits, he is somewhat a man of mystery; more than once he has suffered from unscrupulous gentlemen who impersonated him—one of whom murdered a wife and was subsequently shot by the police, luckily after losing his alias.

The real Bedford-Jones is an elderly man, whose gray hair and precise attire give him rather the appearance of a retired foreign diplomat. His hobby is stamp collecting, and his collection of Japan is said to be one of the finest in existence. At present writing he is en route to Morocco, and when this appears in print he will probably be somewhere on the Mojave Desert in company with Erle Stanley Gardner.

Questioned as to the main facts in his life, he declared there was only one main fact, but it was not for publication; that his life had been uneventful except for numerous financial losses, and that his only adventures lay in evading adventurers. In his younger years he was something of an athlete, but the encroachments of age preclude any active pursuits except that of motoring. He is usually to be found poring over his stamps, working at his typewriter, or laboring in his California rose garden, which is one of the sights of Cathedral Cañon, near Palm Springs.

Bedford-Jones has written stories laid in many corners of the earth, but among his most popular tales were the John Solomon stories which started many years ago in the *Argosy*.

Made in the USA
Middletown, DE
25 February 2022

61818611R00116